DICK CLUSTER

for Betty,

Dick Cluster

· E. P. DUTTON 🅓 NEW YORK ·

Published in the United States by E. P. Dutton,
a division of NAL Penguin Inc.,
2 Park Avenue, New York, N.Y. 10016.

Published simultaneously in Canada
by Fitzhenry and Whiteside, Limited, Toronto.

Library of Congress Cataloging-in-Publication Data
Cluster, Dick, 1947–
Return to sender/Dick Cluster. — 1st ed.
p. cm.
ISBN 0-525-24690-8
I. Title.
PS3553.L88R48   1988   88-10097
813'.54 — dc19   CIP

Designed by Steven N. Stathakis

1   3   5   7   9   10   8   6   4   2

First Edition

For Nancy

Joan Goldberg has always generously shared her medical knowledge; Jim Campen introduced me to the arcane world of money market instruments; and Nancy Falk pointed me toward Alex. For these contributions, and many readers' comments on my writing, I am grateful.

1

Tough Nut

Through millions of revolutions, shaft and nut had clung tightly to each other. Now, Alex Glauberman's wrench and forearm could not persuade them the time had come to let go. With a certain fondness, Alex wiped oil from the shiny, machined Swedish steel. Gently and carefully he attacked both camshaft and fastener with a propane torch. When the steel began to glow a faint, hot red, he shut the torch off. This time the nut spun easily under his wrench.

Alex drummed with greasy hands on the front bumper. His hands echoed the New Wave beat pulsing from the radio.

"All right now," the deejay exulted, "and that was the Cramps. It's exactly two-thirty-five on Friday morning, and I'm the Manic Insomniac, with you till four to put a little fun into your perfect life. You know me, and I know you, so let's not pretend otherwise. Now I'll shut up and play music for twelve full minutes. Then we will converse again. . . ."

"Not me," said Alex. He left all the Volvo parts spread neatly on the floor, punched his antique Bendix time clock, shed his overalls, and headed for the shower in back of the shop.

The warm water felt like summer rain, the abrasive soap like the brand-X face in an old Gillette ad. Alex dried himself on the only towel and stepped into a pair of cutoff jeans and a Royal Shakespeare Company T-shirt, a gift from Meredith that had arrived, airmail, only a week after she left. He hit the off switches on radio and lights and the down switch on the garage door mechanism. He let himself out the street door into the warm, quiet, late-September night.

It would take him half an hour to walk home. Alex wished he got more exercise, somehow. Not for his figure—his metabolism had always kept him thin, even cadaverous. It was more a question of keeping all the moving parts lubricated and fit. He did ski, in the winter, and he kept up with a nine-year-old, half the week. He played some first base on a softball team, but this summer he'd been forced to put himself on the disabled list. So he walked home. He wondered who else in the city was awake now, and why. He hoped the walking, and the wondering, would help him sleep.

It took a Dalmane to put Alex out. Then he slept solidly till ten-thirty in the morning, when an electronic beeping busted up his dream of hunting elephants. He'd been attacking the sad, lumbering, gray beasts with a flamethrower. He knew it was his job, and no one else's, though he couldn't remember why. He knew it was for their own good, but didn't know the why of that either. He only knew the tears coursing down his cheeks, the solid feel of the flamethrower in his workmanlike hands. The roar from the weapon and the roaring of the dying animals flowed together into a tight, unyielding knot that only the intermittent insistence of the alarm could finally pierce.

Massacring elephants. Mercy killing. Jesus Christ. Alex felt the pillow to make sure it was not really drenched in tears. He might stay up till three and sleep past ten, but his subconscious remained on duty, reminding him of what needed to be done. He slid back into the T-shirt and cutoffs and shuffled to the kitchen.

A high counter separated cooking space from dining space. On its ashwood top were two bottles of pills, one round and one square. Alex poured himself a glass of orange juice and used two gulps to down three prednisones from the round bottle. These were steroids, high-dose synthetic hormones. They were what kept him up late at night. He put whole wheat bread in the toaster-oven, deposited Cheerios, milk, and banana slices in an orange plastic bowl, and made sure the half-smoked joint was still in the glazed purple bowl his daughter had created in day camp two months ago. By now Maria seemed to have settled in with her new third-grade teacher, which made this as good a time as any for Alex to take a vacation. But which vacation—from whom or to whom, from what or to what? Alex had been around that circle several times the night before. He passed it up, this time, and ate the toast and cereal in the same orderly manner with which he'd handled the flamethrower. He lit the joint, which lasted for six drags.

Speedy at night, groggy in the morning, then get high. Getting high was supposed to keep the nausea down. Drugs and counter-drugs, winding up, winding down. Stay on this cycle for one week, then lay off it for two. The whole procedure, Alex liked to say, made him into a kind of human yo-yo.

It was lucky, at least, that he'd always been fond of that particular toy. In college, he'd once kept a yo-yo in motion for three hours without rewinding, though he hadn't told a soul. Now he exhaled a last long, smoky breath, scratched about in his curly black beard, and brought himself to uncap the square bottle, the one that had remained untouched. He counted out thirteen chalk-white tablets, laying them on the counter like files of toy soldiers. The soldiers waited in ranks of two, with a lone leader at the front.

Soldiers about to invade, Alex thought. Crusaders, out to burn the infidels and recapture the Holy Land—and none too picky about who or what they might loot and shoot along the way. He imagined the Manic Insomniac making a wee-hour pitch for the thrill of cyclophosphamide: "Take took much of this, boys and girls, and you can kiss your white cells and your platelets good-bye. Instant immune deficiency. Instant hemophilia. By prescription only. See your druggist *today.*"

Alex grimaced and reminded himself that he was only a machine. Last night he had found a chipped tooth on a timing gear. If you let something like that go, more teeth would chip off, and sooner or later the engine would stop running. So you pulled the pair of gears and replaced them. You dealt with the minor dysfunction. You didn't worry about the rest of the car.

If, inside your body, certain cells multiplied out of control, you did your best to remove them before they got seriously in the way. You didn't worry about the rest of the machine. To prove that this strategy was working, Alex felt the flesh below his right ear. He could not feel any more tumor there. He slid off the stool and ran cold water into a tall glass, and then he swallowed the baker's-dozen pills. Two at a time, and one at the end.

Twice, when he felt a gag coming on, he closed his eyes and breathed deeply through his nose while clamping his jaw shut with his free hand. When all the tablets rested safely in his stomach, he rested his head in his arms until the sensation of draining blood was gone. Then he rolled another joint, took two drags, replaced it in the little purple bowl, and went back to bed. Propped against the pillows, he dialed Kim.

"It's Alex," he said. "I got up, I did my drugs. I'm going to sleep some more, and write Meredith, and stay away from the shop until the buzz hits tonight. Do you want to go to an early movie?"

"Don't you want to talk before you write?" Kim asked. Her tone was helpful but not really pressing. Alex imagined her in patched jeans and a smeared workshirt, paintbrush in hand, smothering her irritation at being interrupted.

"No. I want to go to a movie after I write."

"Okay, Alex," said Kim cheerily. "Do you want to be fed or anything? Or I'm available to stay over, if you want company. Maria's room is up for grabs, right?"

"No, thanks, Kim. I'm doing okay so far. Can I call you like sixish?"

"Okay. You're the boss. If I'm not quite home, the machine will be on. Or Sally will be here."

"Okay, thanks."

"Good luck."

"Yeah. See you."

The Boss. It occurred to Alex that, in the dream, he had held the flamethrower very much the way, on the cover of his retrospective album, Bruce Springsteen stood and handled his

4

guitar. That was not, however, the reason why this week he was the boss.

Any other week, Kim would not have let him off so easily. As matchmaker, she had a proprietary interest in his relationship with Meredith. She had fixed them up in the winter, under the guise of recommending a mechanic when Meredith's fuel pump gave up the ghost on a five-degree morn. Meredith had promised that if her car purred like a kitten when she turned the key, she would take the mechanic to dinner—an offer no one had made before or since.

Now, three seasons later, Meredith was away in England, their first lengthy separation. They'd planned for Alex to come to London to meet her—and her family, and her friends. But just now Alex did not want to go on that sort of pilgrimage. What he felt was, he supposed, a version of the old cancer-patient cliché: what would you do if you were told you had only six months to live? Alex was confident, almost always, that he had many more months than that. Yet the kind of pilgrimage he wished for, deep down inside, was the kind that went with that *x*-months-to-live loosening of life's regular ties. It was an adolescent, knight-errant fantasy, he told himself severely. Springsteen again: No Retreat and No Surrender.

But there it was, and the visit to Meredith just did not fit. He knew that Kim could not be happy about his canceling the trip. And Kim was not normally reticent about her views. During his weeks of medication, though, what Alex said went. That was one of the luxuries that came with his condition. So, left to his own devices, he hung the receiver on the phone and shoved the phone on the floor. Within minutes, he was asleep. The crusaders did their killing without bothering their host. The flaming elephants did not come back.

2

Regulations

The match seethed before going out. Angry bubbles hissed on its short, round stem. Like lava, cooling on contact with Alex's rapid explosion of breath.

Seethed? Alex shook his head and curled thin lips at the corners. He blew quickly on his singed fingertips. The matches were foreign, made of some woody, quick-burning substance, coated with wax to slow the flame. That was why they bubbled, not because they were angry. Alex took another deep breath of the smoky atmosphere inside the car, then crossed the gritty street and slid into the stale, air-conditioned ambience of the little post office in Davis Square.

The wall clock said he'd made it ten minutes before closing. The nausea that had peeked around corners while he sat at his desk, writing Meredith, had gone for a while. First he had tried fighting it with meditation, letting thoughts and sensations swim by like graceful, placid fish, neither shutting them out nor holding on to them. Snorkeling among them, he had thought, but then realized that was paying attention to the fish, which was wrong.

Alex was getting better at meditation, with practice, but he still had a long way to go. Once he reached the correct state, he was supposed to visualize his medications as friendly creatures, cute little Pac-Men assiduously gobbling up the haywire cells. Alex had no objection to this procedure. But for now, for relief from the nausea, he depended on the dope. Fighting fire with fire, he told himself. An eye for an eye, a drug for a drug. As a result, he now felt pleasantly stoned. He felt giddy and well disposed toward the world—though the world did seem to be something of a spectator sport.

Alex took his place in one of the two lines. He stood behind a teenage girl in a plaid parochial-school skirt. He named her Donna Marie. She looked at her watch, scuffed her loafers on the floor, and leaned out to peer at whatever transaction was stalling the line. She fingered a sky-blue envelope, squarish, addressed in a neat round hand. A love letter, Alex thought. A nice, simple one, unlike his own.

At the head of the other line, a small woman filled out forms in the cramped counter space left by a big box. She wore a sweater despite the lingering summer heat. Snatches of her conversation with the clerk drifted back—return receipt, catalog sale, I knew this would happen, my sister said . . .

Alex wanted to know what rejected, unsatisfactory item lay inside the box. The clerk lifted the package easily to the scale with one hand. Alex closed his eyes, visualizing masses of Styrofoam peanuts protecting a ghastly display of artificial flowers, or a Scandinavian-style wooden light fixture imported from Taiwan. He could ask, he supposed, but then he would have to take on the burden of the woman's complaint. He realized suddenly that, aside from Kim on the phone, he'd talked to no one for the past twenty-four hours. He fingered his own letter, sealed tight against his urge to reread, to edit, to try to explain his decision one more time.

Yes, he had tried to put on paper, I meant what I said on the phone. I am not getting on tomorrow's plane. I am not coming to visit, not now. Because, because I've been working hard and I want my time: a break from the chemicals, a break from the job, a break from my daughter—and I don't want to replace them with you. Let's spend two weeks in London when this is all over, when you can be my guide and not my nurse. Because I don't want you to be my nurse—or, maybe, because I do. Because I don't want to meet your father—not now, not yet. Very much love and equally much stubbornness. See you in November, here, with open arms. Love again, Alex.

It was not the kind of message Meredith would like: it was not logical, nor did it, most likely, show much love or much trust. It did not say whether, or how, his feelings about her had changed in the month they had been apart. But Alex felt, or hoped, that the issue had to do with him, not with her or with them. He wanted just now to be free to follow his own fancies, to find his own fate, without having to demonstrate how these were good for him, without having to explain them to anyone. He hoped that was the kind of message Meredith could accept.

A tentative cough from behind reminded him he was not alone. He opened his eyes to see that a space had opened between himself and Donna Marie. The cough behind him was repeated, less tentatively. He turned, a spectator again, to inspect a balding man in a brown business suit.

The man's suit was soft, almost fuzzy, a subtle pattern of dark brown on light. An expensive suit, a downtown suit, not quite right for Davis Square. The man himself was shorter than Alex, maybe five-ten, neither fat nor thin. He had a pointed chin, sad eyes, and wide, bloodless lips. Sweat glistened on a high, round forehead. It wasn't healthy, outdoor, Marlboro Man sweat. It was cold sweat, giving a sickly cast to the pale skin.

"Oh, sorry," Alex said, realizing he was staring. "You look like you're in a hurry. Do you want to go first?"

The man drew the translucent lips back around the bony jaw. Despite his agitation, his smile was somehow superior —lecturing, professional, something like that. An expensive, downtown sort of smile that irritated Alex. Here in the Davis Square post office, it aroused his curiosity as well.

"Thank you, young man."

The voice was softer than Alex had expected. The man's eyes flickered over his. It wasn't what people called a flicker of hope, Alex thought. A flicker of appreciation, perhaps. If "young man" had been intended as a compliment, Alex didn't

8

take it that way. Almost forty, he was mourning the time when being considered young had been a matter of right. He dropped his eyes to the floor and noticed that the creases of the man's pants landed just at his shoelaces. It had been a long while since Alex had bought a suit, and he wondered whether this was the fashionable length. It used to be, he thought, that the crease was supposed to buckle. The shoes were old-fashioned wingtip dress shoes. The swirls of holes punched into the leather reminded Alex of his father, who had worn shoes like that to funerals, or to the theater. Churchgoing shoes, only his father had not been one for going to *shul*.

The man passed by Alex to take his place behind Donna Marie. He held a flat corrugated box, about the size of a ream of paper, under his arm. At the head of the other line, the small, unsatisfied woman turned and left. A younger woman, tall and better dressed, dropped a heap of bound bundles of envelopes on the counter. She said, "Another day, Sal."

Sal was beefy, white, middle-aged. He left his uniform shirt open at the collar. He said, "Yeah, another dollar." At the head of Alex's line, Donna Marie licked a stamp, left her letter, and hurried out. The clerk who had sold her the stamp, a light-skinned black man with a pencil mustache and a tightly knotted government-issue tie, said mechanically, "Can I help you, sir?"

"Yes, you can," began the man in the soft, expensive suit. "I have an overseas package, for Germany. I'd like it to go by registered mail."

Most overseas packages from Somerville, so far as Alex had noticed, went to relatives in the old country—to Italy, Portugal, Greece, sometimes Haiti. This man spoke with a trace of New York, an accent familiar, even Jewish perhaps. A package to Germany . . . why? Alex leaned to the side to check the clerk's reaction. The clerk frowned and pointed at a rack full of forms on the counter by the window. "Fill out one of those," he said. He looked pointedly at the clock on the side wall, hands nearing five o'clock.

The balding man followed the finger and the eyes. He smiled sadly at Alex, shrugged as if to say "Regulations!" He glanced out the window, took a pen from the inside pocket of

9

his jacket, and began to write. The secretary who had left the bundles of letters passed between him and Alex. She looked over her shoulder and gave Sal a quick wave. She said, "We'll see you, Sal." The other clerk said to Alex, "Can I *help* you, sir?"

"Oh, um, yeah, this is airmail. To England. Nothing special, just airmail." As he dropped his letter on the counter, Alex found that he was still unsure he really wanted to send it. "Um, just weigh it and give me the stamp, okay?"

"That's what we always do," the clerk said shortly. End of the day, Alex thought. A black public official in a white town had to stand on his authority—especially if it was limited. Suddenly the man in the brown suit pushed in beside Alex. His superior smile was gone, and a beseeching grimace twisted his pale lips. His eyes danced crazy little steps, and more moisture stood out on the back of his bare, pallid head. He dropped the box on the counter, covering the edge of Alex's letter, as if to say in a children's pushing match, Hey, I was here first. His fingers pressed into a half-completed form and a twenty-dollar bill. "It's all written on the package," he said. "Please take it, I have to leave."

"Soon as I'm done with this customer," the clerk told him. "Just finish the form, please. . . ." He plucked Alex's letter from beneath the package and dropped it on the scale. Though Alex hadn't had much to say, it had taken him an ounce of pages to say it. "That will be eighty-eight cents," the clerk declared.

The balding man looked at Alex, that quick flash of appreciation suddenly showing as his eyes, for a moment, stilled. "You'll do it," he said. "You will. Here. Keep the change." He didn't wait for acknowledgment. As he brushed past, he wiped his brow quickly with pale, spotted fingers.

Alex stared at the clerk, who placed his own fingertips flat on the counter and said nothing at all. Alex said, "Just a minute," and left his letter to Meredith sitting on the scale. He crossed to the counter by the window and watched the man in the suit walk away down the sidewalk, toward the square, between two other men. These men also wore suits, but their suits were plaid and much more shiny. They seemed to keep the balding man between them, matching their steps to his. Or so Alex thought, if he wasn't imagining things.

Alex quickly completed the form: a local return address, a destination in Berlin. The paper was damp with perspiration, and Alex touched it with a mixture of sympathy and distaste. He waited what seemed a geologic age for the clerk to weigh the package, total the price, attach and stamp the necessary papers, and hand back the change from the twenty plus the carbon-copy receipt. In the meantime, Alex stuffed his own transatlantic letter into his back pocket. He wanted to know whether he was imagining things or not. He had a curious, romantic feeling that fate had just beckoned in his direction. If so, for the moment anyway, the way fate beckoned was the way he was going to go.

3
Mortality

The Commonwealth of Massachusetts respects certain traditions. The baseball team plays on real grass. No bottled or canned alcohol can be sold in a store on the Sabbath. The representatives to the Electoral College are the only ones never to have voted for a President who subsequently resigned. Any place where more than two streets come together, in any town in the Commonwealth, memorializes someone. Such an intersection, whatever its shape, is referred to as a square.

In Davis Square, Somerville, six streets and the ghost of a railroad track came together in the pattern of a deformed asterisk. The steel rails had been driven underground, to become part of the latest extension of the metropolitan Boston subway system. In Alex Glauberman's youth, this system had been made famous by the Kingston Trio. Only four stops away, in fact, lay the very Kendall Square Station where poor old Charlie had, in all innocence, handed in his last dime to ride on the MTA.

Times change, however. Scollay Square—where Charlie's wife brought the daily sandwich to the man who never returned—had long since been renamed Government Center. Just now, a minor battle raged over the authorities' move to change the name and image of Kendall Square Station to Cambridge Center/MIT—a semantic skirmish in a larger struggle between residential neighborhoods and the wizards of high-tech. In any event, the subway had come to Davis, and in place of the old railroad track it had brought a quaint, bricked-over park in the off-center hub of the asterisk.

The park was furnished with old-fashioned wooden benches and decorated with life-size statues in out-of-date dress, all of which gave it a certain spooky charm. On one of the benches Alex spotted the man whose package he had mailed. He sat wedged between the two men, younger men, who had surrounded him on the sidewalk. They sat straight up, but the balding man was doubled over, his head dangling limply toward the ground.

Though the square was full, no one except Alex appeared to notice this particular tableau. Alex edged closer, stopping by one of the statues. It was a boy with bat and glove, walking home forever from a summer game. On the other side of the bench, an elderly couple stood frozen for posterity with shopping bags in their arms. Alex latched on to the baseball bat with one hand. He held the receipt from the overseas package crumpled in the other.

The two men's dark plaid suit jackets were buttoned over dark shirts and light ties. If the man in the brown suit might be a professor, or an executive, then these might be contractors, or aldermen. They might own bars, or be lucky playing the dogs or horses. But Alex could not mistake the way the balding man slowly straightened up, from the waist but not the neck, his head still hanging in either pain or shame. He had to be recovering from a rabbit punch, a chop with the edge of a hand, a quick needle in the thigh.

When his head did come up, finally, he stared at Alex. He fixed Alex with his sad, watery eyes, betraying neither recognition nor surprise. All Alex could think of to do was to let the man know that at least his package had gotten off. Alex flashed the receipt, and then it occurred to him that he could also leave it in a post office box, so to speak. The balding man could collect it later if that was the way things worked out. So, as the man watched, Alex stuffed the flimsy paper into the opening where the statue-boy's mitt hung from his bat. The balding man blinked, and then one of the younger men rose, holding him solicitously by the arm. The younger man led him slowly past Alex to the curb where a taxi sat idling. Alex noted the company—Green Cab.

The pair disappeared inside, and the third man climbed into the front seat. The cab jerked its way into the clogged traffic. It drifted past the beauty salon and then the sandwich shop, and then the angle of the buildings caused it to vanish from Alex's view. Alex watched it disappear with a feeling that a curtain was dropping, slowly but inexorably, in front of a play that had hardly begun. He was not going to run after the taxi, nor was he going to sit in the little park breathing exhaust and hoping for one man, and not three, to come back. He did, though, remove the receipt from its hiding place and recopy the addresses onto the back of the envelope holding his letter to Meredith. He thought a moment and then added a short message to the bottom of the receipt: "Petros's Coffee Shop, Central Square. Till seven tonight." Then he wadded the receipt up once more and stuck it back into the crevice between glove and bat.

A note in a bottle, that was what he had just sent. Crossing from the park to the subway station, Alex could not guess whether his note would be read. He could not even be certain that he hadn't, wishfully, read romantic significance into a perfectly ordinary incident. In any case, he was not really sure where in the incident he stood. He still thought of the frightened, balding man with ambivalence. This might well be the sort of odd, lonely creature, the person on the next stool at the bar or beside you on the bus, best left to his or her own devices, to his or her own extrication or demise.

But all these questions were beside the point, because what Alex had just witnessed spoke to him in a voice that he could not deny. The voice said that fate, once he or she beckoned, did not fuck around. The note was for this voice, more than it was for that man.

14

The new subway sometimes pushed Alex to think about mortality. This was because, as Meredith had pointed out to him, four men had died in cave-ins and crane accidents to bring better access and higher property values along its extended route. Unlike Alex, Meredith followed such news unflinchingly.

That was a quick death—a sudden squashing out of life under a careening crane. Quick and shocking. "I'm sorry, your husband/father/son/brother won't be coming home from work today." Not like a cancer. With a cancer, there could be a long time between the shock and the death.

Alex told himself to knock it off. Anyone could die, anytime. Besides, relatively speaking, Alex was one of the lucky ones. Statistics said this. So did the personal grapevine that had materialized like magic when he'd received his diagnosis—so-and-so's Aunt Helen, so-and-so's friend Larry, so-and-so's ex-boss. With proper care, and a good attitude, his number was not likely to come up very soon.

Still, Alex felt different from other people. What made him different was not his knowing that he was going to die. Everyone knew that. It was knowing more fully what was likely to kill him. He not only knew it but, unconsciously massaging the back of his neck, he could feel it.

It was Meredith who had discovered the knot there, during the third night they spent together. She had insisted he get it checked out, and that was how he'd learned he had swollen lymph nodes all over his body. Then it had become her task, as well as his, to wait out the winter and the spring until his tumors got to the point where they required treatment. She'd stayed with him, an anxious onlooker, for his first week of medications and the weeks while his body and his blood supply recovered to the point where they would tolerate going through the cycle of medications again. Then she'd left, at his insistence, to fulfill the half-semester teaching fellowship in London that she'd accepted long before. It was an important academic opportunity and, for her, a free visit home. She would be back to Boston by Thanksgiving. And by turkey time, more or less, Alex should be cooked. By Thanksgiving, he should be as normal as he was ever going to get.

Alex pulled the envelope from his back pocket and smoothed it gently on his knee. Normal, but cheated of the time the beginning of their relationship should have been. They had enjoyed one surprising dinner, the pair of them thrown together by Kim's machinations, warm and soaking up together the glow of hot food and wine after trudging like awkward storks through the icy Cambridge streets. The surprising dinner had continued on into a surprising night and then a bright, sunny day out skiing across the clean, powdery snow on a frozen river not many miles from town. They had shared some talk about books read, places been, past lives followed or abandoned, and (wrinkling noses) marriages walked away from.

Meredith possessed a self-assured, no-nonsense, things-in-their-places outlook that Alex found powerfully attractive, though he had not thought he was in the market. And Alex, Meredith said, was older than she without being terminally stuffy. On the clean, frozen river she had held him by the beard and examined him again. She had declared him to be a rather cockeyed, unexpected sort of a man.

Yes, it had been a nice start, a lovely, no-questions-about-the-future, opening-up couple of weeks. Then she'd come to Alex's apartment, through wet, chilly slush, the evening after his diagnosis. She'd listened as Alex explained just what the pathologist had found on the slide, the wrong kind of cells on a thin but representative slice of Alex's tissue. She'd asked a few technical questions, and hurled a glass ashtray to bits on his new kitchen floor. Much later that night she had asked whether the chemotherapy made men sterile.

"Somewhat," Alex had told her. "The doc pointed out the option of opening an account in a sperm bank for a few hundred bucks, as a precaution. But the effect is generally just temporary." He'd stroked her hair and run his hand all the way down her spine, and up again. He'd rolled away from her, and then snuggled back, and finally said, "Meredith . . ."

"Yes?"

"I've got one kid already, and I won't take bets about getting to her high school graduation. I don't know who's going to pay for her college, but it's not likely to be me.

Also, I'm only just beginning to know who you are. But that was—is—a very nice thought."

"I didn't mean it to be nice," Meredith had said. "I'm just trying to understand what's changed."

Now Alex looked over the words and numbers he had copied from package to postal form, and from postal form to his letter to her. The balding man's writing had been fine and precise. Alex's was more like a monkey's scrawl. "Sender: G. Meyer, 91 Old Mill Circle, Melrose, MA 02176. Recipient: C. Meyer, Gasthaus am Mockernstrasse. 58 Mockernstrasse, West Berlin 61." Wife, brother, daughter, son? He wondered what Meredith would have to say about this man G. Meyer. Would she have invited him to sit over Greek coffee in small, hand-painted cups to explain what had frightened him, and why? She might have, but only if she could say it to his face. Leaving a note in a bottle, dropping bread crumbs like Hansel and Gretel along the path—these would not have been her parson's-daughter ways. She might have laughed, and Alex liked making her laugh, but Alex did not want to be laughed at just now.

The thing was, Berlin fit. Berlin was redolent of decadence, iniquity, intrigue. It made some sense of G. Meyer's half-concealed desperation, his need to get rid of that package right away. Berlin meant hard-edged syllables, postcard images of new neon jungle and the old Brandenburg Gate. Shadowy, trench-coated figures crept though back streets and lurked, waiting, beneath a looming Wall.

Alex's ancestors were Russian Jews, not German ones. To his parents, Berlin meant the headquarters of the Holocaust, nothing more or less. But Alex had a curiosity about the Berlin of Bertolt Brecht as well as the one of Adolf Hitler. He indulged a fantasy of himself and Meredith, a tall, bearded Semitic Holmes and a red-haired, not-at-all comic, female Watson. Strolling down a cobbled street, peering and trading guesses as they passed Number 58 Mockernstrasse, wherever that might be.

4

Family Pictures

At Central Square, Cambridge, Alex climbed into the sunlight. He had to end up here anyway if he was meeting Kim, who lived nearby. Petros's, two blocks down the street from where he stood, was simply the place—a place some distance from the scene of the crime—that had popped into his mind to suggest to the man he now thought of as G. Meyer.

It was Friday afternoon, five-thirty. Alex stepped down Mass Ave through a jumble of nurses' whites, students' chinos, assorted T-shirts and jeans, suits male and female, denim vests, colorful tank tops. The staccato of jackhammers punctuated speech in English, Spanish, Creole, and further tongues. At Petros's, about half the dozen tables were filled. Regulars argued in Greek over papers from home, spread out between them. Young, rising professionals networked busily over coffee or tea. Alex claimed the sole no-smoking table— an unhealthy contradiction in terms—and waited for the man who most likely would not come.

Alex was good at waiting. He figured that he'd inherited his mother's mouth and his father's patience. The mouth came in handy very often, but he valued the patience more. Possibly that was because his mother drank too much, while his father did not. On the other hand, Meredith told him it was because boys worked at being like their fathers, while they took after their mothers without knowing it. He asked the waitress behind the counter for tea and spinach pie.

They served excellent coffee at Petros's, but coffee of any sort was not something his insides could tolerate this week. That was the cyclophosphamide; it chewed up his stomach lining because it couldn't tell one kind of rapidly dividing cell from another. It chewed up the nascent blood cells of the bone marrow for the same reason.

When his food was served, Alex took the teabag out of the pot right away. He chewed and swallowed his pie, but as the dope wore off, the food did not sit very well. The wheeze of the ineffective air conditioner irritated him, and the circling of the ceiling fans did not help. He nursed his cup of weak tea and waited longer. He opened and reread his letter to Meredith, less sure about it now. If he really wasn't going, he ought to call and cancel his reservation, which he had not yet done. He ought to call Kim, anyway, and tell her he had gotten himself tied up till seven. But Alex did not step out to make either of these calls. He waited, in a kind of suspended animation, as if he were playing a game of poker and had called the bluff of a teasing opponent *fate*. Now she would show her hand, and he would see whether there was anything in it or not. Many questions he wanted to ask of fate could not be answered. This one could.

It was getting close to six-thirty when his man walked in. The jacket of the brown suit was gone, and so was the tie. In shirtsleeves, Meyer looked poorer and sadder—like a washed-up accountant, or a pawnshop manager who'd seen too may sad cases in his time. He walked haltingly, as if something hurt at every step. He didn't display broken thumbs or a mouth relieved of teeth, but there was dried blood on his lip and a blotchy red mark on his temple. Yet, when he slumped into the chair opposite Alex, his look of fear or desperation, or whatever it had been, was gone. He pulled back his membranous lips into one of those superior half-smiles, and said, "Good to see you again, young man."

"Good to see you too, Mr. Meyer," Alex replied. The voice speaking was his own, and he was in control of it, but he felt as if he were acting in a different realm. He felt very lucid, and at peace. As if he had stopped time, had willed the yo-yo to hold still at the top of the string. "I wasn't sure you were going to make it."

Meyer looked away quickly, but then looked back and spread his hands philosophically. He picked up the big shaker of sugar, cupped his hands around it, and put it down again. "Oh well, " he said finally. "So often the imagining is worse than the event."

With an obvious effort he stood up again and, still nodding at Alex, crossed to the counter. He turned his back just long enough to place an order. Alex realized that Meyer had been as doubtful about finding him truly waiting as he had been about Meyer showing up. Meyer seemed concerned that Alex might prove to be an illusion, and disappear.

"Very nice place," Meyer said as he sat gingerly back down. "Since you seem to have had dinner, I've ordered us Greek coffee and baklava for dessert. I'm Gerald Meyer, as you guessed. And you are?"

"Alex Glauberman."

"I appreciate the favor you did me, Mr. Glauberman. And I wonder what you intended by inviting me here." This time Meyer wagged a finger at Alex as he spoke. Again Alex noticed brown spots, age spots, standing out on the skin. "I assume a suppressed longing for adventure is what stands behind your note."

"I don't know," Alex said. "When I see something, I like to understand it. I like to take things apart and figure out how they work."

"Indeed," Gerald Meyer said. "Do you mind telling me what you do for a living, then?"

"I fix cars." Alex pulled out his wallet so he could hand Meyer a business card.

"'Blond Beasts,'" Meyer read out loud. "'Northern European Motors Repaired.' Very clever, Mr. Glauberman. Tell me, how much do your patrons normally pay you for your time?"

"Thirty an hour. About what they'd pay a dealer, and half of what they pay their shrinks."

At that rate, Alex made a decent living. The main drawbacks about being a self-employed sole proprietor were the lack of company life insurance, which for his daughter's sake he wished he had, and of a company pension, which these days he didn't expect to need.

"And I noticed you were mailing a letter to London," Meyer said, with the eyebrow next to the bruise on his temple slightly raised. "I take it you have friends there?"

"Mm-hm," Alex said. "Tell me, Mr. Meyer. Why all these questions for me?"

The waitress set down two coffees in small, attractive, rounded cups on matching saucers. She brought two helpings of pastry, and Alex asked for two glasses of water. He noticed that, for the moment, all of his nausea had gone.

"Well, Mr. Glauberman, I'm wondering whether you might be interested in doing one favor more. You see, that package you mailed for me—what I'd like now is to get that package back."

"Get it back?" Alex asked. "Wouldn't it be sent off by now? Property of the Postal Service, mountains of red tape?"

"Oh, even if he were still sitting behind his counter, that officious man wouldn't return my mail. I mean I'd like you to get it from the person to whom it was addressed."

"C. Meyer, Gasthaus am Mockernstrasse, West Berlin?"

"My . . . my eldest daughter." Meyer sipped the scalding coffee, winced, and added, "I'd pay you for your time and your travel, of course. You're self-employed, and you could visit your friends in London on the way back."

It was Alex's turn to raise an eyebrow. Was Meyer serious? And did he read minds? Alex raised both brows and stroked his narrow, hairy chin. "What was in this package?" he asked.

"Pictures, mostly. Pictures of my daughter. A large collection of family pictures, baby pictures. The day she first sat up, her first solid food, that sort of thing. Do you have children, Mr. Glauberman?"

"One."

"Ah." Meyer frowned, which meant that the lines on his

21

forehead changed their pattern. The bruise on his temple seemed to darken. His nostrils flared to give out a little snort. "And a wife?" he asked.

"Divorced."

"Ah." The frown abated. "Well. So am I. Twice, which was enough." Meyer puffed up his throat and recited some lines with mock grandeur, lines that apparently were supposed to demonstrate the point. "'Here I do disclaim all my paternal care,'" he quoted. "'Propinquity and property of blood, and as a stranger to my heart and me hold thee from this forever.'"

"Did you make that up?" Alex asked. Shakespeare, he thought. Meredith would know it.

"No, not I. King Lear spoke it first, to Cordelia. In my case, the result was not immediate tragedy. We just all went our separate ways."

"Gasthaus am Mockernstrasse," Alex said, emphasizing his German pronunciation. "Berlin."

"Exactly. The Gasthaus is a sort of pension that my daughter from my first marriage runs." He narrowed his eyes at Alex's long, narrow face and profuse black hair. "I assume you're Jewish, incidentally."

"Lapsed Jewish, I suppose."

Meyer nodded "Well, in Germany that wouldn't have made any difference. I was there just after the Nazi period, with the Occupation forces. When I came back home, I left a wife and child behind. The wife is dead. The daughter would be about your age."

Something made Meyer's lips twist then, some reflex emotion that he couldn't control. He glanced down into his cup while it lasted, closing his hand into a fist beside his plate. That made the spots stand out sharply on the taut skin. Afterward he drank slowly. When he set the cup down, grains of coffee stuck to the scab forming on his lower lip. He pushed the empty cup aside, poking at the muddy residue with a spoon. Alex took both glasses of water and slid the second coffee across the table. He sliced off a piece of baklava with the edge of his fork.

"You'll have to drink my coffee for me." He pointed apologetically to his stomach. The pastry was too sweet, but he found himself taking another bite right away. During his weeks on drugs, his cravings were apt to be sudden, and odd. Grease and salt, often, and sugar as a result of the marijuana. He generally explained that he had the cravings of a pregnant woman.

"Ulcers?" Meyer inquired. His sparse eyebrows rose skeptically.

"Chemotherapy," Alex said. He watched the man's deep eyes take their time again over his tangled hair and beard. These had not thinned much with either the passing of his thirties or the coming of treatment. That little shine of appreciation was in Meyer's eyes again.

"The treatment's on the light side," Alex explained. "As these things go. My hair's not going to fall out on the table. I do worry about my kid pulling at it, having too much come out in her hands." He felt sorry for Gerald Meyer, and thought someone else's troubles might console him. And besides, he didn't want Meyer to think he was incapacitated. He didn't want anyone to think that.

"I see." Meyer busied his hands centering the second cup in front of him. Alex worked at the baklava, paring off thin sticky slices with the edge of his fork and depositing them automatically in his mouth.

"How well do you know London, Mr. Glauberman?" Meyer asked finally, as if picking up where he had left off.

"Tourist's acquaintance, that's all."

"Well, there is a place called Threadneedle Street, in the City—the financial district, you know. On business days, there's quite a crush. Otherwise I don't think Jack would have recognized me."

"Jack."

"Yes, a man named Jack Mazelli. Or Moselle. He changed it. I don't see what difference it made. We were both posted to Berlin during the Occupation and fell in together at the time. Meyer and Mazelli. Jerry and Jack. Berlin fascinated both of us, if for different reasons. Or the same reasons, God knows. He stayed, though, much longer than I."

"Did he marry a German too?" Alex asked.

"Marry? Jack? Jack never thought of marrying. Jack only fucked. He was a black marketeer, a brilliant one. He

23

didn't waste time on nonessentials, luxuries. Food and building supplies, that was all. It was the perfect market. You had Berliner demand that could never be fully met, and army supply that never failed. Jack's only weakness was a tendency to take sex as payment. But it wasn't just sex. He liked keeping people on a string. I suppose that's why he recognized me. This was many years after Berlin, but quite a few years ago, by the way. We went for drinks, caught up on our lives. He told me he was making deals, the same as always. His empire was rather broader, that's all. In fact he buys quite a high class of friends, today. But he operates on the same old principles. Don't we all, though?"

Alex assumed the question was rhetorical. He couldn't begin to say what principles he was operating on, just now. He couldn't say, either, why Meyer was telling him all this. So he shrugged, while Meyer picked up the second cup and drank. Meyer seemed more comfortable now.

"Very nice coffee," he said. "Well, then he told me he had stayed in touch with my first wife and daughter, which I had not. 'I fixed them up, Jerry,' he said. 'You weren't going to do your duty, Jerry. I thought I should.'"

Imitating Mazelli-Moselle, Meyer assumed a nasal tone and a sneer. That wasn't right, Alex guessed—the effect ought to be smoother, more buttery. Meyer respected Moselle's abilities, clearly, but couldn't relinquish a certain snobbery. Alex wondered how he handled it face to face.

"He told me my daughter had actually lived in the States for a while, but by this time she was back in Berlin. I was divorced again myself. I wasn't much closer to my American daughter than my German one. So I was curious, when Jack picked me up in London, to get some news about Cynthia. . . ."

Meyer's lips twisted once more, again seeming to do it of their own accord.

"Not a very *echt deutscher* name, is it—Cynthia? A bit hard to pronounce, over there. Not *ganz yiddishe*, either, for that matter. Where did I think we were, naming her that? Some damn Walter Scott castle? Anyway, Jack said he kept tabs on her. 'Regular wild oat she is,' he said. 'Quite a bombshell, and practically a commie, too.' He said he'd be happy to keep me posted on her, in the future. 'Now listen, Jerry,' he said. 'Can you do a favor for me?'

"So Jack and I became partners again, in a small way. Since that time Cynthia's settled down a bit, I gather. That's given me a certain settled feeling as well. Recently, though, Jack and I had a, well, a falling out. It looked as if our partnership were dissolving. And Jack, you know, wasn't one to just let matters drop. No more quid, no more quo. And in touch with Cynthia as he was, I expected him to distort a good many things. I decided I'd better strike the first blow, so to speak."

Alex had the distinct feeling that Meyer's story was making less and less sense. "Which was?" he asked.

"When I left Germany, you see, I wasn't intending a final break. Quite the contrary. I was planning, foolishly, on bringing my German wife and daughter home into the bosom of my Jewish family. So, among other things, I brought with me the photos I mentioned and some other mementos. I always thought she might resent my having, shall we say, stolen those moments away with me. Yesterday I gathered the things up and spent a long time deciding what sort of a note to include. Finally I put together some thoughts, some feelings, and sent off the package—today, you understand. But now—I've changed my mind."

Alex did not understand, and he doubted that he was supposed to. However, he saw that Meyer's monologue had come full circle.

"And that's why you want me to help you get it back."

"Why, yes. I'd like you to get there before the package, if you can. And persuade my daughter that it would be better to let you bring the package back to me. Then we can leave our lives as separate as they have been, up until now."

No one can will his life not to change, Alex thought. It doesn't work that way. But Gerald Meyer truly wanted the package, perhaps even enough to send a random Alex Glauberman chasing across an ocean to get it. "You mean," he asked, "you really *do* want to send me to Berlin?"

"That's what I said, isn't it?" Meyer snapped. "Mail won't be moving very fast over the weekend, work incentives being what they are not, these days. Do you think you could arrange to be there by, let me think, Tuesday? I will pay for transportation and expenses plus, let's say, an honorarium for the auto-repair business you'll have to postpone while you're away. I assume you'll agree with me in costing that out at a total of two thousand five hundred? Dollars, that is, not marks or pounds."

Could a person broadcast his fantasies, was that it? Alex thought. Broadcast them to someone who had the right antennae with which to pick them up? Separately, neither would amount to much. Together, like the twin windings of an ignition coil, they could pack a pretty big punch. Meyer's offer still made very little sense, but Alex felt the jolt a spark plug must feel, on the receiving end of those quick ten thousand volts. He attempted, despite this jolt, not to translate it immediately into flame.

"Twenty-five hundred dollars for family pictures, Mr. Meyer? And those guys you left in the taxi with . . ."

"Family matters are not necessarily either simple or peaceful, Mr. Glauberman," said Meyer sharply again. "I've made you an offer. Take it or leave it, as they say."

Okay, thought Alex. Confession time is over. If I ask you more questions, you'll tell me more lies. His thoughts raced until they came to rest on one thing he could do about that. He sliced baklava with the edge of his fork, lifted it, felt the heavy sweetness, and rested his head on his hands for a moment.

"Excuse me," he said afterward. "Could you maybe tell me a little more about this Mazelli? Why does he care whether you send baby pictures back to your daughter?"

"I didn't say he did, Mr. Glauberman. Also, I don't think anyone would benefit by my telling Jack's story out of school. If you'd like to approach him directly, you're free to try it en route. He's the president of an enterprise that he styles Interface, Incorporated. I believe his door in London would be opened by my name."

"Interface," Alex said. "Computers?" But Meyer only shook his head, flared his nostrils again, and blinked his sad eyes. Alex scooped up half the remaining pastry and swallowed it quickly, gagging at its heaviness. Then he let a pained look cross his face, bending over the table again, and pushed the remains of his pastry away.

"Well, Mr. Meyer," he said. "That's all very tempting. But I'm afraid I can't make up my mind right away. You have my card. I'll be working later tonight. Why don't you give me a call there, say between ten and midnight? I'll tell you then what I decide."

"I suppose." Meyer wet his lips and gave Alex another disapproving look. "Would you mind giving me your home number also, just in case?"

Alex was the only Glauberman in the telephone book. His name was a rare one, stemming—so family legend said —from the occupation of a particular ancestor back in Russia. So it could do no harm to tell Meyer what he could so easily find out. Alex shrugged, took out his pen, and began to add his address and phone to the ones on the card. When he got halfway through, he let another pained expression cross his face.

"Excuse me," he said quickly. "But I'm afraid the Greeks haven't got a bathroom for me. Would you mind waiting while I run to the place next door, where they do? I'm very glad to do business with you, Mr. Meyer. It's just that I'd rather not vomit on what's left of your suit."

5

Stuck in His Thumb

The scent of hot Szechuan cuisine made Alex feel almost as faint as he had claimed, but he sprang in two strides to the pay phone, dropped in coins, and dialed Kim. He needed to know more about Gerald Meyer, and this was the only plan that had come to him. Luckily, this week, he was the boss.

"It's Alex," he said. "Look. I can't explain this now, but I'm with a guy. An older guy in a dress shirt, no tie, face is a little banged up. At Petros's. I'm going to hold him there as long as I can. I need for you to follow him."

"*Follow* him?"

"Yeah. I'm not kidding, and I'm not feeling as crazy as I sound. Don't talk to him or anything, just see where he goes, and call me at home as soon as you get a chance. Get here as fast as you can. Let's see. Drive. Double park, keys in the tray. I'll pick it up and drive home. Okay? Kim?"

"Okay, Alex. I guess. Follow him. You bet."

"Thanks. But look—one thing. If you see anybody else following him too, then forget it. Like two slick younger guys—or anybody."

"Yes sir. Call me Girl Friday. No, Officer Friday. Just the facts, ma'am. Into the valley of death rode the six hundred. I'll be there as soon as I can, Alex. I'll see what I can do."

From the phone, Alex could watch the street too. Meyer hadn't left the coffee shop, but if his suspicions were aroused he might soon either split or follow. Alex gambled on the latter. He fled to the bathroom, leaving the door unlocked, and bent over the toilet.

The toilet was clean but stank faintly of disinfectant. Alex visualized hospitals. He visualized a particular hospital. He saw himself waiting for a CAT scan—chipper, knowledgeable, explaining medical facts to the relatives of confused, frightened patients. He remembered a particular patient, an older woman, clasping a hospital cloth to her throat. Her daughter, exasperated, said she was gagging on the dye she had just drunk. But Alex knew that she was gagging on helplessness and fear. If you didn't speak the doctors' language, no one told you shit.

Alex remembered the woman, unreachable, dribbling slowly and ceaselessly into the cloth. He pictured the bitter orange liquid filling her stomach and intestines; the needle in her arm, the cold, ghostly iodine creeping through her veins. For Alex she had represented, in external form, all the fears he had managed to comprehend and to master. Now he pictured her covering her face from the world, as alone as if she were already dead. This time, visualization did the trick. He was in a suitable condition a minute later, bent with his head in the toilet, sweating and retching to beat the band, when Gerald Meyer knocked. Getting no answer, Meyer walked in. Alex did not have to visualize anything anymore. He just let a wave of timeless helplessness wash over.

Behind him, as in the post office, Meyer coughed.

"Excuse me," he said. "I wanted to see whether you needed any help."

The wave broke slowly, and receded. Alex took his time flushing the toilet, spitting, blowing his nose, and flushing again. The tank had not filled, so bits of escaped vomit danced together and apart in the bowl. The smell, he assumed, was in the air as well as in his nostrils. *Stuck in his thumb,* Alex thought, *and pulled out a plum. And said what a good boy am I.* He tottered to the sink, rinsed his mouth, and splashed water on his face.

"No," he said finally. "Really, you wanted to see whether I had run out on you. Let's get out of here before we get busted for indecent acts, okay?"

Alex led the way past diners and waitresses who paid them no mind. Outside, on the sidewalk, he stood leaning weakly against the wall. The air had cooled already, yet the smells of urban evening and auto exhaust were still heavy, almost visible, like a curtain drawn around Gerald Meyer and himself. A green Ford was double-parked halfway down the block, but no blue Rabbit.

"That doesn't happen too often," he apologized. "But it will be over after Sunday. So it wouldn't interfere with my doing that job, if I chose."

Meyer wiped his hands on a handkerchief but seemed otherwise undisturbed. His skin was tinted the palest pink by the illuminated sign proclaiming the Pa-Kua Restaurant. His suspicions, if any, were voiced with a courtly irony.

"No, I wasn't concerned it would interfere. Your condition is singularly disarming, as I assume you are wise enough to know. I paid the bill for our little meal, by the way. So, if you're all right now. . . ."

"Yes," Alex said. "A lot better. I was in the middle of giving you my address. . . ."

Meyer gave him back his card. Alex wiped his hands on his pants and finished what he had begun.

"Ganz gut," he declared, "if that will make you happier. I do speak some German, by the way."

"By the way of Yiddish?" Meyer asked. He did not seem to be in a hurry. Again Alex felt that Meyer wanted to hold him, just as he wanted to hold Meyer.

"No, by way of Kafka. I don't know. By way of Brecht. I studied some German literature, once upon a time. Before I got kicked out of college." Alex shrugged off this past tragedy grandly. "Sixties," he added. "You know. Then there was a German Volkswagen mechanic who taught me my trade. In Nebraska. His name is Hans Heidenfelter, if you'd like a reference. He loved it out there, on the plains. I sort of wanted to love it too, but I guess I was already hooked on cities. I grew up in New York. Did you?"

Meyer nodded but did not speak, while Alex was fast running out of things to say. Just then a tall, striking white woman with short black hair walked past, hesitating on the corner. She was not in paint-spattered jeans but in black velvet slacks and a black cape that the weather did not require. A little conspicuous, Alex thought, but he forgave her this foible.

"Well," he said heartily. "Call me tonight, Mr. Meyer."

Meyer nodded again and walked past the hesitating woman. He still moved stiffly, but maybe not stiffly enough to be noticed by anyone who hadn't seen him escorted away earlier in the Green Cab. He crossed the side street and kept going. Alex walked the other way, not looking back, until he spotted Kim's Rabbit parked neatly in front of a fire hydrant across the street. He collected the car, turned the radio up loud, and made his way home. He found that, not only from chemical causes for once, he was high as a kite.

Alex's apartment was on the first floor of a regulation North Cambridge two-family house, two stories plus attic. By the time he reached it, he had sobered. From the front porch he could hear his phone ringing, but when he got his key in the lock it stopped. He went into the bathroom to brush the lingering sour taste from his mouth.

The face that looked back from the mirror did not look very much like his image of a disreputable confidential agent. The pouches under the eyes were all right—they might come from strung-out exhaustion and stale coffee and all that. The untrimmed beard, though, the unruly hair, the long nose never broken on the police force or in the ring. . . .

Alex rinsed his mouth once more. So he was out of his depth. So what? The fact remained that this was the kind of story one cherished to tell one's grandchildren—in the unlikely event, for Alex, that he lived to see any. If not he, perhaps Maria could do it. He pictured his daughter, who loved to tell a story. Out of parental generosity, he gave her a fireplace, a rosy face glowing from the flames, a nice pair of breasts beneath a soft sweater with sleeves pushed up over her elbows. He gave her two wide-eyed children and a figure in the shadows that might or might not be a husband.

What story, though? What story would explain why a well-mannered, bloodless, professional sort of man would offer him twenty-five hundred cash for this seemingly pointless errand? Baby pictures or no baby pictures, the package was on its way to the daughter, and it was the daughter's to keep if she didn't want to give it up. Sending Alex after it didn't get it back for Gerald Meyer, or keep it out of the hands of an alleged Jack Moselle or of the two men, unnamed, in the shiny suits. The only story that would explain Gerald Meyer was the story of a man who is sinking, grabbing at any floating object within reach.

When Alex got tired of looking at his face in the mirror, he came back to the living room and dropped into a soft armchair whose cushion was shedding bits of feathers as usual. On the opposite wall, over the couch, hung a few of Kim's paintings: abstract, textured, mostly blues and whites and grays. Just now they seemed a little too . . . vacant. It was one thing to dip his own inquiring toe into the well of Gerald Meyer's affairs, but he wished now that he hadn't pushed Kim in headfirst. He struggled out of the chair and went to the kitchen to answer his empty stomach's craving for grease and salt. He put Tilsit cheese and Genoa salami on the butcherblock section of the counter and sliced himself a tentative piece of each. When those went down okay, he poured himself a glass of milk and sliced some more.

The kitchen cheered him, perhaps because he had redone the room himself. The LaFarges had been happy to give him a rent reduction in return for his labor in putting in the shining wood floor, the counters and cabinets and racks for showing off cookware. There was no doubt the kitchen would enhance the apartment's rental value, or its sale as a condominium someday.

But Alex could have the place as long as he wanted, Anne LaFarge had assured him. She was an admirable landlady, who knew an amazing store of neighborhood babysitters. She had even tolerated the women Alex had allowed to drift in and out of his life in the years since he'd moved in.

She was enthusiastic about the staying power of Meredith—despite the liability of Meredith's being a Brit. Mrs. LaFarge was French Canadian by marriage, and Irish by birth. But she declared that she knew a good woman when she saw one. If Alex didn't get on that plane for London tomorrow night, he knew he would have to bear the unspoken accusation in Anne LaFarge's eye. Afraid to get tied up again, it would say; once bitten, twice shy. Well, whatever Declaration of Independence he was making, if he ran Gerald Meyer's errand, he could keep his London date without compromising his flexibility. See his mate, and leave her too. Saturday Boston, Sunday London, if this is Tuesday it must be Berlin. But, shit, why didn't Kim call?

It didn't seem like Meyer, to be pacing endlessly along the city streets. He ought to come to rest someplace, allowing Kim to phone. Or was it Kim who couldn't stop, because she was pursued rather than pursuer? Was she being asked, right now, to explain her interest in this affair? Or would the phone ring, and a gravelly voice tell him, Okay, Alex, here's what you've got to do now, if you want to get Kim back?

Alex kept slicing, mechanically, and eating, and not-trying not to think. That was the trick of meditation—not trying. This was a meditation on the sound of a telephone not ringing. There were no more rolled joints, and just now he did not feel like rolling one. When he needed something to focus on, he focused on that little refrain: Saturday Boston, Sunday London, Tuesday Berlin. Then would come London again, and Meredith, and then he'd come back home and take care of Maria and have his lumps checked and his blood checked, and then the whole cycle would begin again. And, shit, why *didn't* Kim call?

6

Tell Alex

What rang, finally, was not the phone but the doorbell. Kim flung her purse and cape on the floor and slumped into the chair that was losing its stuffing.

"You owe me thirty-three dollars and seventy-eight cents," she told him. "Plus you pay the ticket for parking at a hydrant, if I got one. And that doesn't include compensation for my valuable time and the creeps I had to fend off."

"Creeps?"

"In the bar by United at the airport. Including your friend."

"He spotted you?"

"Uh-huh. Have you got anything to eat? I'm starving."

"There's cheese and salami on the counter. Frozen chicken nuggets in the freezer, Maria's current favorite."

"Shit, Alex, don't you believe in vegetables?" Kim stretched her long legs before heading into the kitchen to forage. When she came back and settled her full plate on her lap, she demanded, "So? You first." Alex stood, back against the wall, as he explained. Kim listened, knitting heavy brows

34

and grinding the heel of her leather boot into Alex's old braided rug.

"His name is Gerald Meyer. He went to the post office to mail a package to his abandoned daughter in West Berlin. Two guys appeared from somewhere and scared the shit out of him. I mailed the package—I was in the post office—and arranged to meet him later. Now he wants me to help him get it back. I wanted to know more about Mr. Meyer. Who else would I have called but you? I shouldn't have done it, but I did."

Kim was not above flattery. She and Alex had known each other since college, a small liberal-arts school in the Midwest. In fact, they had left there together, keeping each other company until they reached the Pacific. They'd kept in touch through subsequent changes and crises—his wandering about the country and her coming out of the closet; his putting down roots, not all of which took; her putting in a decade as a high school teacher and now struggling to re-emerge as an artist. She smiled, then caught herself.

"Help him how?"

Alex didn't smile back.

"By going to see the daughter in Berlin, standing under her mailbox, and telling her everything might be better if she stayed abandoned. For that, he's willing to pay two thousand five hundred bucks."

"Uh-huh. Well, report first, questions after. Your Mr. Meyer took the subway to Harvard Square. He showed some hesitation at the entrance. I don't think he knows his way around here, or else he's above the subway. That's a pun, Alex, laugh. He walked into that new hotel. Goddamn, what a place—smallest lobby I ever saw. It's a cross between a basement and a boutique, plus a few gold-plated elevators. Meyer went up in one of the elevators. I sat in one of the few chairs, feeling like everybody in uniform was glaring at me, till he came down again. He had on a new suit and was carrying a briefcase. He got the doorman to put him in a cab to the airport. I got the doorman to put me in a cab, too." She gave Alex a quick, mocking smile. "Same cab," she added.

"Kim!"

Kim tossed her head like a stamping colt. "I'm an amateur at this, you know. What was I s'posed to do? Jump in the next one and say, 'Follow that cab!'? Anyway, don't you know what it's like at Logan on Friday night, Alex? It was arrive in the same cab or good-bye, Johnny. Jerry. Whatever his name is. I thought I'd see what plane he took, or met, and that would be that. When he said he was going to United, I said, 'Me too.'"

Alex slid to the floor, propping his back against the wall under a poster, another gift from Meredith: Greenham Women Everywhere. The poster celebrated resistance to American missiles in Europe.

"I went in first and stood around studying the TV screens, you know. He went past, and headed into the bar, so after a while I did too. He drank pretty steadily. I sipped and fended off creeps, the last one of which was him. He came over to me and sat down, drinking without saying anything, looking in his glass and giving me a pickled eye. Finally he kind of oozed across the table and said, and I quote, 'You're pretty obvious, honey. I suppose Mr. Glauberman fancies himself a detective?' I didn't answer, so he said, 'Get out.'"

"And you got?"

"No, I was cool." Kim drew herself up and looked down her nose in imitation of being cool. "'Want to tell me what you're doing here?' I said. 'Just so I can tell your Mr. Glauberman.'

"'Sure, sure,' he said. 'I'm picking up a lovely lady. Sadly, it's not going to be you. Now go. Not all my friends are gentlemen, if you know what I mean.'

"'Right,' I said. I remembered your advice, and I decided my job must be over. Only then he held on to me. He covered my fingers on the table with that cold-fish hand of his. 'Wait,' he said. 'Honor among thieves, if nowhere else. Tell Alex I've got a little riddle for him. Tell Alex I once met the lady in the company of Jay Friedhoff, in Berlin.' So there's your message, Alex. I got my hand back and caught a cab."

"Uh-huh." So, truthfully, Kim had been in danger, Alex thought. And now Meyer was somewhat the wiser, and Alex might be, or might not. "Listen, Kim. How did he seem?"

"Creepy, I told you. He'd had a lot to drink, and he was

kind of woozing over me, so I was trying not to look in his face. He sounded . . . I guess sorry for himself would be the best way to describe it. It's a common tone in the mouths of intoxicated men. He seemed pleased to take that out on me or you."

Kim drifted past Alex toward the kitchen with her plate. He heard her washing the plate and silverware and, from the sound of it, his too. When she came back, she bounced on the balls of her feet as if she wished there were more busywork she could find to keep herself in motion. She stopped bouncing, and now it was the toe of her boot that she worked into the rug.

"What's it all about?" she demanded.

"Do I know? Wait, sit down. He told me a lot of stuff about his life, but along the way he made a point of bringing in a wealthy ex-black-marketeer in London named Jack Moselle. Moselle runs some kind of business empire called Interface. Sounds very eighties, doesn't it? Only the guys who more or less kidnapped Meyer, earlier, seemed to come from this Jack. The only thing I know, really, psychologically, is that Meyer is a man with a habit of changing his mind. The reason he has this abandoned daughter is because he married a German woman. He claims, anyway, that he planned to bring wife and daughter back here, then backed out. He implied that his family here—Jewish—wouldn't tolerate them. The way my mother hit the roof when I told her I was fixing Volkswagens, only more so."

"You ended up working with your hands like your father, Alex. Your mother would have hit the roof if you had been fixing Chevys. Are you asking me what she would say about you getting involved in this?"

Alex stood up, stung, then sat down on the couch under Kim's paintings. "Maybe he's scared off now. If he does call me, maybe I'll just say no. I want you to understand the temptation, though. Suppose some gangsters offered you two thousand to, I don't know, decorate their boardroom with a pornographic mural?"

"If I knew where to find somebody like that, I'd say four thousand and get to work. But painting doesn't have quite the same lure of illicit adventure. This came to you on a platter, that's the point, and things that come to you on platters you don't like to pass up."

Kim stopped there, pressing her lips together as if she'd said enough but wanted Alex to know she could say more. She bent to pick up her purse and cape, slung them both over her shoulder as she stood. She paused and looked at Alex on her way to the door.

"Spit it out," he said. Kim worked her boot into the rug some more.

"It's terminal behavior, Alex, to get mixed up in something like this."

Alex nodded knowingly. That was an accusation he'd learned how to handle. "Look," he said in his most reasonable tone. "It's not so unlike me to explore it a little. Right now, I don't even know what I'm getting mixed up *in*. So I mess around. I try this, I try that. I see what makes it work."

Alex remembered explaining himself in almost the same words to Meyer, when Meyer had told him he must be looking for adventure.

"What does that have to do with what I just said?" Kim demanded.

Alex shrugged. "Terminal is just being yourself," he said. "Only more so."

"Oh shit, Alex." Kim scowled and kicked viciously at the rug. She examined the rip she had made, then bent to smooth it out. "Okay, what the hell else am I supposed to say to you? How did my car sound, anyway?"

"Valves are a trifle noisy, that's all. Listen, thanks a lot for what you did, following him. I couldn't have done it half as well. Can you drop me at my car, on your way home? I left it by the post office."

"When is old fishy Meyer supposed to call?"

"Tonight. I told him I'd be working, finishing up. Listen. I've got Maria in the morning—we're going to the country with Bernie and his kids. I'll call you in the afternoon, okay? One way or the other, will you promise to let me tell Meredith about this in my own way?"

Kim glanced toward Meredith's poster, hanging between

a pair of stereo speakers. She seemed to be asking Meredith to speak.

"I will expect you to do just that, Alex," she said finally. She frowned. "And how about locking the door to your shop while you work?"

7

Without Warning

Kim dropped Alex at his car just before nine. Alex drove thoughtfully down Somerville Avenue and parked just before Union Square. If Meyer lived a short commute away, in Melrose, he wondered, why was he staying in an expensive Harvard Square hotel? There was a North Suburban directory in his shop. The first thing he would do was to look Meyer up.

Freddy's Liquors, next door to Alex's shop, was doing the regular Friday-night party business. Alex stuck in his head to keep up good relations with Freddy, who was watching the ball game on his little nine-inch TV. The Sox were two runs behind Toronto, Freddy said. What else was new?

Inside the shop, nothing was: old furniture, old parts, old clothes, old tools. The front of the Volvo still rested a few feet off the ground. Minus its grille, radiator, fan, water pump, and gear cover, it looked like a patient sliced open and ready to have his or her guts fixed. Alex knelt in front of the exposed ends of the engine shafts, methodically screwing the three arms of the puller into the threaded holes of the upper gear. Then he twisted the center rod of the puller with a Vise-Grip so it pressed against the camshaft end. Like a cork from a bottle, the gear slid slowly toward him.

Alex found an inexorable, simple-laws-of-physics assurance in this. He examined the broken fiber tooth. Volvo used fiber rather than steel to cut down on noise. It was a wonder this didn't happen more often. He got out a smaller puller and repeated the process on the steel-toothed crankshaft gear. Then he slid and bolted the new set nice and tightly into place. He replaced all the parts he had removed, and finally slid down under the front end of the car to tighten up the oil pan. Head resting on the cushioned end of the creeper, he tightened the last bolts, wondering where Meyer and his dollars might be now. While he lay there, the nightly prednisone rush came. Alex didn't know why the three steroids he took first thing in the morning always hit him this way, at ten at night. But he'd been through it enough by now to know that they would.

The rush came on greased, silent wheels with an acceleration like lightning. Alex slid out from under the car and quickly let down the front end. The pure fact was that, effects on his schedule aside, he loved this part of the drug. The onset of the effect was, like most drug rushes, a time not only of excitement but of confidence and internal power. There was a down side to come, a few days hence, but for now Alex looked neither forward nor back. He checked the exhaust hose, started the car, and let the rhythm of the engine carry him along. Good as new, it sounded. He turned the key, punched the clock, made out the bill, and headed for the shower. The phone jangled, stopping him in his tracks. Meyer. The clock said ten minutes past eleven.

"Alex Glauberman?" It was a male voice, muffled. "This is Meyer. You forget all about what I told you today. Just forget it, you hear?" Then the phone clicked dead.

Alex stood still, listening for any more sound, but the phone yielded nothing more. He couldn't say for sure whether the voice on the phone had belonged to Gerald Meyer or not. He'd forgotten to look up Meyer in the book, but now he thumbed through the pages, leaving dark grease spots all over the Ms. There was no Gerald Meyer listed in Melrose, or in

Malden (where more Jews lived), or in any of the surrounding towns.

Being told what to remember and what to forget always rubbed Alex the wrong way. Just now, flying and knowing that his night was young, it rubbed him very wrong. He decided to go pay a scouting call, what could that hurt, to the return address that was supposed to belong to Meyer. In the shower, with warm, heavy rain falling all around him, he decided to call on the neighbors, delivering flowers.

The night air was comfortable and auspicious, but if there were florists open at eleven o'clock between Somerville and Melrose, Alex didn't know where to find them. He left the client's car, with bill, on the street as promised. He locked up securely, and drove his own car to the all-night supermarket on Winter Hill. There he bought a nondescript $7.50 house plant and a roll of green ribbon. He tied the ribbon around the wide part of the pot with a big bow and followed the thinning traffic down the hill past the housing project and up onto I-93. A few minutes later he pulled off the interstate at the exit that led past the Metropolitan District Commission Zoo. Alex had been to the zoo often, but he'd rarely explored the bedroom communities nearby. Now he saw himself padding quiet suburban streets with the restless, implacable prowl of the big Siberian tiger. He hoped the tiger wouldn't, opening his mouth, sound too much like the Manic Insomniac instead.

A gas-pump attendant directed him to Old Mill Circle, which turned out to be three sides of a square. Cruising slowly, Alex picked out a few small, old cottages among the newer, larger homes. Maybe there had once been a mill here, when the town had really been a town. Some houses were dark, but most still showed lights behind curtained windows. It was a family neighborhood, not a place for lonely, twice-divorced old men.

The lots were of a medium size, with grassy lawns and straight walks from front door to street. Number 91 was written out in wrought-iron script by the door of a two-story home with yellow aluminum siding. No watchers slouched in parked cars outside. Except in the blacktopped driveways, Old Mill Circle contained no parked cars at all.

The second time around, Alex parked in front of a brick house with its porch light extinguished, across the street from number 91. He wasn't sure he wanted to barge in on Gerald Meyer tonight, but he did want to know whether Meyer could really be found behind that yellow siding. He hoped that nighttime flower delivery was the sort of part-time, no-benefits job going begging these days. He hoped the people who took it didn't need to wear uniforms, or shave, or have their names printed on their coats. He hoped it was okay for them to drive around in '75 Saabs.

There was no name on the door of the brick house either. When he rang the bell, Alex got a quick response and a suspicious look from a man about his own age. The man had disheveled red hair receding from his temples.

"Olympia Florists," Alex recited officiously through the screen door. "Sorry to disturb you so late, but I've got a real rush delivery here. Gift for Mrs. Meyer, if you'd care to sign for it."

"No Meyer here, Mac," the man said.

Alex consulted his clipboard full of car-repair orders.

"Mrs. Gerald Meyer, 91 Old Mill Circle," he said in a brusque, confident tone.

"This is 94."

"Oh, well, my mistake, then, sir. I couldn't make out your number from the street. Sorry. Can you do me a favor and show me the Meyer house?"

"That's 91 across the street, Mac. All the odd numbers are on that side. If you've got a delivery for number 91, talk to them about it. Otherwise, you ought to call it a night before somebody calls the cops."

"Yessir. Thank you."

Alex marched across the street and up the opposite walk. There was a welcome mat on the concrete stoop, a Melrose Soccer League sticker in the window, but no name under the bell. Alex rang once, took a deep breath, and rang again. At length the inner door opened and a small, dark-haired woman in a deep purple bathrobe appeared. She was a lot younger than Gerald Meyer. She made a point of checking the lock on the screen door, to make sure it couldn't be opened from the outside. Her plump lips pursed in an angry way.

"Olympia Florists," Alex declared. "Gift for you, if this is 91."

"Gift? What are you talking about?"

"It's just a plant, ma'am. A house plant. Olympia Florists."

"It looks half dead," the woman told him suspiciously. She tightened the belt of her robe and peered sharply at Alex through the screen. Her eyes were large and probing, dark eyes that matched her short, sculpted hair. She had a kind of pixieish good looks, but just now—or maybe always—the severity of her expression took over. "Who's sending me junk like that?" she demanded.

Under her scrutiny, Alex felt like a bad little boy caught out in some trick. He held the plant higher as if to examine it. "Should be a card on it, ma'am." He consulted his clipboard and opened his mouth to ask if this was the Meyer residence. A big man, in sweatpants and T-shirt, appeared next to the small woman in the purple robe. Alex had the feeling he had interrupted them just as they were getting down to Friday-night sex. The man stared ferociously at Alex. He said, "What the hell is this, Joanna?"

"Olympia Florists," Alex maintained. "Plant for Mr. Meyer. Is that you, sir?"

The man said "Nope" and started to add something more. The woman turned toward the man, muttering disgustedly. "Jesus Christ," Alex heard her say, "what assholes they got out tonight!" Then her heel slammed the door shut in his face.

Nothing ventured, nothing gained, Alex rationalized to himself as he let out the clutch and eased the Saab away. So Meyer didn't live at 91 Old Mill Circle, Melrose, MA 02176. Why should he make himself easy to find? The florist charade could make for comic relief in the story that he might tell Maria, and Maria might tell to the grandchildren. Comic relief or a shaggy-dog ending.

After Melrose, Alex's own neighborhood felt a little more alive. A few kids were drinking at the playground, and a siren wailed somewhere in the distance. He turned the corner into his own street and found a space a few doors down from his apartment. He wondered whether anyone would know, or care, that he had not obeyed the instruction to forget all about Gerald Meyer. He climbed the porch steps quietly, but saw no one lurking behind the shingled half-wall. No one crouched down below, among Frank LaFarge's rose bushes, either.

No one sapped him with a blackjack in the entryway. His living room was as he'd left it, his kitchen empty and smelling slightly of garbage. The smell hit him as an affront, like the door that had been closed in his face. He lifted the bag from the trash basket and, feeling foolish but careful, snatched up the magnetized flashlight from the door of the refrigerator to light his way to the bins out back. When he opened the rear door, Antoine, the LaFarges' matted old tiger cat, looked up into the flashlight's beam. The cat's eyes gleamed yellow, with narrow slits of pupils, amid its dark, irregular stripes.

"Hey, Antoine," Alex said softly, squinting as he liked to do to cats. He had read that they interpreted half-shut eyes as a kind of communication. "Hey, Tiger. You staying out all night again? Seen anybody suspicious? I'll let you in on some mighty fine catnip if you can finger a guy name of Meyer for me."

Antoine squinted back and returned to sniffing around the garbage cans. "Well, if you change your mind," Alex began, and then stopped. Behind the cans, toward the driveway, the cat had found something that both attracted and disturbed him. He disappeared to sniff it out and appeared again, backing off, near the LaFarges' Chevy Caprice. He sniffed his way toward it, vanished behind the cans once more. He reappeared close to the porch, squinting questioningly at Alex.

"Strange behavior, old guy," Alex said. "You been at the catnip already?" This time he followed the cat and found a man slumped against the row of rusty cans. The man's knees were drawn up against the chest, and his head was slumped down on the knees. What Alex recognized first were the shoes, like the ones his father wore to funerals.

He knelt down to look at the contorted face, paler than

45

ever in the flashlight beam, staring sightlessly at the ground. Meyer's creeping baldness did not stand out anymore, though it came back to Alex with a shimmering clarity that this, in the post office, had been his first impression: a balding man, impatient to get to the front of the line. Now the skull's hairlessness was masked by congealed blood, and overshadowed by the dark, gaping hole where bone had been punched inward like plaster. Inside the hole, and flecking the sticky blood around it, was a kind of nondescript matter, neither liquid nor solid, that Alex realized with revulsion had to be brains.

Without warning, he added to the mess by throwing up his half-digested cheese and salami. He did manage to miss both the cat and the corpse.

8

A White Rose

Alex went back inside, noted that the time was thirty-six minutes past midnight, and dialed 911 to report that he had found a dead stranger in the driveway. Then he rinsed his mouth, blew his nose, and dug a pair of winter gloves from the bottom drawer of his bureau. He pulled the wool liners out of the leather. He wanted another look, but he did not want to take the chance of leaving his fingerprints behind.

Kneeling in the dark amid the smell of garbage and vomit, Alex trained his light on the man's brown suit jacket. He tried to fight off the compulsion to take another close look at the mystery of death, but could not. This time the hole and the brains did not come as so much of a shock. Alex recoiled not from the gore but from the fact that this leak, this blown seal, this injured part had suddenly, perhaps even instantly, caused the whole machine to stop functioning—for good.

The back pants pockets were jammed under the dead man's rear. Alex let them alone. He searched the jacket pockets, inside and outside, and the front pockets of the pants. All were empty. Someone had done this searching before.

Alex played his light around the ground near the body, but found nothing. He wished he hadn't called the police right away. He needed to figure out how he would explain this. The best explanation would be the closest to the truth. He picked up the bag of garbage from the back porch, climbed down the three steps again, and pulled the big aluminum can toward him as he would normally do. Meyer toppled over backward and to the side, still folded up.

Now Alex wormed his hands into the back pockets, expecting an icy-cold sensation even through the gloves. There was no icy cold, and no wallet—just a feeling of invasion, of being where he shouldn't be. He wondered what people felt like who rolled drunks.

Immobile, Meyer seemed heavier and more solid than he had as an active being. Had he been forced into this compact position before being shot, or had he been arranged this way after?

No sirens sounded yet. Alex made one last circuit around the body with the light, but found nothing more. He was in the kitchen, putting a flame under the kettle, when his doorbell chimed.

The cop sported a broad, sandy mustache on his open, pink face. He seemed very young. He'd left the cruiser double-parked, light still circling. "You Mr. Glauberman?" he wanted to know.

"Yes."

"You the property owner?"

"No, Mr. and Mrs. Francis LaFarge, upstairs. That's their door, right there."

"Okay," he told Alex, "let's go see what you found."

Alex stepped outside, led the cop down the driveway to Meyer's remains. Antoine reappeared but ducked under the car. The policeman shined his own flashlight, touched Meyer's lips, looked at the puddle of vomit.

"That was me," Alex said.

"Yeah," the cop said. "Bullet to the brain. It's ugly. Can we bring the owners downstairs to your place?"

"Sure," Alex said. "Come in, Officer. . . ."

"No, I got to radio. Someone will be along to take care of you in a couple minutes."

Alex brewed himself a cup of weak tea while the patrolman went back to his car. It didn't take long for another cruiser and an ambulance to arrive, sirens blaring. After a few minutes the young cop came back with a shorter, older one in plain clothes. The new one had a thin, combative face and a black mustache that angled sharply down from his nose on each side. It was sort of a Billy Martin face, Alex thought. The young one said, "This is Sergeant Trevisone." Trevisone came in, while the other one rang the LaFarges' bell.

Alex showed Trevisone to the living room, invited him to take the stuffed chair. Trevisone turned toward the couch instead, as if this was something he'd been taught in Questioning 101: never take the seat that's offered, keep them off their guard. His eyes took in Kim's paintings, above the couch, before he sat down.

"Anybody else in your apartment besides you?"

"No." Alex stayed on his feet, expecting Frank and Anne. Anyway, he was too jumpy to sit. "I mean, I have a daughter, but usually she's here only half the week. And this week she's been with her mother the whole time."

"No girlfriend?"

Alex shook his head. "She's away for three months, working, and she doesn't live here when she's not. Would you like me to make some coffee or tea for everyone?"

Trevisone shook his head, looking around the room without comment. He took in the stereo system, the antinuke poster, and the worn rug. On the wall opposite him, on either side of the chair he'd turned down, were a full bookcase and a set of mounted photographs. Alex had the feeling the sergeant was cataloging the book titles and committing the photos to memory, one by one.

A lot of cops lived in the neighborhood, and Alex knew some of them to say hello to. But no police had ever been in this apartment before. For the first time Alex wondered about the wisdom of putting his life on display. He felt the pictures behind him, travelogues of his own journeys. His parents posed in front of the elephants at the Bronx Zoo. Hans Heidenfelter towing a wreck out of the Platte River. Alex himself in full hippie regalia, under arrest in the Nation's Capital, chatting with a crewcut national guardsman about when they might both get to go home. Maria dressed as Rosa Parks for a school play—eyebrow pencil all over her face, peering out the front window of a refrigerator-packing-box bus labeled "Montgomery, ALA." Meredith and Maria, backs to the camera, feet in the Atlantic, looking east from Cape Cod. Bernie in a three-piece suit, caught at lunch hour on State Street. Bernie and Alex, on the ski slopes at Wildcat. The pictures that weren't there were of Alex and Gerald Meyer: in the post office, in the little park, in the coffee shop, on the street outside. No photos, but witnesses to these meetings there would probably be.

Trevisone sat and watched until the uniformed cop ushered the LaFarges in. "Thanks, Al," the sergeant said. Al left again, presumably to help with sizing up and removing the corpse. Alex offered Anne the armchair and sat himself cross-legged on the rug. The sergeant invited her husband to take the other end of the couch. He balanced a small notepad on his knee, clicking a blue ballpoint a few times.

"What happened?" he said.

A simple question. If Alex told the truth, his part in all this would be over. Alex felt the skin of his own fingers crawl as he remembered Meyer's fingers trembling on the package, remembered shaking Meyer's more confident hand. But he wasn't ready to hand this thing over—not now, not yet.

"I was working late at my shop, till about midnight." Alex got up to offer another of his business cards. "I came home, went to the back to put out a bag of garbage. When I moved the can, he, uh, fell over into sight."

"You always put out your rubbish at midnight?"

Alex shrugged and sat down. He folded his legs again. "Sometimes. It was kind of smelly after the night air. . . ."

"Okay, never mind. What time was that?"

"Just before I called. I was here for dinner, say from six-thirty to about nine, but I didn't hear anything then. I went out the front door. I park my car on the street. He might have been here already, or not."

"And you haven't got any idea who the guy is?"

Alex shook his head piously.

"Never saw him before, around the neighborhood, on the T, nothing like that?"

Alex shrugged. "I don't think so. Didn't you find any ID?"

Trevisone looked through him and then turned to Anne, and then to Frank.

"How about you folks, did you hear anything?"

They hadn't. Frank had brought home a videocassette, and they'd watched it till eleven, watched the eleven o'clock news, and then gone to bed. If they'd noticed Kim's arrival, they didn't mention it. Trevisone took down names and occupations and other details, while the first cruiser and the ambulance left. Another cop came in and checked out the walls, photos included.

"I'm afraid I've got to ask you two to take a look," Trevisone said to the LaFarges. They went out with the third cop, came back looking shaken and puzzled.

"Okay," Trevisone said. "That's it. I could, probably might, have more questions when we find out who he is. Any of you planning to go out of town or anything?"

Mrs. LaFarge glanced quickly at Alex and then away. Alex coughed.

"Actually, I have plane tickets to London tomorrow night, I'm afraid." He shrugged in an embarrassed, self-effacing way. "It's my vacation, Sergeant. It would be awfully difficult, really, for me to rearrange."

Trevisone looked again at the British antinuke poster, but he smiled for the first time.

"Your bonnie lies over the ocean, huh? How long a vacation?"

"Two weeks," said Alex, holding up that many fingers together, like a Cub Scout.

"Well, look, I don't promise, but that ought to be okay. Come down to the station to give a deposition, tomorrow at . . . let's make it four."

"Okay," Alex said. "Thanks."

Tenant, landlord, and landlady engaged in the necessary headshaking.

"Mugger or the mob," Frank LaFarge insisted. He was a short, stocky, friendly man with a pleasant hint of a Quebecois accent. "Either way, why did they have to pick my backyard?"

"It's odd, though." Behind that deceptive, middle-aged angel face, Anne LaFarge was quick and logical. "Somebody like that, wandering around our neighborhood. Maybe he has a kid like you, Alex, renting an apartment around here."

"A kid like me, with forty breathing down his neck?"

"Well, a student, maybe."

"Maybe he got put here at random," Alex insisted. "I wonder what time it happened, though."

"We were up with the TV on all night. We were up there watching, and here was this man getting murdered right below."

"Yeah," said Alex. He shook his head, stood to indicate that it was time to wrap up the wrap-up. "You going to tell Donna about this? She used to love a good murder."

"She can have them in the movies," Anne said on the way to the door. Their youngest daughter had gone off to U. Mass. in Amherst two weeks before.

"It's a good thing none of us saw it happening," she concluded. "For us. Not for him."

When they had gone, Alex plucked an atlas from the bookcase and tried to calculate the time difference between Boston and Berlin. Ninety degrees of longitude equaled a quarter of the way around the world. Six hours later, then, or almost 8:00 A.M. He carried the atlas to the kitchen counter, nibbled cautiously at crackers and cheese. He picked up the phone and told the long distance operator he needed to know the number for the Gasthaus am Mockernstrasse in West Berlin, and needed to know how to dial it direct. Scribbling on the margin of the Mercator world, he pushed fourteen digits and listened to the sound of a phone ringing in a blank place. Finally a thin but musical voice said, *"Gasthaus hier."*

"Uh, *moment bitte.*" Alex groped, unprepared, for his German. He felt he was about to toss a penny down an incalculably deep well.

"Ich wünsche mit, um, Fräulein Cynthia Meyer zu sprechen. Bitte. Ich telefonier . . . ich rufe aus die Vereinigten Staaten, aus

Amerika." In the days when Alex had been studying German, no one had taught him how to say *Ms.*

"*Ja, ja,*" the thin voice said. "*Cynthia kommt in eine Stunde zurück.*" Meyer had been right about the mess he'd made with his daughter's name. It came out something like Tsin-tia, halfway Chinese. "*Wer ruft?*"

"*Ich heisse Alex Glauberman. Ich bin ein Freund.*" Alex stopped. Was he a friend? Hardly. How the fuck did you say *acquaintance*? "*Ein Gekennte,*" he tried without much hope the word was right. "*Ein Erkentnis ihres Vaters.*"

"*Vater? Sie suchen nach dem Vater?*" The tone, Alex thought, held a measure of hostility overshadowed by surprise.

"*Nein, nein. Ich bin, ich habe einen*—shit, oh, sorry, I can't say it in German! *Sprechen Sie Englisch?*"

"A bit only. She comes in one hour back, and speaks good English. *Sie heissen Herr Glauberman?* Your telephone number, please."

Alex gave it. "*Danke sehr,*" the voice said noncommittally. "*Bitte,*" Alex replied.

In one hour. If not, he'd call again in the morning, Boston time. At two-thirty, though, he decided the time had come to call Meredith. He pushed another fourteen digits, and prayed in an agnostic but fervent way that he would hear her clipped, warm tones. The man who answered instead identified himself as Mark. Alex felt his heart sink like a torpedoed vessel, all at once.

"She's left to give her seminar at university," Mark said. "It's a morning one. She won't like missing your call, Alex. We've heard so much about you."

For no reason, Alex disliked the man already—a social service bureaucrat, if he remembered Meredith's rundown correctly, married to Meredith's old friend, now seeing her every day in a scene Alex did not know. Well, not for no reason, then. He disliked Mark because he missed Meredith. "Look," he said, "could you tell her I'm coming? Yes, arriving tomorrow morning, at Heathrow, same old ticket, as originally planned. All reports to the contrary are canceled."

"So, that's good news, Alex! I can look forward to meeting you, then?"

"Yeah," said Alex. "Yes. But tell her I'm probably going to do some traveling by myself on the Continent, okay?"

"Yes, of course. *Ciao,* Alex."

"Yes, of course," Alex repeated. *"Ciao."* He drank a little milk, set out his medications for the morning, and shut off the kitchen light. In his bedroom he began tossing clothes into a pile to pack. He took a quick shower, pissing out dead cancer cells and other debris. He took a sleeping pill and got himself horizontal for what was left of the night. The phone rang just as he felt his nerves begin to let go.

"Cynthia Meyer here," said a voice different from the one that had answered his call to Berlin. This voice was fuller and less musical, more businesslike and in-a-hurry. Yet it was a welcoming voice. Perhaps that was a professional trick, Alex thought, that went with the innkeeper's trade. Alex tried to sound professional himself.

"Cynthia. Ms. Meyer. My name is Alex Glauberman and I'm calling from the U.S. I don't know how to explain this, but I was instructed to visit you, by a man who gave his name as Gerald Meyer and said he was your father. To be honest, he hired me to be his representative with you."

To be strictly honest, he had only *offered* to hire Alex. Hiring, as Alex's friend Bernie would no doubt point out in the morning, meant that money exchanged hands.

"Representative?" Her tone grew colder, more correct. "Are you a lawyer, Mr. Glauberman?"

"No, no, not me." Alex sat up and got ready to give the news that it had fallen to him to give. "I'm not a lawyer. I fix cars."

She laughed.

"The world would be better off with fewer cars and also with fewer laws. Why would this father want to pay you to visit me?"

"I don't know. But now he's dead."

"But now he's dead," Cynthia repeated. "Am I supposed to mourn?"

"He was murdered. I feel responsible for carrying out his last wishes, more or less. Also, I'm hoping you might be able to explain some things about his death."

There was a long pause during which Alex tried to picture the woman at the other end, who she was and what she might be doing. He got only a black-and-white image of Marlene Dietrich in some war-ravaged basement. That would be her mother, not her. He substituted a leather-jacketed punk, but realized he had skipped a generation. Gerald Meyer could have been Alex's father—a thought he preferred not to dwell on—and so his daughter would be someone his own age, in fact slightly older. Someone dealing with the fact that if she looked back, her view was blocked by the crest of the hill.

"He was murdered," she said, "and you fix cars. All of this is a little hard to understand. When and where would you like to meet?"

"I'm arriving in London Sunday, but, um, I'd rather not leave there right away. Would it be convenient to see you any day during the week?"

"I'm traveling too, as it turns out, so I won't be available immediately myself. Hm. But that means I could meet you en route, somewhere. Suppose we find each other on the Ost-West Express, Tuesday night's train. I'll be boarding in Hannover."

"Hannover?"

"Look on a map, Mr. Glauberman. It's the last major city before the DDR, the East German border. I will carry. . . ." She laughed again, a more pronounced laugh that was both mocking and amused. "I will carry, for sign and countersign, a white rose. And you?"

"A bewildered look. A black beard and a hook nose. I don't know. I'll be coming from England, like I said. Is there something I can get you there?"

"A record of reggae music? I leave the choice to you. We meet, let me look, it is actually Wednesday morning, about three A.M. If you take the boat-train from London on Tuesday, you will pick up the Express in Aachen. You will see— it's done all the time. Like the murder of one's long-lost father. I don't know what to make of you, Mr. Glauberman. But I do appreciate your call."

"One more thing," Alex said.

"O, ja?"

"Depending on when you leave, you might receive a

package in the mail first, from Gerald Meyer. It was his strong request that you shouldn't open it until we've had a chance to talk."

"Really? Well, perhaps. I will see you when I have said, by Hannover. Get yourself a ticket through to Berlin."

"Right," said Alex. He sank back onto the mattress, and set his alarm for ten. He wondered how much it cost to buy a ticket on the Ost-West Express from London to Berlin.

9

You Pick 'Em

This time the electronic beeping dragged Alex, hand over hand, out of a deep and dreamless place. It was ten, Saturday morning. He was due to pick up Maria in an hour.

Alex wolfed down prednisone and orange juice, starting two eggs frying and whole wheat bread toasting. While breakfast cooked, he finished packing. When he was done, the toast had popped and grown cold. The eggs weren't bad, if a little crispy around the edges. Burned-over animal fats probably contained more than one form of carcinogen, but they did not stack up as something to worry about just now.

By the time he had mopped up the last of the eggs with the last crust of the toast, Alex had considered and rejected the idea of telling all to Sergeant Trevisone. Aside from how it would feel, there was the fact that, if he did, Trevisone would never allow him to make his plane.

Clear on that point, he fished his dope supply out from the box of crackers where he'd stashed it after dialing 911 the night before. He rolled a fresh joint, smoked half, and again laid out the thirteen chalk-white pills totaling 650 milligrams of cyclophosphamide. This was his fourth day out of five. It was possible to take the whole five days' worth in a single intravenous administration, but the reaction was more intense. Anyway, Alex liked to receive his drugs from his own hand.

He swallowed the pills without trouble, cleaned up, showered, and was dressed by the time his doorbell rang. That would be Bernie and Bernie's two children, ready to go apple-picking as Maria and Elizabeth, Bernie's oldest, had decided earlier in the week. The weather forecast called for ten degrees cooler than the day before. It was a perfect day for apple-picking, no doubt about that.

The man at the door wasn't Bernie. He was younger, and dressed in an old-fashioned khaki uniform with a uniform cap—just the sort Alex had wished for when playing Olympia Florist the night before. "Messenger service," he said, consulting his clipboard just as Alex had done. "Glauberman?"

Alex laughed—he couldn't help it—and felt a resilient wholeness ripple through the muscles from his belly to his face. He signed and was given a manila envelope, nine-by-twelve, that bulged slightly. The messenger got back in his van and sped off. Alex shut the door and opened his present. Inside the envelope were two rubber-banded bundles, each wrapped in white writing paper, labeled simply **ALEX**. He unwrapped one bundle and thumbed quickly through twenty-five likenesses of Ulysses S. Grant. Some were crisp, others worn. Behind the two bundles rested a brief handwritten note. The writing came in a neat, precise hand he recognized from the day before. *Dear Alex,* it said. *Here is your fee. Best of luck. G.M.*

Alex rewrapped the bills and re-closed the envelope in a careful way that came naturally to a man who took things apart and put them back together. He finished just as Bernie's new BMW did indeed drive up. He stuffed the envelope in his carry-on bag, and threw bag and suitcase into Bernie's trunk.

Elizabeth, Bernie's daughter, was Maria's best friend. Bernie's son, Matthew, was three years younger than the girls. They were all going to swoop up Maria for the expedition, and drop her back at her mother's afterward. She would stay there through Alex's two-week vacation and then his next week of drugs. After that, Maria was supposed to return to her accustomed schedule, splitting the time between her two homes.

Alex chatted with the kids until they pulled up in front of Laura's house near Fresh Pond—not far away, but both literally and figuratively on the better side of the tracks. Maria was ready to go, in blue jeans and sneakers plus her new red, purple, and blue vest. She ran to the car to conspire, leaving Alex the customary minute to deal in logistics with his ex-wife on the porch.

"She's in good shape," Laura said. "She's been nicer than usual with Sarah, even found her blanket for her. What time do you think you'll be back?"

Sarah was the baby—toddler, actually, by now—Laura and her new husband's kid. The new husband was a software designer and in general an intelligent, reasonable man. Two seaworthy, even-keeled, unadventurous craft, Alex thought, joining together for a voyage when they were old enough to know that about themselves. If that was so, he couldn't ask for a better conveyance for his daughter. Still, it always surprised and saddened him to be reminded how little he and Laura could find to say.

"My flight's not till eight, but I've got to be somewhere by four. So suppose we get back around three?"

"I guess so. Are you going anyplace besides England?"

She meant, Alex suspected, *Are you going back to Paris?* That was where Maria had quite probably been conceived.

"Germany, I think. I've got somebody to visit in Berlin."

"Oh. Berlin should be . . . interesting."

"I guess so." He tried to be businesslike, but thought he succeeded only in being brusque. "So we'll be back at three. The medical report is generally sunny with patches of fog. Tomorrow in London is the last day of this round. I'll call in the next few days, to tell her myself that I've finished the pills and stuff."

"Okay, Alex. Take care."

"You too."

Bernie already had the three kids belted in the backseat, but he left it to Alex to keep up running banter and guessing games for the half-hour drive to the you-pick-'em orchard. The cooler day and distance from the city made everything suddenly feel like fall. Air and fruit were bright and crisp. Alex organized the girls to clamber among the branches and toss the reddest apples down to Matt; then he started to tell Bernie about the post office and everything that followed, but Bernie interrupted.

"Is this because you're chasing death, Alex, or are you finally getting tired of the shop?"

Uh-oh, Alex thought. "Kim called you?"

"Of course. We care about your health, not just your disease."

Of course was not exactly right. Kim and Alex were kindred spirits, which accounted for the length and depth of their friendship. Bernie was much more a case of the attraction of opposites. He was a lawyer downtown now, and Kim considered him a stuffed shirt. He'd grown richer and fatter since he and Alex had met, but the two men had grown ever closer. Alex didn't know who he'd talk to if he didn't have Bernie, and vice versa. For Bernie and Kim to line up against him was unusual.

"When did she call you?"

"Last night."

"And?"

"I called a few people about the names you gave her. Jack Moselle is well enough known. Interface is a sizable asset-management firm. That shows you how little he has to fear from anyone, much less a walking drugstore of a nobody like you."

"What do you mean?"

"Alex, how did we meet?"

When Bernie was in his Socratic mode, there was no hurrying him up. Alex yelled praises at Matthew to keep him from rebelling against the division of labor, whether on the basis of age or gender. It was fun being in charge of a little boy occasionally.

"You got me off without a finding when that park ranger didn't like me smoking hash at Plum Island."

"Thank you. And, in general, how do criminal lawyers make at least, say, half of their living?"

"You mean, defending people like me who are guilty as charged?"

"Right. Guilty of being involved, in one way or another, with one of the largest sectors of modern commerce—the world of illegal businesses, less accurately known as organized crime. Drugs are its most popular product, but far from the only one."

"So?"

"So this sector doesn't just need and hire slews of lawyers. It needs all the services that any other business contracts for, and more, and specialized ones."

Matthew experimented with throwing apples back up at Maria, and Alex saw Elizabeth drawing a bead on him in response. He swooped in, scooped the boy up, and lifted him to a low, solid branch.

"Matt's turn to climb. Elizabeth to tally person."

"To what, Alex?" Maria demanded.

"Tally person. Keep track that everybody's picking fast enough. If not, they don't get paid."

"Paid what?"

"Whatever I'm bringing back across the ocean for them."

Alex ducked back out from the tree. Bernie put a hand on his elbow to hold him still.

"Look, schmuck, the point is that these sectors don't exist in isolation. Money, supplies, personnel, credit, political influence, you name it—they all have to flow back and forth. Somebody has to be the link."

"The interface," Alex translated. "You mean this Jack Moselle launders money?"

Bernie scowled. "Launders money, maybe, and dirties clean money that wants a good return, and introduces people that need to be introduced, and suggests the shadiest trial judges and the most discreet shipping firms, contributes to political campaigns, prepares analyses for potential investors. . . ."

"You're telling me Jack Moselle sits way up high in a bank building in London and does all that?"

"How should I know? I'm telling you that all those functions must get done by somebody. He's the honcho of Interface, and the people I talked to said that both he and it have popped up in scandals connected to racketeering. And I asked one guy, who ought to know, if he would screw around in those waters without a damn good navigation chart. He said not unless he was planning a trip to Davy Jones's locker. So don't do it, Alex."

"Yeah," Alex said, his eyes on a squashed, discolored apple rotting its way back into the earth. "Well, guess what? Meyer got that trip, sometime between nine and one last night. Somebody called me at my shop and told me to forget all about him. His corpse ended up outside my back door, for me to find. So listen. After we drop Maria, I'd like a ride to the police station. I have to make a statement there, to a Sergeant Trevisone. I'm not going to volunteer any of this information if I can help it. I think I'm safer, and everybody connected to me is safer, if I'm out of here while everything sorts itself out. Once I'm in the air, you can go to the cops, or Kim can, anytime either of you feel it's necessary. But not till I can look down at the icy North Atlantic. No way, José."

Reaching up for a live, growing apple, Alex tossed it in a lazy arc toward Maria's section of the tree. He yelled, "Bernie, cut that out." Then he dashed thirty feet into the lane between the trees and began slinging fallen apples at his friend and would-be keeper. Bernie, his face red, unleashed a vicious pitch at Alex's head, which Alex ducked, and another, at Alex's crotch, which Alex turned his ass into. "Ow, shit," he cried. "Hey, girls, I need reinforcements."

Soon he had Maria and Elizabeth in his corner, while Matthew worked his own way out of the branches and dashed in and out from behind them, dodging and throwing. When Bernie's anger had cooled, Alex declared a truce. He took Maria's hand in his and led her off to check out the rest of the orchard. Under a Yellow Delicious tree he rubbed toxins off the skin of a pale apple and sat his daughter on his lap, facing him, for a farewell address. The nausea crept up for the first time in the day. He bit into the first apple, handed it over for Maria to bite, and talked while he chewed. The sweet juice didn't calm him, but it gave the nausea a more interesting edge.

"So listen, kiddo. When you wake up tomorrow, I'll be in England."

"I know that." Maria looked the apple over until she found a satisfactory place to bite. "You'll be with Meredith. Is she really going to take you to meet her father?"

"I guess."

"Meredith's father is a minister. Are you going to meet him in his church? Some of those old churches in Europe have people buried under the floor. And they've got dark corners that are good for people to meet, in secret."

Maria had reached the age where, especially seeing her only half the time, Alex could not keep up with what she was reading. He wished he knew what ideas about crypts and dark places were bouncing around in her head.

"He's retired. I just hope he likes me okay, and doesn't give Meredith a hard time. Are you mad that I'm not taking you?"

"Well, not mad exactly. But I'm jealous that you're getting to go and I'm not. If Meredith keeps getting work in England, then you ought to go again, and take me." She handed the apple back, and watched her father take a bite. "Will you get blood taken in London?" she said sternly. "You always get your blood taken after you finish your drugs."

"I can get blood tests anywhere. Tomorrow is the last day of the medicine for two weeks, at least. I won't take any more till I get back." Alex paused, worrying about the unwashed skin of the apple. He took another bite anyway, and added, "So I'll feel pretty regular during my trip."

"I want an excellent wool sweater," Maria declared, cutting off further discussion just as she'd brought it up. "I want some punk posters, too, even though I don't exactly know what it is. I mean, would you call Madonna punk?"

"Soft punk, maybe. Tell you what, I'll do the best I can. And I'll call you, too, at your mom's. And I'm going to miss you while I'm gone."

Maria took back the apple, studied the inside, and said nothing. She could plunge deeply into stoic silence when it suited her.

"You'll owe me a lot of help with homework," she told him. "And you better get Mrs. LaFarge or somebody to water my avocado."

Alex agreed and rose up with an effort, lifting her to a branch from which she could collect a few more apples. He told himself that, at any rate, he was a better father than the late Gerald Meyer. Even if he was being a pigheaded or foolhardy one.

10

Time to Kill

At Bernie's house, Alex dressed for the police out of his suitcase. He picked one of his few pairs of creased slacks, and his sole corduroy sport jacket. In the car he chatted with Bernie about the Sox. Outside the police station he shook Bernie's hand warmly but formally. He got out, then bent through the window to plant a light kiss on the top of his friend's expensive haircut.

"You're one of a kind," he said.

"You should talk," Bernie told him. "And I mean that both ways."

Sergeant Trevisone and a stenographer took Alex's deposition in a room furnished with an insurance agency calendar, a desk, and two chairs. The only decoration was a sign reading, WILL THE LAST PERSON TO BE LAID OFF PLEASE TURN OUT THE LIGHTS?

Alex answered questions dutifully if not truthfully. The sergeant told him to wait for the statement to be typed, after which he could sign and head for his plane.

"Do you have any idea what the guy was doing in the LaFarges' backyard?" Alex inquired.

Trevisone ran his thumb and forefinger down the two sides of his mustache. He reminded Alex of a whippet, small and lean and fast.

"His name was Meyer and he worked for a New York bank. His pockets were stripped, so we have to consider robbery as a likely motive. He wasn't moved after being shot. Anything else I tell you is strictly off the record, you got that?"

Alex nodded.

"A contact shot in the head is a hell of a way for a robber to panic and commit murder. That's one thing. The other is that Meyer was staying at the hotel under an alias, and paying cash."

"That's interesting," Alex said in a tone he hoped was bemused. "What name did he use?"

"Diebstahl. G. Diebstahl. That mean anything to you?"

It did, in a way.

"Yes, actually," Alex said. "Not personally, but—"

"But?"

"It's a German word, that's all. Thief-steal, literally. Larceny, maybe. And maybe *G* for *gross*—big, grand. Grand larceny."

Trevisone stroked his mustache again and got up from the edge of his desk. He looked curious.

"You're German, Mr. Glauberman? I thought . . ."

"No, you were right the first time." Alex smiled. "My name is Yiddish, more or less. I don't know if my German translation's any help to you, but there it is."

Trevisone didn't tell. He walked to the doorway and then turned. The rest of what he had to say, he delivered from there.

"It's most likely the victim was running from his assailant, and that's where the assailant ran him down. On the other hand, Mr. Glauberman, it might have been an execution. Then I'd say the location could have been picked as a warning. A warning to someone in the neighborhood, or the occupants of that particular building. I'm not asking for testimony now, just for a little brainstorming. You've lived on those premises for quite a while. Also, it's true that you and the victim both hail from New York, though I grant you so do, what is it, eight million other individuals. Now there I go again, running off at the mouth. Before you catch your plane, can you think of any reason why anyone might want to give that kind of a warning to you, or to Mr. or Mrs. La-Farge, or to any of the neighbors? I'll be back in a little while with your deposition to sign."

Alex picked out the pieces of new information as quickly as he could. Meyer worked for a bank. Meyer had been involved in something secret and/or illegal, possibly theft. Meyer had been killed on his way to see Alex, or else he'd been forced there to make it look that way. But he'd sent the fee earlier—or instructed someone else to. Anyway, someone had ordered him down the driveway and shot him there, with a pistol up against his head.

When the sergeant returned with Alex's statement, Alex said that he hadn't come up with any more theories. The sergeant asked where Alex could be reached in London, and Alex told him.

"When are you on duty," he added, "in case I do think of something important?"

"Eight A.M. on, next week." Trevisone stroked just one side of his mustache now. "Somebody else can have the midnight murders."

Alex picked up his two bags and took the subway and shuttle bus to Logan Airport, the world's seventh busiest, or so the sign used to say. The international terminal was a cavernous, skylighted structure with Tinkertoy architecture high above the floor—lots of round, off-white beams converging at circular joints. Shiny, globe-shaped public-address speakers hung like spiders from skinny metallic threads. The whole thing reminded Alex of the models of molecular structure that had been such a fad in his childhood, when anything that smacked of atoms had been a harbinger of the bright technological future. The Brussels World's Fair, for instance, had been housed in a building shaped—somehow—like an atom.

The place oppressed him. He had long outgrown any fondness for the atom. In this space he felt at once exposed and dwarfed, and he knew, without wanting to dwell on it, that he had good reason. He wanted to smoke the one joint he'd packed in his travel bag, nestle into the aluminum-and-plastic tube that would ferry him across the ocean, and be gone.

It was Saturday evening, though, and the lines were long. All the carriers seemed to have transatlantic flights leaving. The lucky passengers who'd disposed of their luggage rode skyward on two-tiered escalators toward the departure lounge. Alex made his way to the British Air desk at the far end of the building, separated from Aer Lingus by Alitalia. Alex wondered whether British Air security was particularly tight, here in Irish Boston. At length he presented his ticket and his suitcase to be checked. The clerk—a woman in a uniform vaguely reminiscent of the Royal Navy—peered at the computer screen between herself and Alex. Alex expected suddenly to be told he was grounded, sequestered, he didn't know what, material witness, his passport revoked.

"Your seat has been selected already," she said with a tired smile. "Boarding is in one hour, but on international flights you are requested not to leave the terminal between check-in and boarding."

Alex extended a hand for the boarding pass. Then he dropped into a black plastic chair and placed his carry-on bag on the dark tile of the floor. Cigarette smoke swirled toward him from two businessmen talking to his left. His throat constricted—they could poison themselves, but he had all the poisons he could use—and he moved a few seats away. From the envelope in his bag he extracted ten of the fifty-dollar bills.

Had Meyer been so sure Alex would do the job? Or had Meyer had money to burn, and not cared? Or had Meyer known that he had only hours to live, and Alex would be his last chance? It did not appear, given the delivery of the money, that the man who had phoned Alex at the shop had been Meyer. Or, if it had, he hadn't meant for Alex to believe what he said. Alex supposed the money was his own now, whatever happened. And the money meant he could go where he wanted, and hang the expense. He found it also made him feel perversely loyal to Gerald Meyer's last request.

Nearby, opposite the escalator, was a small currency-exchange booth enclosed in bulletproof glass. As Alex approached, the glass reflected his figure and those of the people passing behind him. At the base of the elevator stood two men in uniform. Alex turned and gave a quick once-over to the state trooper and the airport security man chatting on their way up. The trooper, his motorcycle pants tucked into shiny black boots, packed a pistol just below his leather jacket. The security man, puffing out his chest in a pale blue short-sleeved shirt, toyed with a walkie-talkie. Alex turned his back and bought two hundred dollars' worth of pounds and three hundred dollars' worth of marks. He kept his eye on the glass, but saw no more uniforms, and also no men with dark shirts and light ties.

He put the foreign currencies with the American bills, and walked quickly to the space hollowed out under the escalator which contained two rows of pay phones. He called Kim, but got her machine. "Hi, it's Alex," he said. "I hear you talked to Bernie, and I guess he's given you the update by now. I don't know what to say, so I won't. Um, Meyer came through with the money after all. I'm almost off now. I'll give your love to Meredith. 'Bye."

Almost off, but still time to kill. He looked up the messenger service that had delivered Meyer's envelope, and called, claiming to have gotten a communication that needed a reply but had come with no return address. The service was proud of its data bank and happy to tell him the address. Mr. Diebstahl, Charles Hotel.

Diebstahl, larceny. If Meyer had a thing about arch, German-derived aliases, what was one supposed to make of the message sent via Kim? I'm meeting a lady, whom I met in the company of Jay Friedhoff, in Berlin. *Friedhof* meant "cemetery." Or, Alex supposed, it could actually be a name.

Between the two sets of telephone booths stood a double row of directories, hinged so you could flip up whichever ones you chose. Alex remembered that these included not just local directories but also books for major U.S. cities. He wanted to know what he would find in the way of real-life Friedhoffs.

There were none listed in Boston, but the next books yielded two in New York and four in Los Angeles. It was a real name, then, or it could be. As Alex reached for Chicago, a hand touched his left shoulder. When he began to swing around, the hand gripped tight and held.

A voice, quiet but deep, talked into his left ear. He could feel the breath, unpleasantly warm. He felt a dull fatality, an inevitability, about the grip that held his shoulder. He told himself to keep calm, but the truth was that he was calm already. Only he felt weary, felt a sinking in the pit of his stomach that sank and sank as if it would never stop. That's just the drug, he told himself. He started to turn his head.

"Easy, Mr. Glauberman," the voice said. "Don't do that. You're trying to leave home with too many questions unanswered. So I want you to look straight ahead, and walk real slow and easy the way I point you. Else you end up like Mr. Meyer."

Alex made his shoulder relax under the grip. Across the stand of directories, a woman talked into a phone with her back to him. She had straight, chestnut hair that reminded him of Meredith. Next to her a fat man faced Alex, waving a lit cigar in the air as he talked. His eyes met Alex's, and moved away. Alex swallowed hard and turned the way the hand pushed him.

He felt rather than saw his assailant, just behind and to his left. The hand on his shoulder was the man's right hand, a right hand like iron. The palm propelled him forward, out from the telephone area, toward the passengers lined up ten deep at the Air Canada desk. A tall man, all in black, with a long white beard, a Hasidic Jew with a flat-crowned black hat, seemed to stare straight at Alex. The stare was an illusion, though. The Hasid turned away toward the desk.

After eight steps, the hand on Alex's shoulder turned him left, toward the exits. Alex could see the glassed-in exchange booth, the open rent-a-car booth to its right, the plate-glass windows revealing cars, buses, cabs, and crowd outside. The sinking stopped, replaced by a rising, honest, healthy fear. Alex felt his heart beating faster, and much too loud.

"How far are we going?" he asked. "I've got a plane to catch."

"For a little ride. If you talk fast, you might make it. Who knows?"

"You took Meyer for a ride," Alex said. "Davis Square? He talked fast, didn't he?"

Turning his head slightly to the left, he could see the sleeve of a sport jacket, a blazer this time, blue, unremarkable, with a plastic button, colored gold. There was a gold ring on the little finger, too. The man said quietly, "Worry about what's in my other hand. And keep your eyes on the floor."

Alex was tired of disembodied voices. Nonetheless, he did what he was told, so he could think. Firing a gun in an airport lobby was a dangerous game. He remembered watching in amazement, on TV, the number of automatic weapons that had appeared out of nowhere when John Hinckley took a shot at the President, out of doors. He could imagine how many plainclothesmen were assigned to the average international departure lobby, these days. Neither of them would make it very far.

Alex watched his sneakers move slowly but steadily along the floor. The plastic tiles, rough-surfaced, gray mixed with black, were like cracked, fossil-bearing rock. He thought, irrationally, that only ages hence would anyone bother to look here for his tracks. When he didn't show up in London, and Meredith called, and then she called Kim. There would be no reinforcements today. He counted twenty more steps, coming to a decision. Gerald Meyer had gone for one ride, and survived at some cost, still unknown. Then he had gone for another, a little walk down a dark driveway to a place where it ended in rubbish and yellow-eyed cats. Better not to go that way. Better not to get started. Better to break the momentum. When he judged he ought to be even with the base of the escalator, he fought the grip on his shoulder, twisting around.

"I've got a plane to catch," he repeated. It seemed preferable not to say the word *shoot*, or *gun*. His heart hammered away. "All I've got to do is yell 'Long Live Kaddafy,' and we'd have security swarming all around. I'll have time to yell that, and take me with you, before I die."

The man dug his thumb into Alex's neck, just below

where one of the remaining tumors, shrunken in half from what it had once been, pressed out. Alex winced and avoided any sudden moves, but he looked the man in the face and insisted, "I'm going up."

The man had a rat's face, lean and sharp-nosed, with protruding teeth. Alex could see how the teeth were clamped shut by the taut muscles of the man's narrow jaw. His chin was close-shaved, smooth, his eyes small and blue. He let Alex turn the corner, let go with his right hand, and moved up close behind so that Alex could feel the hard object in the left pocket of his jacket. It pressed into Alex's kidney.

The escalator step, emerging from the floor, carried Alex up and away from the gun. Still, it would take a bullet only a fraction of a second to pierce his back and do its work inside. He thought of the single hole in Gerald Meyer's skull. He pictured Maria, right now, snuggled with a book, or playing with her toddler half-sister, or in front of the TV. He pictured her at his funeral, in a dress-up dress, some hurriedly bought black shoes, her hand in Laura's, her eyes wide. His only consolation was that this was a scene he had imagined more than once before. He rode upward. He waited.

The first escalator led to a landing, a narrow mezzanine overlooking the ticket counters, and then to another escalator of equal height. At the top of the second one, orange letters glowed. SECURITY CHECK-IN, they said. CENTRAL. WEST. EAST. With arrows, pointing appropriate ways. *Stairway to heaven,* the words formed in Alex's brain.

For the moment, he and the rat-faced man were alone. No one was in earshot on the moving steps above or below. Figures and faces passed going down, unreachably far, a yard away. Another security man—or was it the same one?—held his walkie-talkie with an air of authority as he slid by. "Next stop," the low voice said, "get off. We talk there, or you never talk again."

The landing came. Ten paces to the next escalator. One. Two. Three. Four. Five. The gun pressed against him again, now under his ribs, from the side. Alex imagined it angled up, the trajectory straight toward his heart. He moved faster, oozing sweat now, aching to run but not daring to. Too much challenge, too much pushing the gunman to the point of decision. Best not to force him. Besides, Alex did not know what a pistol could do, from how far.

Shotguns and rifles, he'd learned to handle those during his time in Nebraska—blowing cans off rocks, hunting rabbits and birds. But handguns remained one of those shadowy myths of city life. Always imagined, one in every passerby's pocket on an empty street at night, one behind many a door. A fast death, at close range. Shot by her estranged husband, during an argument in her home. Shot by a hold-up junkie, in the store the old man had tended thirty years.

Six paces covered. Alex kept going. The hard barrel of the pistol followed him. So did an image of cans, felled by shotgun blasts, on the edge of a cornfield. The cans jerked upward, then rolled on their sides, pierced all over. Seven. Eight. Nine.

Ten. The last escalator lifted him free of the barrel, but the gun's owner cursed him softly from a few inches behind and below. "Now you're gonna get it, smartass cunt. Think you're gonna be a hero." The voice, no longer calm, was getting a nasty edge. "I'm gonna wipe your ass off the planet, cocksucker."

He's working himself up to it, Alex thought. Not good. Still, they kept on rising toward the orange letters, in stately progress under the white Tinkertoy-molecule beams. Alex's heart drummed against his ribs, hammering out seconds, half-seconds, too many and too long. "Jesus," the voice complained, "who the fuck do you think you are. . . ."

Alex sprang forward, away, tossing his bag to the top of the moving stairs, flying after it out of his assailant's reach. But not quite. The man's free hand closed around his ankle with that same iron grip. Alex toppled, knees painful against the point of the ribbed steel step, hands going forward to break the fall. He watched his hands glide toward the escalator's mouth, where the stairs flattened and pinched and disappeared. He kicked backward and forward with his caught leg, lifting his hands to grab the moving handrails as they moved toward the floor. He grabbed as high as he could reach, braced the foot of his free leg, and hurled himself forward onto the dark, rocklike floor. He felt freedom, grabbed up his bag and ran, like any passenger late for a plane, stumbling in his haste and then sprinting for the gate.

He turned sharp left toward the door labeled WEST SE-CURITY CHECK-IN. One of the blue-shirted security men lounged against the partition that cordoned off the waiting area from the rest of the upper lobby. It was more thick glass, bulletproof, like that which surrounded the exchange booth. At the entrance Alex stopped, huffing, and pulled open the glass door. He flashed his boarding pass at a small, fattish gatekeeper. This Saint Peter was as good as any—an old man, Italian, East Boston, in a bright orange jacket. He might have been an usher at Fenway Park. Alex slid the bag containing Gerald Meyer's legacy onto the conveyor belt and stepped through the metal detector, while the glass door closed behind him with a satisfying soft sound. Turning, he saw no rat-faced man.

11

Caverns of the City

.

Alex paced the length of the lounge, searching for his attacker through the transparent wall. It was not so much that he wanted to capture the man's features as that he wanted to see him whole. He needed a real person, vanquished, not a disembodied threat still at large. But the man with the iron hand was gone.

Within the security area, Alex crossed to a pay phone and dialed the Cambridge police. Trevisone would be off duty, according to what he'd said. That was just as well. Alex delivered his tip to the police-station operator.

"Never mind my name," he said quickly. "There's a guy got killed, Meyer. I bet you his blood was pickled in alcohol. If you want to know where he did his drinking, he was out at Logan last night. Yeah, drowning his troubles in the North Terminal bar. Waiting on a United flight, maybe. Find out who he left with. It might do you some good."

Then he went to the men's room, bolted himself inside a stall, and smoked his last joint this side of British customs. Not many minutes later, strapped securely in his jumbo-jet

75

seat like a patron in a cramped modern movie house, Alex smiled at the thought of Trevisone receiving his message. Maybe it would be possible to work out a long-distance relationship with the sergeant—you scratch my back and I scratch yours. As the jet taxied into line, Alex felt ready. Not confident, exactly, not like he had all the threads in his hands. Chastened certainly, warned, somewhat humbled by what had just occurred. But not intimidated. In a word, ready.

He knew this feeling, recognized it immediately, because it was a feeling he had come to value very much. This time it did not come as a surprise. The first time, it had. That had been eight months before, seated on the only chair in the small office of the unfamiliar woman armored in her white coat. She had given him, without fanfare, the pathologist's verdict on the swollen nodes in his lymphatic system. In the privacy of this isolation, receiving his diagnosis, he had been surprised to feel neither rage nor fear nor depression sweep over him.

Alex always found it difficult to explain this. Or, as he saw it, other people always found this difficult to understand. No denial, no paralysis, no trembling, no "Oh, God, why me?" One inadequate way he tried to explain it was to remind people that he did love to ski. He tried likening his emotion to what he felt before pushing off at the top of a steep, swift run. That emotion was a challenge, not to undersand or justify or explain what had brought him to this pass, but a powerful urge to get on with doing it. He felt challenged to go where he had not yet been, to put his skills to work, to handle in his way something that many people might confront and handle in their own ways, well or badly, but that perhaps no one else had handled in just his particular way.

Alex had been extremely happy that he could stand there on the snowy summit and look down without an immobilizing vertigo. In the time since, there had been many moments—in fact, most moments—when he had no conscious sense of being or ever having been on that mountaintop. But now, as the jet taxied and then rose, buoyed even more by the sudden thrust of the big engines, he knew, once again, exactly what he was doing.

He was racing down that icy mountain, yielding to gravity in order to fight it, fighting it in order to yield, riding the mountain in a state of controlled excitement, taking the ride however it developed—and knowing all the while that sometime, not soon, he hoped, but sometime, it *would* end. Then, in a peaceful moment, he would walk triumphantly through deep, powdery snow, perhaps arm in arm with someone, to a place where he could sit and gaze back up and say to himself, "Wow. I did that."

Seven A.M. Sunday, Greenwich Mean Time, was still 2:00 A.M. Saturday night as far as Alex's metabolism was concerned. He had barely slept, and the confining plastic cabin had pressed in on him. Euphoria had faded into a nagging, persistent nausea, a *yecch,* like a case of guilt or a pulled muscle—oppressive not in itself, but because it was so hard to shake. He had tried but failed to concentrate on the Japanese slugger Sadaharu Oh's book, *A Zen Way of Baseball.*

All told, he felt like a poor specimen, though a hardy one, when Heathrow Airport presented itself as a mass of nylon and gabardine, denim and leather, all moving too fast. However, his spirits lifted when Meredith Phillips stepped out of the swirling crowd. Her autumn-leaf hair dangled to the shoulders of a leather jacket, equally if differently red. Alex felt a rush of happiness break through the yecch. He hoped that he was not going to be driving her too nuts.

Meredith took him in her arms until he dropped his bags and kissed her as it ought to be done. "I've got a car," she said. "Do you want to go home, or out?"

"Out, please. I want to walk empty streets, with you and nobody else. It's Sunday, right? The City will be empty."

Meredith eyed Alex curiously but only said, "Wherever you'd like." She took his hand and carry-on bag and guided him through the pathways of Heathrow Airport, to a garage where she tossed the bag into the trunk of a Ford Fiesta. She took the suitcase from him and added it too. Alex had landed in Heathrow before, a decade ago, but could summon no visual memory. Once into the light stream of inbound traffic,

Meredith said, "You look good. Have you done the final day's medicines yet? How do you feel, Alex?"

"I feel like we're driving on the wrong side of the road. I want to keep going, while I can. I want to walk and talk, and then go eat Indian lunch. That'll be breakfast, according to my body—I can take the pills then. After that, I'm ready to go home, meet the family, and collapse."

"I understand. And I'd better warn you right off, we're lunching with the proper family on Tuesday. The Reverend Phillips desires to meet his daughter's lover. I thought by Tuesday you'd be settled down, you know."

Alex swallowed. "Um, by Tuesday I'm planning to leave for a detour to the Continent. That's what I want to walk and talk about. But I think if it can be breakfast it should work out. Or brunch, maybe. I have to be in Hannover by late Tuesday night."

"Hannover," Meredith said. "The duchy that gave us Georges number I through III, among others. What is all this on-again, off-again about? And why do you feel you need to declare your independence from me? Your marijuana is in the glove box, by the way."

The parson's daughter, as usual, was nothing if not direct. Alex had once told her she was a walking carpenter's level. She'd replied in all seriousness that she was so pleased not to be compared to a dwell meter. A level was an old-fashioned, logically comprehensible tool—the sort she respected. Alex put a joint, already rolled, into his mouth and ignited it with the lighter.

"In Hannover, I'm supposed to see the daughter of a man I met in the post office. I went there to mail you the letter explaining that after this go-round with the chemo I needed some time to myself." He inhaled a deep breath of smoke and watched West London glide by, not quite ready to take it in. "Footloose time. No-schedule time. Remember-who-I-am time. Then I met this man, and now the man is dead and I'm knee-deep in his shit. I don't know what's happening, exactly. Whatever it is, though, I'm in it and I don't want to let it go."

"I see," Meredith said, though possibly she didn't. "And the medical news?"

"Good," he said. "Here—feel the change."

He took her left hand off the stick shift and put it first below his ear, and then to the back of his neck.

"One's gone," she said, resting her hand a moment longer on his neck. "Isn't it? And the other's down significantly. What does the doctor say?"

"To see her when I get back. She expects she'll want to hit them twice more while they're down. By Thanksgiving I should be as normal as I'm going to get."

Thanksgiving was when Meredith was due back in Boston. With luck, Alex would have no more tumors and be done with medication. But he still might not be the man she had fallen in love with—that was what he meant. He would still be a man with a kind of monkey on his back. He could be expected to go through the whole thing again within five years, quite possibly less. With luck, again, the cancer would not have developed much resistance to the drugs. Nodular lymphoma, Alex's disease, was a relatively domesticated cancer—but not, in the current state of medical science, a curable one.

"How's the teaching?" he asked.

Meredith shrugged, and returned her hand to the wheel. "I'm nearly halfway through, and the work makes me feel professional, competent, insightful, and sometimes gifted. Or, to put it another way, I am surrounded by panting groupies who look at me like I was Simone de Beauvoir."

"A link to lost feminist generations, you mean?" Meredith had come to the States originally to research a book on a writer from the twenties, Susan Glaspell. She was also an acknowledged authority, at thirty-two, on Virginia Woolf.

"I suppose." Meredith kept her eyes on the road, but grinned. Alex marveled as usual at this parson's daughter with the dark red hair, cat's eyes, and alive, inquiring face. "What I meant was someone who seems to them old, wise, and sexy. The students are all very bright, but I have the feeling that for a lot of them it's basically a game."

They sped along the Embankment now, toward central London, then drifted up Whitehall in the sparse early-Sunday traffic. The sights came back to Alex as if from a dream: not quite real, but nonetheless already observed. At Trafalgar

Square, Meredith pointed out South Africa House, where Alex had missed a large demonstration she'd attended the day before. She turned right on the Strand, toward the financial district. Alex kept silent as they reached the canyons formed by incessant construction of newer and sleeker skyscrapers.

"Thatcher's miracle," Meredith said. "The rest of the country can rot, but the sun never sets on British finance capital. Deserted today, as you say. Now, Alex, what brings us here?"

They walked hand in hand through vacant streets, while Alex told Gerald Meyer's story, and his own. Meredith let him tell it, but from time to time she stopped and looked away, up at the distant sky, in mute exasperation. "So, somewhere up there," he concluded, "is Moselle's castle, and I'm down here like David with his slingshot. The thing is, it wouldn't surprise me if something in that package belonged to Jack. It wouldn't surprise me if Meyer knuckled under to those two guys, and told where it went. Maybe that's why he wanted me to get it back. I want to go see Moselle, like Meyer suggested. I want him to think I'm happy to be his pet retriever, to bring it back and drop it at his feet."

"Are you happy to?"

"I guess that depends on what's in it. Possession is nine points of the law. And on Cynthia—it's her inheritance, in a sense."

"What about the fact that Moselle may have killed Meyer, or had him killed? And that he may have sent that thug after you, as well?"

"I'll have to keep my eyes and ears open. That's all I can say."

Meredith stopped and stood her ground. She gave him the carpenter's-level stare.

"You're determined to keep your rendezvous with *Tochter* Cynthia, then?"

Alex took back his hand, in fact put both hands in his back pockets. He was still wearing the outfit he'd put on for the police, and he felt not quite like himself. He nodded.

"Well, what can *I* say, then? I can't say that I like it. I've had to grow accustomed to the idea of your disappearance, in an ultimate sense. That makes me more sensitive, I suppose.

But I won't nag or bluster where I can see that others have already failed. So Tuesday I cancel my morning seminar, we meet Father, and I kiss you good-bye at Victoria Station."

"But?" Alex said.

"But—I love your enthusiasm. You're tenacious, and I love that too. You've embarked on this, and I don't want the role of making you give it up. What scares me is your impulsiveness. Someone makes you an attractive offer, and off you go. It's not the waving good-bye, but never knowing which way you might be turning next. After Hannover, for instance."

"On to Berlin, apparently. With Cynthia. Does that bother you?"

"In the short run. A strange city, a mission, a mysterious woman whom you've traveled four thousand miles to meet. In the long run, I'm more concerned about your safety. Now we're taking the tube to Soho, and a very good little Indian place on Gerrard Street. We'll pick up the car on the way back. Are you sure you want to be doing this to your stomach?"

"Hot spiced *brinjal* and greasy puffed *poori*, with Cytoxan and steroid for chasers. I've got the cravings of a pregnant lady again."

Alex regretted those words as soon as they left his lips. They were a stock phrase for him, but not one he used with Meredith when he could help it. Meredith had been pregnant only once, at twenty, and only briefly then. She'd been married later, but she claimed to have seen clearly that the marriage wasn't good enough for kids. Now, with Alex, it wasn't a question of good enough or not. The half-stepmothering of Maria was all she stood a chance to get. Alex wished he could take back the sentence, but more he wished he could take back and rearrange all the events of the past nine months.

Meredith took no notice, overtly at least. "I've got the cravings of a woman who's been sleeping by herself too long," she said. "Let's get you your food, though. First things first, on a Sunday morning."

12

Hackney Carriage

Meredith was staying with friends in Hackney, East London. On the way home she swung by the local open-air market, set up on a dead-end street. The vendors—Asian and Caribbean as well as English—displayed clothes, cosmetics, record albums, hanging poultry and meat, and unfamiliar fish on ice. Meredith bought a big fish to contribute toward dinner —a whole one, gray-blue, filleted on the spot. From a skinny, dreadlocked Jamaican youth, Alex picked up a UB-40 album to smooth his meeting with Cynthia Meyer. He asked whether Meredith knew of any special symbolism attached to a white rose.

"Purity, for one. The House of York as opposed to Lancaster, also. And it was the emblem of a German anti-Nazi youth underground, during the war."

A few blocks from the market, she pulled up in front of a three-story row house of chipped brownstone. A big, hearty man burst from the house, with red cheeks and a broad chest like a Scandinavian logger. "Here," he insisted, exchanging glances with Meredith during the opening of the trunk. "Here, Alex, let me take your things."

"This is Mark," Meredith said. "You spoke on the phone."

Alex could not work up much interest. Yes, Mark from the phone, married to Janice, Meredith's old schoolmate, now a free-lance TV producer. They shared the house with a medical student, an exiled painter from Chile, and some offspring, though Alex couldn't remember whose.

Inside, the grownups were gathered around tea and toast and beer. The lived-in living room was scattered with newspapers, glasses and cups, and a pile of Legos in disarray. Alex, at a loss, wished he could plop down and build something out of the bright plastic blocks. Maria had lately been outgrowing hers.

Janice brought him beer but looked him over coldly. After a while the beer took its toll, and he felt it was okay to plead exhaustion. That was more polite, certainly, than pleading discomfort, or boredom, or a-month-since-we-last-fucked. Meredith showed him to the third-floor room she was using, still in the process of renovation. The steep roof was covered only by foil-backed fiberglass and gray plastic sheeting, but on the floor rested a new, thick, double mattress. Alex plunged happily onto this bed, managing to strip off the clothes he'd put on the afternoon before. "Ugh," Meredith said. "If you want to take a bath, I'll be here when you get back."

Alex took one, in an old claw-footed tub with a makeshift shower dangling precariously overhead. He nearly fell asleep, but revived and returned to slide gratefully under clean sheets and a musty comforter. He watched Meredith undress, began to relearn after absence the freckled shoulders, breasts rosy and gentle, hipbones almost sharp, legs not long but trim. He could barely keep his eyes open, but he had a fond reawakened memory of warm skin on skin. He could think of nothing more important, right then, than being made love to.

When he awoke, in pitch dark and cold, he could dimly recall the feeling of mouths and tongues and hands and genitals all seeking mutual reassurance, of coming inside Meredith and of her coming on and around him. Now he was alone, and what had awakened him was not a warm lover beside him, but the nightly rush of lifeless steroids within. He rummaged, shivering, bouncing from one foot to another, to pluck clean clothes from his bag. He found underwear, jeans, and a sweatshirt, and tiptoed downstairs.

In the strange house he felt like a burglar — nerves zinging and alert for sounds. He tiptoed down past a darkened second story till he heard voices from the kitchen below. "What *I* know," Janice was saying, "is that you seem to be in love with the man, Professor Phillips. And it's been quite a while since that was true. You may not trust your feelings, but I do. What I'd *like* to know. . . ." Janice paused, and Alex, sensing the drift of the conversation, began to ease his feet guiltily back up the stairs. "What I'd like to know," the irritating, self-assured accent trailed after him, "is whether the man plans to stick with you, once you've got him past the transition you're seeing him through."

"Yes," Alex whispered piously. "Yes, the man does." And he meant it. But after that he forgot Meredith, forgot her housemates, forgot the Legos and his daughter far away. He began to imagine what it was going to be like to confront Jack Moselle. The high-powered prednisone had whisked him through eight or ten scenarios — some triumphant, some disastrous — by the time Meredith returned. Then Alex was content to be talked into a sleeping pill, to drift somewhat more slowly, and at last to sleep.

In the morning — Monday morning, it was — Alex woke up late, and once more alone. When he stood too quickly from the mattress, he saw spots and immediately sank back down. That went with a generally pale and washed-out feeling, yet he was pleased. Today he did not have to take any pills.

In the empty kitchen he found dirty dishes in the sink, and a telegram addressed to him, unopened on the table. For a while he let the sleeping telegram lie. He washed red wine residue out of a pair of long-stemmed glasses. He rinsed dregs of cornflakes and milk from a jumble of breakfast bowls. He put the kettle on for tea. Then he opened the cable, which turned out to be from his local police, dated Sunday night. He was urged to contact Sergeant Trevisone right away, or face extradition proceedings. He crumpled the telegram into the trash, took a deep breath in and out, and checked the London phone directory for Interface, Inc. Asking to speak to Mr. Moselle got him as far as a secretary who wanted to know whether Mr. Moselle was expecting his call.

"He might be. Could you tell him it's Alex Glauberman?"

"Certainly, Mr. Glauberman," the secretary said, meaning *maybe*. "And from what firm?"

"Blond Beasts, European cars."

"I see. He's not available, but if you'll leave a number, Mr. Glauberman, I'll see that he gets your message."

"No, I can't. My office is in America. I'm just passing through. Could you please tell him that Gerald Meyer sent me? If you could do that, I'll wait."

"Then wait, please, Mr. Glauberman."

On hold, Muzak played a very dim reflection of "Light My Fire." Alex could not find any oolong tea, but there was a good assortment from India. He opted for Darjeeling, brewed weak. "Penny Lane" followed as he slouched in a kitchen chair, sipping the pale, warm liquid. He knew from past experience that this was going to be a day of feeling fragile. The feeling resulted from going off the whopping dose of steroid, cold turkey.

"Yeah?" In Alex's ear, a man interrupted the syrupy strings.

"Is this Jack?"

"This is Jack."

Alex sat up. "My name is Glauberman. Alex Glauberman. I'm passing through London, today only, and wondered whether I could meet you. Gerald Meyer especially wanted us to discuss something."

The answering voice showed neither surprise nor alarm, but perhaps a trace of caution: "Say that again."

"My name is Alex Glauberman. I'm passing through London, today only, and Gerald Meyer especially wanted me to talk with you about something."

"Jerry's a sad old man, but he's got nerve. Alex, is it? Why should I see you, Alex?"

Moselle's accent was undoubtedly American. It had a thin overlay of what Alex pigeonholed as middlebrow British inflection. Not BBC, not cockney. The British equivalent of Omaha, if there was such a thing.

"Jerry's dead," Alex told him. "I thought maybe you'd know."

"Is he? Okay, Alex, I've got a light morning today. Suppose you come by at noon. Listen, where are you located, anyway? Why don't I send a man around to pick you up?"

"No, thanks. I can find my way. Should I come to this address in the book?"

"Nope. I'm at my secret hideaway. It's—you in East London, by any chance?"

"Yes," said Alex. East London was a big place, covering what must once have been five or six separate villages.

"Good, then. 23 Romney Road, Bethnal Green. Wait till you see it. Looking forward to our chat, then, Alex."

"Yes," Alex said again. Noon did not give him much time. He slurped his tea and dashed upstairs for suitable clothes. Near the top he fought off a sudden wave of faintness, gripping the bannister tight till he regained his balance. The corduroy jacket for Trevisone would have to do for Moselle as well. Plus the striped tie he had brought, in case of forced attendance with Reverend Phillips at church. He stuffed his wallet with a wad of Gerald Meyer's pounds, but left his passport and other ID behind. He took the stairs more slowly on his way down, found a street guide in the bookcase, made sure the front door clicked shut behind him, and began to jog through a gray London day. The idea of hailing a cab in Hackney was appealing.

A half-block toward the business district, he slowed thankfully as a black, hunchbacked London taxi slowed for him. The driver, Indian or Pakistani, headed back in the direction from which Alex had come. "Bet'nal Green," as the driver put it, lay south and east, toward Stepney. The route carried Alex past old row houses like the one Meredith's friends were remodeling, newer concrete housing projects, and occasional workers' apartment blocks, dark brick, from an earlier industrial era. SHEARLING COMPANY, said the chiseled inscription on one of these, with the date 1895.

Bethnal Green turned out to be a rundown former town center, and Number 23 Romney Road to be a red-brick firehouse, recently renovated.

Alex gave the driver a twenty-pound note to cover fare plus tip. He stepped out and took time to look around. The ground floor of the old building now housed a pub, a pastry shop, and an herbal tea and medicine store. Upstairs, the firefighters' quarters had been remade into offices. A round brass-cage elevator carried visitors up and down a transparent shaft of glass or Plexiglas. Through the middle of shaft and elevator ran a gleaming brass pole. Descending passengers apparently could hook their arms around the pole, if they liked, and play fireman. Alex browsed among herbs till noon, then rode up the pole. The ascent had an Alice in Wonderland quality. Up the beanstalk to meet Jack, thought Alex, mixing metaphors. A young female receptionist in suit and tie directed him to Mr. Moselle's office, where she said he was expected.

If he hadn't known better, Alex would have taken Moselle for fifty. His hair was handsomely gray and all in place. His cheeks were clean-shaven, but he wore a trimmed beard and mustache that made him seem like a man trying to look older rather than younger. His rangy good looks were, well, easygoing and American. Black-framed glasses added a touch of gravity. He stood from a shiny steel and vinyl armchair to shake Alex's hand.

"What do you think?" he demanded proudly. "Quite cozy, isn't it?"

The office was big. It had probably slept half a dozen firefighters once. White walls were interior-decorated with colorful prints. The armchairs and a tiled mosaic-topped coffee table made up a sort of living room area. To the left of that was a workspace dominated by a big, dark, antique desk.

"Let them handle all the paperwork on some fortieth floor," Moselle continued. "Give me a room close to the ground and quiet." He pointed Alex to another chair, identical, at right angles to his own. "I bought the place for development, originally, but then I couldn't let it go. Drink, or coffee, or a sandwich?"

"Very nice," Alex said, saving his words. "Weak tea and a sandwich would be fine."

Moselle issued orders into a speakerphone on the tiled table. Eventually Alex made out the initials JM, subtly displayed in the pattern.

"Well," Moselle said, sitting. "Jerry Meyer sent you to talk to me."

"That's right. He appointed me ambassador to his daughter."

"To his daughter." Moselle scratched behind his right ear. "Now, what daughter is that?"

"Cynthia Meyer. I hope I'm not taking your job away."

"Oh, Cynthia. I thought maybe you meant the other one."

Moselle gave Alex a sudden searching glance, like steel, but to that comment Alex could think of nothing to say.

"Well, Cynthia. I'm more like an uncle than an ambassador to her." Moselle dissolved the stare and waved at his surroundings as if these might sum something up. "An ambassador has to go to the right schools."

"I'm supposed to see her, collect something Jerry sent her by mistake, and bring it back."

"Tough job, if that's not the way she's inclined. Especially if Jerry's dead—assuming she knows that."

"She knows it," Alex said. "I told her."

"Honest man, are you? And what is it you're supposed to get back?"

"Family pictures, according to Meyer."

Moselle smiled, white teeth. "Family pictures. And what does any of this have to do with me?"

"That's what I came here to ask."

"Afraid I haven't got any answers, Alex."

Alex felt his will to keep up repartee draining away, slowly but regularly, like oil from the pan. He shook his head irritably, tried to make a motion of rising from the chair.

"Why did you waste your light morning on me, then?" he demanded.

"Keep your shirt on." Moselle held up his hands like the

victim of a movie holdup. "This ain't New York. We do things a little bit slower. You haven't even had your sandwich. Sure you don't want a drink? I've got Jack Daniel's, which you can't get anyplace else in this country, believe me."

"In my tea," Alex said. Somehow he couldn't bear to plead a ravaged stomach lining to Moselle, the way he had to Meyer. "I'd appreciate some in my tea."

The receptionist came in with the tea, plus cheese and onion sandwiches on a pair of dry rolls. From a cabinet, Moselle fetched Tennessee whiskey, ice, and a glass for himself. He added a slug to Alex's white china cup.

"How well do you know Jerry Meyer?" he asked.

"I met him for the first time Friday. He needed someone to stand under his daughter's mailbox, and I happened to be heading the right way. Why did you call him a sad old man?"

"Isn't he?"

"*Wasn't* he, you mean. I told you, he's dead."

Moselle winked. The wink was so quick, behind the eyeglass lens, it might have been a tic. Alex thought it was a wink of complicity, of welcome to the fraternity of those in the know.

"*Wasn't* he, then?" Moselle corrected himself.

"His eyes were sad. His life sounded sad. I don't think —having talked to him once, more or less just like this—he took much pleasure in life. But I'm not convinced he had given life up, just because he didn't enjoy it."

"And how did he end up being dead? You haven't told me that."

"Somebody put a bullet in his brain. Somebody roughed him up a little, to get some information I guess, and then a little while later somebody shot him. So here I am, kind of operating on my own."

Moselle nodded finally, raising his glass to Alex. "I'll drink to that." He did, and hissed out air between his teeth. For a minute he savored whatever it was that his homeland's corn liquor did for him.

"You know," he said, "Jerry always attracted calamities."

"And calamities wash off you?"

Moselle raised his glass again.

"Like booze off a duck. That tea can be fatal, if you

drink it too straight." He poured another slug into Alex's half-empty cup.

The speakerphone buzzed. Moselle leaned forward to press a button, then said to hold calls and visitors for another ten minutes. The whiskey was washing into Alex, not off, but it gave him a temporary lift. Moselle turned back to Alex with a nod that meant it was time to stop fucking around.

"Well, I tell you," he said with no smile but evident sarcasm, "I'm not very interested in family pictures. Do you know what Meyer did for a living?"

"He was a banker."

"Not quite a banker. Middle management in a bank. A cog, not a mover and shaker. Now suppose I asked you what a bank employee gives out and then wants back. Any bank, anytime. Not pictures."

"Money," said Alex. He took what he told himself would be the last sip.

"Good boy. Now, I don't know what your business is. You said something about cars. Right now I want to know about your deal with Meyer. Just tell me, in dollars, how much was involved."

"Two thousand for me."

"You bring me back that package—without disturbing the contents, and believe me, I'll know if they're disturbed. You do that for me, and I'll match his payment."

Alex put his cup on the table, where the initials swam slightly.

"One condition."

"Yeah."

"I need to know what's in it too."

"Why?"

"Suppose it wasn't something I'd want to bring across customs?"

"You mean narcotics?" Moselle's white-toothed smile returned. "Come on, Alex! Jerry Meyer?" He put his own drink down, leaning forward, hands on his knees. "Do you know what a banker's acceptance is?"

Alex didn't, and decided this was no time to be a wise-ass.

"Frankly, no."

"Well, it's worth a lot of money, but it's as legal as you and me. Now, do we have a deal?"

"Yes."

"By the way, did Jerry send you on any missions to anybody besides me and Cynthia?"

You asked, thought Alex. Does that mean you know what I'm going to answer?

"Yes and no," he replied, as ingenuously as possible. "He did mention something about calling on a Jay Friedhoff, in Berlin. But he didn't give me any address. In fact, I don't know for sure if it's *J-A-Y* or *J* as an initial. Does that mean anything to you?"

Moselle stood up and turned toward the window behind him. His fingers pressed apart the slats of the Venetian blind so he could peek out on his patch of East London. Alex wondered whether that brought him closer to his roots in South Philly, or wherever.

"Man or a woman, this Friedhoff, did he say?"

"I don't know," Alex admitted.

Moselle turned back to Alex. He blew on his finger, looked for any remaining dust, and didn't find any. Most likely someone cleaned and dusted this place every day.

"I like a man who says when he doesn't know. Now Jerry, his trouble is—was—that he would always overreach, you know what I mean? A little razzle-dazzle exactly where it didn't belong. Sure, I can get you in to see Friedhoff, for what it's worth. Not in Berlin. A stone's throw from Westminster Abbey. You want to give me another call in, say, a half hour?"

"Okay."

Moselle downed his drink and stood, extending his hand down to Alex. The cuticles and nails were immaculate, the short hairs plentiful and black.

"Glad you came around, Glauberman. Take your time over lunch. How soon do you think I can expect delivery of those items, by the way?"

Alex shook hands without standing. "Give me a week," he said. Moselle stepped briskly out of the office, leaving Alex to pick at bits of cheese and discard bits of onion. He had nowhere to go in the next half hour, and no one had asked him to leave. He decided, from inertia, to see what happened if he stayed where he was.

He knew the inertia was a cousin, chemically, to the washed-out feeling with which he had woken up. The receptionist came in to clear away lunch, glanced at him curiously, but said nothing. When she had left, Alex sipped cold tea and whiskey, despite his earlier resolve. He hadn't done a bad job, all in all. He tiptoed over to the antique wooden desk, toying with the idea of taking a peek inside.

"Excuse me, Mr. Glauberman," the receptionist said, wide-eyed, advancing from the door. "Mr. Moselle left this address for you." She waited for him to leave the desk and come to her. "Barton Street," she added, more relaxed. "It's right by the Abbey. It's very posh, scads of condos now. He says to go right on over, she'll be expecting you. She's a dear old puss, you know."

"A dear old puss?" Alex looked down at the slip of paper in his hand. Lady Jane Friedhoff, it said. "Oh, of course. I see. Dear old Lady Jane."

13

You Are the Dead

Outside the elevator, Alex noticed, was a square set of nine pushbuttons like the ones on a telephone. Inside, below the big silver buttons marked 1, 2, and B, was a similar set. Security system, he thought. Not just anybody gets upstairs to see Jack whenever they want. He felt again like somebody of reasonable importance, who could congratulate himself on a job well done.

Outside, the afternoon was grayer still, but so far it had remained dry. Alex traveled downtown by Underground, dozing and thankful for the doze. He woke in time for Westminster, where he fell in behind assorted tourists, German, American, and Japanese. He left the other visitors as they entered the holy place where martyrs to empire rest, and kings are crowned. He found Barton Street on his right.

It was a street of town houses, Porsches, and Mercedeses. Through half-curtained windows he caught glimpses of hanging plants, new wood, and bright Formica. Halfway down the block a plaque announced the house that had once harbored T. E. Lawrence, though whether before or after Arabia it did not say. If Alex harbored doubts about Lady Jane Friedhoff—and he did, rather subliminally—some of them were dispelled when he found her name neatly hand-lettered on a white card next to the bell for a basement flat. This must have been the service entrance. It represented a comedown, literally speaking, for a member of the nobility. Still, he would be willing to bet Lady Jane had paid quite a price for her basement flat. He was disarmed completely by the small, spry, white-haired lady who responded to the bell. She offered him his choice of sherry or tea.

"I hadn't expected company until our mutual friend called," she added, "but I did unearth some biscuits in a tin." She pointed him to a wooden armchair in her neat front parlor, and opened an illustrated can of sugar cookies that sat upon a doily on the table.

"Just tea would be fine," said Alex. "If it's no trouble. The fact is, Gerald Meyer more or less asked me to see you."

"So our friend told me." Lady Jane remained standing, seeming to bounce on her toes like a friendly but skittish little mountain goat. "Gerald Meyer. The poor man. I wonder why. I haven't seen him in forty years."

"You haven't?"

"No. I'm British, you understand. Leo—that was my husband—escaped from Germany in the twenties. Well, you don't want me to go on about family history. After the war—I became a nurse, did I say?—Gerald was a young American GI. . . ."

"Did you know anyone from that time who might still be in contact?" Alex asked. "I believe he wanted you to point me toward someone else. Someone he met in your house, maybe, or at least in your company?"

"Really? Did he say so? I don't know. . . . I used to look in on Cynthia, the daughter, in her house—when I would visit Berlin. She wasn't keen on it, though. I don't think she liked the English-speaking nations very well."

"She lived several years in the States, according to her father."

"Is that so?" Lady Jane Friedhoff smiled brightly as she shook her white head. "There, you see, I hadn't even known that. Gerald Meyer. He meant well, I think—with his mar-

94

riage, I mean—but when it came time to bring the poor girl over . . . well, he just couldn't face it, you see. Now, you take your pick of these biscuits, while I see about that tea."

She disappeared through a doorway toward the kitchen, leaving Alex nothing to do but sit and take his pick. No, Gerald Meyer had not been able to face it, that was clear. To stand up to the outrage a Jew would get for bringing home even a "good" German in 1945, love or no love, was not the kind of thing a man who changed his mind about sending packages could manage.

Nibbling at a stale cookie, Alex wondered just what he had expected to learn here. He was chasing a rambling comment from a morose, drunken Meyer in the Logan Airport bar. This was a wild-goose chase with which Jack Moselle had been only too willing to help. Still, he supposed it was better than being at home, sleeping the day off. That would be just ducking his head against the onslaught of the chemical-imbalance depression that he knew was coming. Better to be out and about, making forward motion, however small. Some tidbit about the young Gerald Meyer might prove useful. What, though? The brand of cigarettes he smoked, Camels or Luckies? The way he earned his pocket money? At the sound of a muffled voice, Alex stood up, but the sprightly if vague old Lady had not returned.

"Excuse me?" he called out. "Did you say something?" He got no answer, but he heard a key turn in the latch of the street door behind him. The door admitted a tall man in a dark cloth cap, a dark suit, and an open olive-green poplin raincoat. Under the cap, he had a soft round face with sharp eyes.

"Come with me now, Mr. Glauberman," he commanded. "Right quick, too. No getting away this time. You're interested in motorcars, they say. I've got a right nice Jag. Step lively now."

The tone was bored, but the man's bearing was alert. He looked like a crafty choir boy, except for the lines and the deep pouches under the eyes. Beneath the left pouch an old white scar stood out, reaching all the way to the soft chin.

Alex turned toward the doorway through which his hostess had left. She was in it again, but only said, "Better do what he says, dear. The tea will have to wait for some other time."

"Lady Jane Friedhoff," Alex said. "Well, I should have known. Okay, Mr. uh . . . whoever. Let's go take a look."

Alex did not attempt to argue or to run as the big man followed him out the door. A cold drizzle fell on his head. The Jaguar, double-parked, was a deep maroon color. Inside, it had plush upholstery to match. The driver was just a kid himself, hatless, with short, razor-cut hair. He pulled away as soon as Alex and the man giving the orders were seated in back. A tape player emitted soft sounds from four speakers. A piano and a bass did something between kitsch and jazz.

"Take off your jacket," said the man in the cloth cap. He went through the pockets methodically, removing airplane napkins, half-chewed toothpicks, two ballpoint pens, the London street guide, and the slip of paper from Moselle's secretary. He said, "Empty your trousers and let me frisk you."

Alex handed over his wallet, the spare key to the house in Hackney, and some loose British change. He knelt awkwardly on the floor so the man could satisfy himself that this was really all.

"Don't carry much but the genuine item, do you?" Cloth Cap said in the monotone to which Alex was getting accustomed. "I'm lifting twenty quid to pay for my time. Don't look as though you'll miss it." He closed the wallet with a sharp snap and handed it to Alex. "Smart," he said, "leaving your passport home. If I nicked it, that would cost you a couple of days. No London address, neither—just this key here." He tossed the key up and down in his wide, creased palm, then returned it and the spare change as well.

"Now see here," he added. "We're both of us armed, Pete there and me. And I'm going to put this pair of cuffs on you to keep you from getting notions about taking off." He held up a pair of plastic handcuffs like garbage-bag ties—the kind police used for making mass arrests. Alex turned and put his hands behind him. The plastic cut into his flesh.

Mass arrest was not an experience Alex had gone through recently. But what he felt now was something he recognized from an earlier era. He accepted the cuffs much as he might have if he'd chosen to sit down in a singing, chant-ing crowd and then, finally, been dragged off to jail. It was the same feeling of being one moment big, bombastic, and the next moment small, a fly in a web. The same sudden realization that now, stuck, you lacked any resource at all except patience.

The driver came to a stop in a no-parking zone beside the Thames. Through the droplets on the window Alex could see a tour boat going by. He told himself that he wouldn't have been honored by lunch with the big boss, if his fate was to be dumped in the river by the hired help. He twisted his bound hands into the corner of the seat for comfort.

"Good," Cloth Cap said. "I like to see who I'm speaking to. Now. Suppose you're walking down a street like this, mate, after visiting the nobility and all. You expect the law and the Iron Lady and the Queen are behind you. Then some bloke nudges you into a car and takes you for a ride, and nobody lifts a finger. Gives you a nasty shock, don't it?"

Alex wanted to say that he didn't put much stock in the law or Mrs. Thatcher, but he couldn't guess what the man's politics might be. He couldn't summon up the nonchalance, either. A contorted shrug was the best he could do.

"Your friend Meyer tried to pull the seat out from under his old friend's arse. He tried to take away a businessman's protection under the law. That weren't fair play."

Alex nodded. A little information was better than none.

"What exactly did Meyer do?" he asked.

"Kinda literal-minded, aren't you?" Cloth Cap tilted Alex's head by the chin as if to see him in a different light. "Not in a place to be asking the questions, either. But now you got us by the short hairs, to a degree. So I'll explain it in words you can understand. Meyer had a bright idea to ball up the political protection."

Ah, thought Alex. A cog. A little tooth that makes a big wheel go round. A high-class bagman, working through his position in a very legitimate bank.

"So you got the idea now, do you? Now, the next idea is that you got nothing to do with that big boys' game. If the daughter's got something belongs to us, you just go and bring it back like a gentleman. Otherwise, we've got other means. Do you read me now, mate?"

"I think so."

"Good. 'Cause there's limits to our patience. Now, I don't know what the lady got out of you, but I'm asking you straight. Who the devil are you, and what other good turns did Meyer hire you on for?"

"I'm a car mechanic. I work in Somerville, Massachusetts. I like cars because I'm curious about how things work. I met Meyer in the post office in that town, this past Friday. I was curious about him. He had a proposition for me."

The big man shook his head, squinting at Alex in a fashion that creased the soft places around his eyes. Then he hammered his right fist into Alex's left cheekbone. Alex's head slammed back against the padded upholstery, just behind the side window. The fibers of the plush maroon ceiling went double before his eyes. The other fist exploded into his solar plexus. His mouth sprang open and struggled vainly to take in air. Instinctively he drew up his knees while he remained helpless, paralyzed, from the waist up. His lungs burned and then they slowly, painfully filled.

"He used to do that in the ring," Pete the driver said. "Think what he could do to your ugly face if he had room to wind up."

Cloth Cap took in Alex's troubles with his canny, deep-set eyes. "That may be the real goods you gave me, and it may not. That's not for me to say. But curiosity is something that you best forget all about. Now, where do we find you if we want you, here in London?"

"Sorry," said Alex. "That's personal."

The right fist hit the same spot again. Alex had the presence of mind to lean away from it. That lessened the shock of his skull against the car body, but it didn't do much for his cheek. This time the punch was like a spike piercing through to the bone. Alex made himself lower his knees, and waited for the rhythmic agony of the two-punch to his stomach or his crotch.

"You want it to stay personal," the man said, "you be a good soldier. If we want to take the trouble, there ain't gonna be much you can hide. Girlfriend, wife, kid, your old ma at home with her knitting. Okay, Pete, let's go. Where was you off to next, Mr. Glauberman?"

Still tensing for the next blow, Alex said as coolly as he could, "Victoria Station. If I'm going to do that job, then I've got tickets to buy."

"Victoria, Pete. Now she was a queen worth writing home about. Showed the fuckin' wogs what for, Victoria did." Alex was glad not to have said anything smart about Thatcher. Pete slid the Jaguar into gear and glided through slow, narrow streets, while Alex turned his eyes to the blurred, watery outlines of stone and brick. When the car came to a stop, Cloth Cap leaned past him to open the curbside door. "Out you go, then, mate. Victoria Street. Station's a block to the left. New Scotland Yard a short piece t'other way."

Alex had one foot out the door when he felt a small tug on his wrists. His shoulders relaxed as his arms fell free. He flinched at the thought of the blade that had sliced the cuffs, but in a burst of bravado he looked back to say thanks. The punch caught him sideways on the jaw and spilled his head out into the rain. Something like lightning against his ribs sent him sprawling on the broad sidewalk. He heard pedestrians *ooh* and *ah,* and sensed them forming a circle around him. The drizzle stung the raw skin of his cheek. He tasted sweet-and-salty blood on his tongue. When his vision cleared, he found himself surrounded by gaping teeth and staring eyes, shop windows full of goods dimly visible behind them. Spread fingers reached out for him.

The sleeve of his jacket had ripped on the pavement. He sat up, vaguely brushing it. His ribs still blazed, while his left shoulder ached dully where he had landed. He swallowed blood and probed through his beard to feel for the teeth on his lower jaw. They were all there. He supposed that had been one last warning he had received. After a few bloody swallows he accepted the hands of a young man in black leather and a woman with a stripe of purple hair.

"A falling-out with my new friend," he said when he stood. He was just in time to see the maroon Jaguar turn the corner back into the maze of side streets.

"Kicking out," said the woman with the stripe. "He kicked you right out. You better stay away from that shit."

The rest of the crowd, seeing someone take responsibility, moved on. Alex said, "Yeah, I'll try." He shook off the helpful hands and made his way, hunched over, fists in his pockets, down to the corner. He felt raw, raging, and foolish, all at once. He walked doggedly but gingerly, head down. When he reached the station, he continued across the big, grimy lobby, past the long trains backed up to the old iron gates, until at last an electric eye slid open the door to the Continental travel office before him.

He found himself in plastic-land, an insulated world of rounded counters and textured pastel walls. Taking a waiting number from beneath a digital prompter, he tried to slump back in an upholstered bench. He winced and stiffened as soon as his ribs took any weight. His mouth had stopped bleeding inside. He could feel the cheek swelling, and noticed that his right eye was starting to close. When the prompter signaled his turn, he presented himself to a long-faced man whose lank, parted hair showed a few flecks of gray.

The man pursed his lips as his eyes flickered over Alex, but when he set to work his eyes quickly veiled over. He guided Alex through the purchase of a second-class ticket to Berlin, via a Channel crossing to Ostend, Belgium. To catch his connection without leaving early in the morning, Mr. Glauberman would have to pay extra and take the jetfoil across. In Aachen, as Cynthia Meyer had said, his car would be tacked onto the Ost-West Express from Paris.

The clerk waited for his computer screen to register Alex's reservation. In the meantime, he told Alex that he might know Aachen by its French name of Aix-la-Chapelle, just as the Germans still knew Liége as Lüttich, no matter what. And both sides were still fighting over Cologne versus Köln. They would fight over it again someday, Mr. Glauberman would see.

When he said "fight," the clerk let his eyes pass disapprovingly over Alex's face. Then he advised him to invest five pounds in a couchette for the night journey from Aachen to

Berlin. It could get pretty grotty, he said, sitting up in a coach all night.

To Alex, none of it seemed the least bit real. He paid cash and left the station, boarding a double-decker bus at random. He rode for half an hour along a tortuous route through a flat, low-slung, endless gray city. This was Orwell's London, he thought. That gray, cheerless city of the grimmest future. It was not in ruins, nor under rocket bombs, but it exuded a cold, crumbling heartlessness from just beneath the surface of things. He remembered a line, perhaps the last one, from the hopeless conclusion of *Nineteen Eighty-four*. Winston dreamed that "the long-hoped-for bullet was entering his brain."

Maybe Meyer had hoped for that bullet, maybe not. Alex remembered making a point of that issue in Moselle's office, though he couldn't say why. From now on—he felt his jaw again and winced—it wasn't what Gerald Meyer wanted that mattered. He wasn't in this anymore to do his client's bidding. From now on, he was in it for lack of a way out.

Alex climbed down, finally, somewhere the driver said was Camden Town. The place didn't matter, really. The point was only to keep personal things personal, and not bring the results of his own willfulness down on Meredith and her friends. The point was to walk a few zigzag blocks hatless through the rain, to make sure as best he could that he wasn't being followed. Then he flagged a cab, telling the driver the neighborhood he wanted but not the address. When they reached familiar territory, he asked to be let off at the outdoor market.

The market had shrunk, most of the stall operators pursuing Monday fortunes elsewhere—or idle, or in the pubs, Alex didn't know. A few lifeless yellow chickens still dangled, and a stranded red fish observed the chickens with sightless, colorless eyes. Alex saw himself as Orwell's hero, Winston, stranded helpless like the fish. What was it the little man from the Thought Police had said?

Of course: "You are the dead."

* * *

Alex managed to take some comfort from the fact that his sentiments did not extend quite so far.

The house was still empty, though a new note from Meredith, in violet felt-tip pen, sat propped against the salt shaker: *Back again at five.* By this time it was too late for Alex to put ice on his bruises. He climbed unsteadily to the second floor and drew a bath, in which he lay submerged, soaking his injuries in the warm, womblike, buoying water.

When he woke the water was cold, and his head ached fiercely. He jumped up and then sat back immediately on the edge of the tub. He felt once again that someone had drained his oil and not replaced it. He stood slowly, dried himself gently, wrapped himself in the towel, and trudged upstairs through the empty house. At last he lowered himself carefully onto the bed, where his mind dragged him painfully around a slow, muddy racecourse, a course that began with Gerald Meyer in a long-ago occupied Berlin.

The course was marked with mileposts, and the mileposts were shattered lives. He knew this was a private tragedy that he had blundered into unasked, but that had opened and made room for him too. Now he was powerless to do anything but follow, and others, in his wake, could only follow him. When he woke again, he found himself sobbing into the pillow. Meredith was sitting beside him, pressing her fingers into the spasmodic muscles of his back.

"I really didn't mean to make things worse for you," Alex blurted out between shaken breaths. "I really didn't mean to be such a fool." Hiding his face from exposure and from contact, he felt Meredith massaging his back and neck, very lightly exploring the bruised surface of his left side, and then slowly stroking his hair. From a long way off, her words carried solace despite a hint of desperation.

"I don't know what happened to you, but this part now, this is only the drug. It's an aftereffect, that's all. Like a bad trip. Remember bad trips? The thoughts are real, but not . . . but not *usual.* The chemistry changes, and the thoughts change. It's the drug, honey, it's left you . . . without your armor. It'll grow back. Shh. Quiet now. It'll grow back soon."

14

Acceptance

Thank God, Meredith announced, for the morning at least there would be sun. She gave Alex a few minutes to study his face in the mirror, where purple beneath his eye seemed to glow eerily next to the darkness of his beard. He looked to himself like something out of a black-light exhibit. Meredith hurried him outside into the fresh air and lukewarm rays. She had on the red leather jacket again—an extended loan from Heloise, the medical student, it turned out.

"We'll go to the Center," she said. "You won't have to talk to anyone but me. And you wanted to pick up some books for Maria, didn't you?"

The Center, up Kingsland High Street, offered services to women, immigrants, and the unemployed. Attached to it was a coffee shop and bookstore that provided some income, perhaps.

. "Not much besides muffins and meat pies to eat," Meredith said on the way, "but those ought to do. There's Nicaraguan coffee without fear of the FBI, if you're drinking coffee again."

The little shop was crowded with mothers and babies, and with lone men and women reading newspapers. It had a few meat pies remaining. Alex felt washed-out still, and quite sore. But he was at home in his mind again. "It was my weakened state," he said with his mouth full. "I fell down the steps. Will your father buy that, would you say?"

"Women who get black eyes from their husbands have used it successfully for years." Meredith's color heightened, and her jaw set. "Father will believe what he wants to believe."

"Uh-huh," Alex agreed. "What else besides my bruises are we going to talk with him about?"

"I don't think it's a question of 'we.' You're the man he's come to see. Finance, government, matters like that will do fine. You know. Man to man. He enjoys showing off his knowledge of worldly things."

"But what he really wants to know is whether I'm planning to marry his wayward daughter. And if so, how I'll support her once I'm dead."

Meredith smiled for the first time. Her green eyes flashed. Her fingers on the coffee cup softened as well.

"He wants to know that, but he won't ask. Deep down, he just wants to know what kind of man you are."

"What kind am I?"

"After yesterday, from the sense you made last night, I'd say you're about as gullible as the average. And like all Americans, you're easily seduced by the prospect of meeting the peerage."

"Ouch. So you think there is no Friedhoff?"

"I doubt it. I think he meant a cemetery, as you said. Only *J . . . J* for *Jewish*, maybe."

"*Jüdische.* The Jewish cemetery, in Berlin?" Alex remembered something he would have been happy to forget. "Last night, in my circles, I was thinking about Berlin. The Reichstag, Hitler's bunker, streets where millions cheered him. That scared me. That's where the thread leads—the one I'm following back." He didn't follow it further just now. "Do you think your father is concerned about you cohabiting with a Jew?"

"Shit, Alex. He married Roger and me in his own

church, and the charm didn't hold. Probably he's happy I haven't come back with an African, or an Arab. Now, if you're feeling so cocky again, it's time for me to stop playing the supportive wife. Why don't you give this up, Alex, before you get in any deeper?"

Alex picked at flakes of pie crust on his plate. He wanted to say that nothing he'd confessed last night should be admissible against him.

"I don't know. I can't. I mean, I don't know how I could convince *them*, even if I did decide to give it up. And there's something about 'If you can't get mad, get even.'"

"So now you have to go," she said crossly, "because now you have something to prove."

"Oh-oh. That I'm a whole person—that I can handle this—that all my faculties are intact?"

"You said that, not I. I meant something sillier, and simpler—like that nobody can beat you up and get away with it."

She let that lie there on the table between them, adding nothing more. Alex offered her a concession, but it wasn't much. He promised to place a call to the Cambridge police that afternoon, as soon as he reached the Channel. Then he chose a book for Maria about a boy and girl in Jamaica living through a hurricane, and another about a strike organized by the animals in the London zoo. He tried not to deliberate too heavily over the selection, though the thought did cross his mind that these might be the last books he would ever buy her.

The Reverend Phillips was not tall, but he stood straight amid the swirling crowd by the entrance to the salad-and-sandwich shop. Brunch was in neutral territory, a pseudo-Continental place by Covent Garden. The old man's pinched face, like the hand he extended, was a pale red that reminded Alex of boiled ham. He'd been in his forties already when Meredith was born, but she swore he was now determined to outlive his children as he'd already outlived his wife. Not that he'd wanted to outlive his wife, but there it was. Meredith accepted his peck on the cheek and led the way inside.

In the stuffy booth, Alex shifted uneasily. Under the guise of stroking his beard, he tested what places he could touch his face without wincing. The Reverend eyed Alex while pointing a boiled finger at the "No Pershing/No Cruise" button on Meredith's purse. His sharp Adam's apple bobbed above his neat navy-blue bow tie.

"What is the sound of one hand clapping, as the Japanese monks ask?" he inquired.

"Excuse me?" Alex said. Judging by the Reverend's eyebrows, the question appeared to be directed at him.

"I favor disarmament in principle," Reverend Phillips explained, "but not unilaterally, like my daughter."

When Alex hesitated, Meredith began an answer about the unofficial peace movements of Eastern Europe. The old man cut her off. "Well, well," he said. "I didn't mean to provoke any disputation." Meredith flushed but took it. Alex hurried to create a diversion by explaining about falling down the stairs. Then, escaping that topic as well, he said he had a financial question on which perhaps Reverend Phillips could shed some light.

"Meredith didn't mention you were interested in banking, Mr. Glauberman." Reverend Phillips raised his brows, wrinkling the skin above. "Are you thinking of investing the proceeds from your business? To judge from my own local garage, automobile mechanics now have the rest of the populace over quite a barrel."

"No. I haven't got that kind of proceeds. But I got into a venture with a client who deals in bankers' acceptances. Would you mind telling me what those are, exactly?"

The Reverend made clearing-away motions with his hands, as if the explanation he was about to deliver were a trifle that anyone could be expected to know. Behind the motion, with a practiced air, he sifted the facts. Perhaps the man's problem was that, in retirement, he missed the opportunity to compose and deliver sermons.

"If I'd understood your interest, I could have brought you a cutting from the *Times*. They published a series on money-market instruments, not long ago. Suppose you wish to buy, for instance, a shipment of new dynamos for those Volkswagens you repair, hm? The dynamos are made by a manufacturer in Frankfurt, who is hardly going to advance any credit to an unknown American garage. An acceptance is a device by which a bank lends its good name to help you. In brief, you approach your banker, who issues a letter of credit promising to deliver payment within, for instance, ninety days. You, of course, must sign an agreement to provide the equal funds to your bank."

Alex nodded. The explanation was rapid and precise. It was the kind of gadget, unfortunately, for which a circuit diagram ought to come along with the text. But probably the gist was all he needed.

"Now that you have this unimpeachable backing," Reverend Phillips continued, "the manufacturer is happy to issue credit, provided he can slightly inflate the price of the dynamo. Because, you see, he doesn't have to wait the full ninety days to collect."

"Because. . . ."

"Because the manufacturer sells the letter of credit to his own bank, for slightly less than the face value. Now this scrap of paper may be sold and resold any number of times until those ninety days are up, at which time it is redeemed for full face value. You, in the meantime, repair the cars, collect from the customers, and pay off your bank."

"I get it," said Alex. This wasn't quite true, but he was at least memorizing the details for future mulling over. "It's kind of like a savings bond, which is gaining value all the time as it gets closer to maturity, only it all happens inside ninety days instead of twenty years. Where does the term acceptance come in?" He watched Meredith catch the eye of a waitress several tables away. Unless he was mistaken, preaching rather than eating was sustenance to the old man.

"There's an ancient convention that letters of credit must be submitted to the issuing bank for acceptance. Your bank would declare the instrument valid, and certify its intention to pay when the note comes due. An officer of the bank must stamp 'accepted' upon it—physically, I believe, though perhaps this now has been computerized. Then the letter of credit becomes an 'acceptance,' which may be traded in the market as I explained."

"So, after it's accepted, it doesn't matter whether I originally ordered a generator from Bosch, or Margaret Thatcher ordered a missile from General Dynamics, or a drug whole-saler ordered ten pounds of cocaine from Colombia, is that right? All that matters is that Bank of Boston, or whoever, stamps 'I accept' in big letters on the back? From then on, it's like a check made out to cash?"

"I believe so. Like quite a large check, of course. Many thousands, much more than the cost of a case of dynamos, in practice."

A piece of the diagram suddenly became clear in Alex's mind. "And what would keep someone who wields that stamp from stamping everything in sight, grocery bills or who knows what? Then he or she could sell them himself or herself, on the market?"

The Reverend frowned. "Almost always male, I should say. You see how this legislated equality is now legislating awkward phrases into the language. The answer would be something about the nature of the stamp or signature, I sup-pose, but more importantly the short maturity. Within ninety days the unlucky purchasers will begin trying to re-deem them. Since no customer will have paid in funds to cover them, an imbalance will rapidly show up on the bank's books. Your, ah, person with the stamp had better have caught a quick flight to Patagonia."

Alex looked meaningfully at Meredith, but she had got-ten the waitress and was now taking it on herself to place the orders. Whatever favors Gerald Meyer had done for Jack Mo-selle, he'd been doing for years, not days. When the ordering was done, Meredith remarked that capitalism, in its centuries of development, had produced truly bizarre and Byzantine ways of getting products from one place to another. Then she prodded the old man to talk about parish matters until fresh salad and not very fresh bread were served. Finally, the Rever-end held up a fork and leveled the tines at Alex.

"Mr. Glauberman. I can't help thinking that you had reasons other than academic ones for asking about bogus bankers' acceptances. Is that so?"

Alex wolfed down raw spinach and hard-boiled egg. No explanation came to mind, but Reverend Phillips's boiled-ham hand continued to demand one. This meeting was primarily a ritual combat, he reminded himself, and the goal was for the two parties to walk away with mutual respect.

"The client I mentioned may have been involved in something like that," he admitted. "The next thing I heard, he had died—suspiciously, perhaps suicide. I'm supposed to explain things to his daughter, in Berlin. That's why I'm in such a hurry today. I'm due at Victoria for my train."

"Ah," said the Reverend, crossing his fork and knife on his plate and then wiping his lips and setting down his napkin with a flourish. This, Alex imagined, was the way he must invite the parishioners to join him in song, if the Anglican church did that. Or it was the way he would gather away the fallen chess pieces after triumphantly crying "Check" and "Mate."

"Well, Berlin is not the city it once was. I'm told the Berliners appreciate a wry comment much more than a prolix explanation. It's been an old cleric's pleasure elucidating this mystery, but in the end, I suspect you're barking up the wrong tree. Mind you take good care of my daughter, when you return."

Alex looked back and forth from father to daughter, knowing better than to step into that breach.

15

White Cliffs

Alex kissed Meredith good-bye in Covent Garden, leaving her to the ministrations of her father. This was not so much to avoid farewells—though there was that—as to appear in the station alone. If anyone was keeping an eye on his departure, however, that eye was professional and invisible. Alex made his way past tour groups and reserved cars to a second-class coach near the front of the Channel-bound train. He sat next to an Englishwoman in a gray suit, who chatted about the theater to an identically dressed Englishwoman opposite. Nothing could be more normal.

The train's departure had the usual magical quality of imperceptibility. One moment the heavy car was stationary, motionless, a part of the scene. In the next its motionlessness was transformed by some alchemy into a slow, gliding acceleration. There was no sound of engines—on the wings or under any hood—no rush down the runway or letting out of the clutch; just a vague cerebral knowledge of a locomotive, pulling, somewhere ahead.

Perhaps, Alex thought, it was this unhurried inevitability of railroad travel that appealed to him. You went where the engine pulled, where the tracks led. You did not concern yourself, and you did not rush. For the two hours to Dover, he mulled over financial intricacies and then slept off the last of the washed-out feeling. When the train reached the sea, he felt that his yo-yo period was over for a while. He sniffed the salt air, then hurried to the jetfoil lounge and grabbed a phone. He had talked Meredith into lending him her credit card.

"Mr. Glauberman." Trevisone's response reached him, via satellite, from the other side of the Atlantic. It was clear, though slightly delayed. "Glad you could fit me in."

"Yes," said Alex. "Did Bernie call you?"

"Bernie?"

"Oh. That's my lawyer. I thought maybe he had called."

"No. It might be that he should. When did you give Gerald Meyer your business card?"

"My card?"

"That's what I said. Where the hell are you, anyway? Are you really in London?"

"I can see white cliffs outside," Alex told him, smart-mouthing automatically while he tried to figure out what was going on. Had the police found the card, in Meyer's hotel room maybe? Wouldn't they have searched the room the first day, before Trevisone had allowed Alex to leave? "When I get on the boat, I'll have a better view."

"Uh-huh. Been there myself. What country are you going to next?"

"I'm not sure, Sergeant."

"Uh-huh. The card had your handwriting on it, and your home address. So now it don't seem like such an accident he got shot outside your house."

"I give out lots of cards," Alex said. "You told me Meyer's pockets had been stripped. Where did you get this particular card, and what makes you think Meyer had it, or that Meyer got it from me?"

"Somebody gave it to us, somebody that wanted to be helpful to the police. It had Meyer's fingerprints on it."

Ah, Alex thought. So that's the way it fits together. That's why Trevisone only sent me a cable, instead of sending a bobbie to Meredith's door.

"Look, if the person who killed him planned ahead, they could easily have set that up," Alex reasoned. He knew the same reasoning would already have occurred to the detective. "Getting his prints on my card, using my house as a red herring. . . ."

"Yeah. But why you?"

"I'll get to that, if you'll give me a minute. Is there anything else that points to me?"

"Yeah. I found out you changed five hundred cash into British and German before you took off. That's a lot of cash to be carrying. And we found the murder weapon."

"You're not going to tell me you found my fingerprints on that?"

"No. It was wiped. But we did find it in the rubbish behind your shop. We're working on a search warrant. Where did you say you were Friday night?"

"In my shop, the way it says in my deposition. Look, Sergeant, that's a very neat picture, but you know it doesn't make any sense: I used my card to lure the guy to my home address, then I shot him, stashed the gun in an obvious place, collected my fee, and fled to the Old World. Then what? I've got a kid waiting for me, and I'll be back in two weeks just like I said. If you want me then, you can have me. The reason I called is because I have some loose ends for you. They aren't neat, and parts are probably wrong. Two guys grabbed Gerald Meyer in Davis Square, out of your jurisdiction, last Friday about five, and took him away and roughed him up. About six I sat and talked with him in Petros's coffee shop, three blocks from your desk. I told him I was going to Europe. He offered me twenty-five hundred dollars to visit his abandoned daughter while I was over here. He wanted me to get back something he sent her."

"Something like what?"

"I don't know, but I have a guess. That would be bankers' acceptances for nonexistent transactions, used to launder money for payoffs to public officials. Do you want me to say that again?"

There was a pause, longer than the transatlantic time delay. The pause ended with Trevisone saying, "Please."

"Bankers' acceptances for nonexistent transactions, used

to launder money to make payoffs to pols. You'll have to check this out through Meyer's bank. What I mean is, he was using his position to deliver bribes. The bribes weren't cash money, but something close to it."

"And why would he be doing that?"

"I don't know, and anyway, that's as much as I think it's safe for me to tell you right now. Somebody knows Meyer asked me to do this. I'm taking a chance by calling you at all. In another day, I might have more news."

"Glauberman, you are a first-class asshole, you know that? You withheld evidence so I'd let you go visit your girlfriend. And you're not visiting your girlfriend, am I right, you're going to see Meyer's daughter?"

"Well, asshole or not, I'm out of your reach. Maybe I've left you out on a limb, but now it's in both our interests to cooperate. Is there anything else it might be useful for me to know?"

Alex was afraid he might be pushing too hard, but apparently the detective was willing to do things Alex's way, like it or not.

"We got a tip that Meyer had been hitting the bottle at the airport," Trevisone said sarcastically, "in case you know anything about that. Anyway, we checked it out, in our jackass, slow and careful way. He tried to pick up a woman but she walked out on him. He left. He came back and tried again, seems like, and did better. He left with the second one. So it could've been a hooker with big ideas, I don't know. His pockets were empty, like I said. But why pull the trigger? And why your house? You know what this daughter looks like, by any chance?"

"She's got an alibi," Alex said. "She was in Berlin. I called her as soon as you guys left my place. I thought she deserved to know he was dead."

"Glauberman, you are the limit. Notifying the next of kin is my job, in case you didn't know. When you called her, she was in Berlin?"

"No, but she called me back an hour later."

"Oh. Right. And you knew her voice, and you could tell she was calling from Berlin. . . ."

"No, you're right, I jumped to a conclusion." He had

liked her on the phone, and didn't want her to be a killer. "I'll try not to jump to any more. Now look. Suppose I call you back tomorrow, about this same time? I appreciate you telling me as much as you have, and I'll try to do the same. Think of me like I'm your lonesome end." Alex laughed. "Or your Wandering Jew."

He heard a soft cough, a clearing of the throat on the other end of the line. "I don't give a fuck how you worship," Trevisone said. "Just make sure you call me back."

"Yes sir," Alex answered, and hung up. The jetfoil didn't board for another quarter hour, and he had one more call to make. He could just catch Maria before she left for school. That would be no help to Laura, trying to get kids out the door, but it would have to do.

Maria's voice was like a stranger's, unaccountably high-pitched and childish.

"This is Tuesday," Alex said. "So I'm on my way to Belgium. What's happening there, much?"

"Not much."

"Did you eat all the apples we picked?"

"I brought a bag to school, to share. Is Meredith with you?"

"No, I just left her and got on the train. Now I get on this jet-powered boat and zip across to Belgium, and another train into Germany."

Maria hadn't asked what he was riding where. She'd asked whether he was with Meredith.

"Probably I'll be with her again by the weekend," he added. "Do you like knowing who I'm with?"

Transatlantic silence greeted that.

"I took my last pills Sunday, so I'm all done with that for now."

"Did you sleep all day Monday?"

"Not all day, but a lot."

"And you were sad."

"Right. But not now."

"I've got to go."

"'Bye, kid. I miss you. I'll see you not this Saturday but the next."

Alex listened to the click of the broken connection.

Good marks on sparring with the sergeant, bad marks with the kid. But he didn't know what else he had wanted to say, or hear. Intimacy was a hard thing to get out of a telephone.

Maybe this place was getting to him. Dover. He'd crossed from here with Laura, a decade ago, on a sunny, early-fall day not too different from this. They'd sat somewhere and read World Series news in the *International Herald Trib*—Yankees demolished, four straight. Alex, Brooklyn-born, had taken it as an omen. He'd been seeking omens anyway, now that the decision was as good as made. On the crossing, they'd bought two small bottles of champagne. They'd gone on deck to drink up, and then they'd ceremoniously launched the empty bottles into the brine. The bottles had disappeared. They'd thrown Laura's diaphragm after.

Alex turned away from the phone and found himself wondering how Reverend Phillips would get on with his father, if they ever chanced to meet. Ira Glauberman had little affection for the Old World, and most likely it would take a wedding to coax Reverend Phillips across the other way. But just supposing. . . . Would Ira enjoy showing his new in-law the better delicatessens of Queens, and the tattered but still magical glories of Broadway?

Not that Alex had any interest in a repeat performance of marriage. Nor did the parson's daughter, as far as he knew. It was children she would have liked, not a ceremony or a title or a ring. He was only thinking these thoughts because he was here in Dover, missing his daughter. And because he was here in Dover, leaving Meredith behind.

16

Hitler's Ghost

The jetfoil might as well have been a 747, for all the sense it gave of being seaborne. Belted into his airliner-style seat, Alex found that the cramped windows and low angle yielded only a small slice of Channel to his eye. His thoughts went back to his father, who had crossed the waters not far west of here, without benefit of a view. His father had been down in the hold of a troopship, with German torpedoes and artillery zeroing in.

The Continent was at peace now, the alliances of nations reshaped. Or, as Bob Dylan had put it, "We for-gave the Germans, and they became friends." In the meantime the difference between war and peace had dwindled down to a question of seconds. Somewhere, in clean, modern underground bunkers, missile technicians sat poised to wage the deadliest of all European wars, and the last.

These dark musings reduced Alex's own murky business —and his bodily ills—to a pleasing insignificance. In Ostend, he stepped briskly off the craft onto a concrete walkway. He glanced backward over his shoulder toward the big jet engines mounted on the open deck. He would have liked to linger in the salt air and examine these machines. Instead, he followed the line of passengers onward into an enclosed, carpeted hallway. The Belgian officials were foppish and comical in their uniforms and braid, like a collection of clean-shaven Hercule Poirots. They asked no questions, stamped no passports, and stared at no bruises on one's face. They waved Alex forward toward his train.

Until darkness fell, he watched the passage of the right, tight green fields and the right, tight picture-book towns. Then night, the lights of Brussels, and darkness again. Sometimes the train plunged in and out of a deeper darkness, roaring through mountain tunnels. The German border crossing, just before nine, sounded a different note. Hearing clipped German commands spoken by young, blondish men in uniforms gave him a chill. Not long after, at Aachen, his car was dropped between platforms, on a middle track. Alex warmed up his dormant *Deutsch* by studying travelers' phrases in a pocket dictionary. *Liegewagen,* couchette car. *Anschliessen* (railroading term), to connect. Yes, he reminded himself, and also (geopolitical term) to annex. The *Anschluss* had taken Austria, if he remembered his history, in a single day.

When the Ost-West Express rolled in, Alex's car was pulled backward to a switch and then shoved forward, to be annexed. The coach passengers looked at their watches and stayed seated, but Alex picked up his things and descended to the platform in search of a *Liegewagen* to match the number on his reservation. He tried to acclimate his ear to snatches of conversation, picking out words as he passed. He found the right car toward the front of the train, the right compartment midway along its corridor.

The compartment was dark except for a reading light on one of the bottom couchettes. A black man, his eyes on a book, greeted Alex quietly in French. Opposite, a white woman, face to the wall, appeared to be asleep. The beds above these two had been folded down from the wall and provided with a sheet and blanket each. The third tier remained folded up against the walls. Only four reservations, then. The fourth occupant, presumably, would be boarding later in the night.

Lifting his bags to the rack, Alex spread out the sheet on one of the empty bunks. He pulled off his sneakers, mumbled *"Pardon"* as he stepped on the edge of the cushion where the man was reading, and pulled himself up. There was a strange, un-American communality about this accommodation. He bunched his windbreaker on top of the detachable armrest for a pillow, tucking his ticket and passport underneath. Then he lay flat, staring up into nothing, as the train pulled off toward the east. It would not reach Hannover until after midnight. He listened to the rhythmic clacking, and tried to conjure some vision of Cynthia Meyer.

All he could summon from the phone conversation was a tone of voice, a kind of mocking tone, mocking and self-mocking. The tone had taken him and his message in stride, and seen something perhaps darkly amusing in them. He wondered whom she might have become, if Gerald Meyer had brought her back with him to grow up in the fabulous fifties.

He could see her in Westchester, maybe, in a hired photographer's touched-up shot, at the bas mitzvah party she would surely have had. An uncomfortable just-teenager, she posed with her father's itchy woolen arm around her bare shoulders, awkward and blushing in a black formal dress against a white tablecloth and a bouquet of mixed flowers. Cindy Meyer. She squirmed in front of the camera with beautiful sad eyes, glowing cheeks, and honey-colored hair.

Alex was nearly asleep when the conductor slid open the door, demanding a ticket. In his best German, Alex asked to please be awakened at Hannover, where he was meeting someone. When he did sleep, the teenager in strapless black stole silently into his dream. She emerged, on Gerald Meyer's arm, from the North Terminal bar. Meyer's arm was around her waist now, and creeping upward in a drunken way to experimentally stroke her right breast. She recoiled, but there was no escaping her father's embrace. Then she stood beneath the living room windows of Alex's apartment, blowing smoke away from the barrel of a little nickel-plated gun. She put the gun into a black patent-leather bag with a silver clasp, which she handed to Alex through the window. There was a right thing to do with it, Alex was sure, but he didn't know what.

He woke with a start, frozen, then breathed and

dropped his head to the pillow and breathed again. He tried to meditate on his breath, matching the in-and-out to the clacking of the wheels. When the train stopped to take on and discharge passengers in Köln—or Cologne—Alex did not notice. He crossed the Rhine bridge in a dreamless sleep. It was much farther on that something woke him. The offending thing bothered his neck just below the Adam's apple. He reached to scratch at it, and then someone hissed curt syllables at him. He froze again.

"*Jud! Still! Schweig!*" Like a train barreling out of a tunnel, the meaning of the hiss loomed up at Alex, big and loud. "Jew! Don't move! Shut up!" It might have been another dream, but Alex opened his eyes into a blinding light surrounded by darkness.

"*Dass ist ein Messer!*" the hiss said. Alex swallowed and nodded a millimeter to show he understood. A knife.

"Passport!"

Alex slowly doubled his left arm back, hand toward his ear, to pluck his passport loose. The light—a flashlight—disappeared from his eyes, but before he could adjust to the change, the blinding circle came back. Alex listened hard to the sounds of breathing. Only one breath was close by, and only that one sounded awake: a lone assailant, with both hands busy.

"American Jew!" the hiss came again. "Where is Meyer? When do you meet?"

"*Wer?*" Alex whispered. He whispered the question so as not to alarm. He kept his left arm doubled back and ready.

"*Der Mischling,*" the urgent voice said. The mongrel, that meant. There was not going to be any reasoning with this man. There were not going to be any guessing games, either.

"Fuck you," Alex answered, in English. His left hand snapped over onto the knife-holder's wrist. It wasn't much, but it was enough to drive the blade away from his jugular. When he wasn't dead, he slammed his hand backward against where the source of the hiss ought to be. Then he rolled off the bed, against something. He butted. His head hit something that was solid at first, and then gave.

The attacker slipped and landed on the sleeping man,

then regained his feet and withdrew into the corridor. The sleeper, no longer sleeping, snapped on the light by his head and said something in French that Alex didn't understand. In the dim glow, Alex saw what he was looking for: a switch-blade, maybe five inches long. A wet dark red was smeared along one of the sharp, symmetrical, converging edges. Alex scooped the knife up with one hand. He explored with the other through a tear in his shirt.

Blood welled over his collarbone. It was a steady flow, but it did not spurt. Alex pulled himself up and stepped into the corridor in time to see a figure disappear toward the front of the train. He sliced off enough of the bottom of his shirt to make a decent compress. Pressing it tight against the cut, he stumbled the way the figure had gone. At the end of the car he flipped the door handle down with the hand that gripped the knife. He hoped to hell his platelets were in good shape. If he needed two hands, the clotting action was going to be up to them.

The door swung open onto the darkened, jouncing plat-form where the two cars met. It swung open, and then it tried to swing shut. Alex threw his left shoulder into the door, turning to brace his right hip against the frame. His bruised ribs complained. Through the opening, he slashed at cold air with his blade. That was stupid. The man had to be behind the door. Alex twisted into the empty space, letting the door shut.

Under his socks the coupled cars shifted, but the footing was not bad. The ends of the cars were covered by a sort of floor, and the rushing world outside was cordoned off with steel and glass. The force that had swung the door back was now a shadowy silhouette against the moonlit window. It became a mustached man in a leather jacket, lunging forward with outstretched hands. Alex swiped again with the blade. This time he connected. The man landed at his feet. Alex dropped on him and swiveled around, riding him like a horse. An exhilaration—a rodeo cowboy's rush—came with ending up on top. A thrill of being in action pounded through his veins, even as he could feel blood dripping out. He pressed the point of the knife to the back of the prone man's neck.

"Dass ist ein Messer," he said. *"Wer ist dein Chef?"*

Chef—the word came out of its own accord. Alex had always enjoyed calling Hans Heidenfelter *Chef.* He had relished the idea of a mechanic as cook—tuning an engine the way a chef might taste and season a soup. In German it meant chief. Boss.

"Who's your boss?" he demanded now. "Who pays you?" He kept all his weight on the man's back, the point of the blade against the short hair below the base of the skull. The man held still.

"Verstehe nicht."

"Bullshit," Alex retorted. *"Du verstehst."* With his free hand he tried to limit the flow of his own blood. But the hand that held the knife was beginning to shake. He forgot about clotting and he gripped the knife harder, with two hands. If the man under him was another messenger from Jack Moselle, Alex wanted to know it. Moselle's tentacles might be many and slippery, but for the moment this one was caught.

"You understand me. Who pays you? Then you can go."

"Gespenst des Hitler," the man spat out. Hitler's ghost. He heaved upward, leaving Alex a split second to plunge the knife in or get out of the way.

A split second was long enough. A quick plunge, a hard plunge between the vertebrae and into the spinal cord, would sever the nerves. It would slit the wires that made the machine work. No more current to the pump, no further instructions to the lungs. All the king's horses and all the king's men could never put little Nazi together again. It would be so clear, so simple, so fairy-tale bright—to kill an evil thing and to leave it behind him, dead in his path. But Alex stood up, the knife extended like a cross to ward off ghosts. In that split second he was both glad and sorry to find that it was one thing to fight, to draw blood, but another to kill for the pure power of it.

The man on the floor wriggled back, his spinal cord intact. He rose warily, one hand gripping the other wrist. As the man got up, Alex felt the train begin to slow.

"Raus," he commanded. He pointed the knife at the far

door. Power was still his, but not so much. "Get out. That way. Now."

When the man stood framed in the doorway, Alex took one hand from the knife to reach behind him for the handle of the door to his own car. He steadied himself, then flipped it down. For another second they eyed each other warily. Alex saw the suspended conflict of hate and fear on the man's face. He was shocked to think that it must mirror what showed on his own. Then the train braked more sharply, the cars shifting heavily underfoot. The attacker turned his leather back and vanished. Alex looked at the blade in his hand and slowly folded it shut against his leg. A conductor called out *"Hannover, absteigen. Für Hamburg, umsteigen. Für Frankfurt, umsteigen."*

Get off for Hannover, change for Hamburg and Frankfurt. Get off, or stay on board through to Berlin. Alex tossed the knife and the bloody cloth into a corner and hurried back to his compartment. The other occupants were wide awake now, and staring, but Alex only reached in to grab shoes, coat, ticket, and passport from the bed. The windbreaker covered his wound. In the corridor, he kept one hand inside, bunching his shirt against the slash as best he could. The train had braked to a slow glide. Station lights showed through the corridor windows. A few departing passengers lined up behind Alex, rubbing their eyes and talking in whispers.

When the train stopped, the conductor opened the door to reveal oncoming passengers waiting below. Only one of them interested Alex—a big woman in loose purple pants under a green, army-surplus-type field jacket. She carried a brown canvas duffel bag slung by a strap over one shoulder. To the strap of the bag was pinned a wilted white blossom on a long stem.

Alex jumped down and took her arm. Her hair was blond, as he'd imagined, though wilder. Her eyes, taking him in, were neither sad nor dark, but frank and blue. He noticed he was holding her arm tightly for support. The one word that came from his mouth sounded more pleading than he meant:

"Cynthia?"

"Alex Glauberman?"

"Yes." He answered quickly but quietly. "Couchette number one-oh-four, halfway down. Please. I've got a soft navy-blue bag, just the one. Get it for me, and come right back. Watch yourself. I met a man with a knife, looking for you. I ought to get to a hospital fairly quick."

17

More to Do with Freud

The matter-of-fact men and women in white cleaned the caked blood from the right side of Alex's chest and took two tubes of fresh blood from his left arm. Then they sewed him up, eight stitches, and told him in German to keep lying down. A while later, a uniformed policeman came in. Cynthia Meyer was with him.

Under the fluorescent surgical lighting, Cynthia's round, pink face revealed its share of wrinkles. Her hands, in fists, rested on wide hips. Her mouth was framed by her father's pale, translucent lips, but she parted them in an inviting, crooked smile that, despite the circumstances, did not appear sad. Alex wanted to ask how the man with the switchblade had known to ask for her, and why.

"I am to translate," she said, in her ironic, American-accented English. "If I give you any advice while I translate, please take it."

The policeman handed Alex back his passport. Cynthia had presented this item to the graveyard-shift admitting clerk when she had bullied their way through red tape earlier. Alex hadn't been able to follow the rapid-fire interchange, but he'd been thankful for the bullying. Before that, on the quick trip to the hospital, there had been just time enough for him to give her his medical data and a quick summary of events on the Ost-West Express. In return she'd told him that, if anyone asked, they had never before met or planned to meet. She was a random Good Samaritan, that was all.

"How did you get this wound?" the policeman asked. He didn't sound particularly curious.

"On the train. Somebody called me a Jew—which I am—and stuck a knife at my throat. I tried to get away, and he cut me. I did get away, but I decided I better get fixed up."

I cut him too, Alex thought, but for the moment, anyway, it seemed best to leave that part out. Alex's own prints would be on the handle of the knife, which someone, sooner or later, would find. A Jew's word against a German's—who had started what? Where did paranoia end, and caution begin?

"Why didn't you call a conductor to help you?"

"I don't know. I wanted a hospital more. I've been taking medications that can have serious side effects on my blood."

As Cynthia translated, the policeman nodded. Presumably the doctor who'd done the sewing would have certified the existence of Alex's extenuating tumors. A man in Alex's condition might be expected to show a few lapses of judgment. Maybe that would explain the bruises on his face, too.

"And you were traveling to?" Cynthia translated that as, "And where was the next stop on your vacation?"

"West Berlin. I'm planning to spend a few days looking around, then make a few more stops on my way back to London. Or I was. Does this kind of thing happen very often?"

The cop shook his head emphatically. "*Nein*. Never, in my experience. Can you describe this person?"

"A man with a mustache—early thirties, I'd guess—brown leather jacket, leather collar. Short hair, kind of light brown."

The description rated a few notes on a pad. "And if the

police in Berlin succeed in finding this man when the train arrives, would you be able to identify him?"

"Yes."

"When you leave the hospital, where will you go?"

"If he is not continuing on to Berlin," Cynthia said, "I will help him to find a hotel." She said it as if she had staked a claim that she was daring the policeman to challenge.

The cop looked her up and down. "Here or in Berlin," he told her to say to Alex, "please keep the police informed of your address. Your inconveniencing makes me sorry. It is very unusual. I really do not think anything like this will happen again."

With that, he turned on his heel and left. Cynthia made a face at him, for Alex's benefit, before she followed. A doctor appeared, introducing himself as Dr. Bazargan, a resident specializing in oncology. The cancer doctor wore thick, heavy-rimmed glasses and a heavily burdened air. His skin was faintly brown, and his accent British.

"I've been summoned from my bed to reassure you," he said. "We won't have laboratory results until tomorrow. But any depressive effect of cyclophosphamide on blood factors usually takes at least another week. It can vary with the kinetics of the patient, or course, but the first effect is on the production of stem cells. Only after a period of differentiation will this result in a depressed white count or subnormal production of platelets."

Alex nodded wearily at the jargon. Dr. Bazargan did not appear interested in conversation. Alex knew the physiology, having absorbed it in doses over the past months. He knew he could possibly have gotten himself stitched up, reasonably safely, without copping to his malady at all. But he feared asking his body to take too much, feared asking for too many favorable rolls of the dice from fate, from change, from God.

"Nonetheless, we want you to remain here until your counts come back from the lab. If you were to show any lowering of clotting or immune function, then we would want to keep you here while you heal. There would be a possibility of internal bleeding and infection. We would want to monitor you for that."

Alex nodded again. That was what he'd come for. Waiting, monitoring, observing—these were all ceremonies in a ritual he'd grudgingly accepted. In this ritual, one did not rush into the ring with cape and spear to do battle with the bull. One led the bull, or followed it, keeping one's distance, by means of a long stick and a ring through the nose. One kept a sharp, doubting eye on oneself, as well as on the bull.

"Well, if you have no questions," the resident went on, "you'll be moved into a regular room for what's left of the night. I'll stop by tomorrow late in the morning, I would guess. Most likely I'll have good news, and say good-bye."

"Oh—and my, uh, new friend?" Alex asked. "The lady who brought me here?"

The doctor—Iranian, Alex decided—delayed going back to bed for long enough to leer conspiratorially.

"I wish I were so lucky in the ladies I met. If you'd like, I will inform her you aren't in any danger. I'll tell her she may come again to see you in the morning, if she desires."

In the morning Alex stared into a bright, unflattering bathroom mirror. His bruised cheek was much improved, but his face as a whole had a pale, haggard look. His hair was full of knots and his beard entangled with bits of lint and some remnants of dried blood. He supposed he must have wiped his hand on it, the night before. All around, he looked like a medieval woodcut of a tattered ghetto Jew. He got back into bed to await developments.

A nurse arrived and pulled back the green plastic room divider to reveal a silent old man attached to too many bottles in the other bed. She rearranged the bottles with a perfunctory greeting. She closed the curtain and told Alex in German that the doctor would be in to see him before too long. Soon afterward, Cynthia arrived without escort by the police.

She had on the same loose deep purple drawstring pants she'd worn the night before. In place of the olive drab coat, she wore a black vinyl jacket zipped halfway up. Under the jacket was a T-shirt with a silk-screened slogan or pattern, Alex couldn't see what. She watched Alex watching her and said, "Luckily I have at least one acquaintance in Hannover, so I managed to beg a bed for the night. Now let's see the damage."

Alex unsnapped his hospital gown at the shoulder. "Eight stitches," he said. The stray hairs below his collarbone had been shaved to sanitize the repair job. His skin looked red, raw, until the black hair began again. Did German men have this much hair on their solid pink chests, he wondered. He wondered whose bed Cynthia had begged for the night. She patted his shoulder and said it appeared he would live. She remained standing next to the bed, loose fists on her hips like the night before.

"Are you experienced at such combats?" she asked.

Alex laughed at the phrasing. His own musings had given him a ready answer.

"I was pretty scrappy growing up, but the last switchblade I handled was the one my friend Tony used to carry on his nighttime adventures into Manhattan. We were fifteen, I think. I never used it. I don't think he did, either. Not then, anyway. I don't know what's happened to him since. Any word on the fellow I tangled with last night?"

Cynthia reached into the purse she'd dropped on the visitors' chair, a patterned woolen bag of what looked like Middle Eastern design. She rummaged as she talked, finally pulling out a small bundle wrapped in white waxed paper.

"Our stalwart police didn't find your alleged Nazi stepping off the train in Berlin. Either he got off there undetected, or he continued eastward out of their reach. So they say you might as well go on your way. And if I know what's good for me, I'll get out of their hair. They don't say that, but by now their computers will have told them something about me. I brought you some pastries. Here."

Alex accepted two sweet, sticky rolls. He wasn't sure he wanted to be mothered, or distracted from his line of questioning. But he was hungry, and there was no indication anyone was planning to serve him breakfast. He doubted that his roommate received any solid food at all.

"There's literally no place he could have got out between here and Berlin?"

"Practically speaking, no. One travels on a sealed train, like Lenin." She smiled the crooked smile again, lips parted over white teeth. Alex took the comment for a test, to see how poorly educated was this American she had been thrown in with.

"The Kaiser allowed Lenin to pass through Germany to Russia," he recited between bites of sweet roll. "The German general staff hoped the revolution would pull Russia's troops out of the war. But they wanted to make sure the Bolshevik leader wouldn't get a chance to infect the Kaiser's army during his passage. By the way, I think it was probably *your* Nazi, not mine. He seemed pretty sure of the fact that I was on my way to meet you."

"Correct about Lenin." She tilted her chin up in a way that implied a certain respect, but warned him not to take on any airs. "So now the DDR parrots the tactics of the Hohenzollerns. They provide a sealed train for the heretical Poles, as well as travelers like ourselves from the West. The Ost-West Express stops in Berlin, East and West, but nowhere else between here and the Polish border. As to whose Nazi, I suspect we may be able to share."

The last word was accompanied by a motion of her hands, coming together with fingers laced, and the index fingers pointed upward like a steeple. Without reason, Alex imagined her wide hips pressed tightly against his, her energetic thighs quivering around him.

"Would you mind showing me your passport?" he asked abruptly.

Cynthia raised her eyebrows, but plucked the passport from her bag and tossed it onto his lap. She sat while he thumbed through the visa pages. She'd been to Italy once—via Czechoslovakia, it appeared. Aside from that, a mass of rubber stamps showed she'd been back and forth across East Germany from Berlin quite a number of times. The stamps bore images of locomotives, some diesel and some steam. She hadn't been to England or America, not on this passport anyway. By its date of issue, it was three years old.

"I used to teach school in Frankfurt," she said dryly. "I still have friends there. That's where I was coming from, if you have to know."

Alex shook his head, but leafed through the passport once more anyway.

"No, there's a police detective who dreamed up the idea that you weren't really in Europe when you and I talked on the phone. I can reassure him, and maybe get some information in return. Now, what about what happened to me on the train? That guy seemed to know something about you, or about your ancestry anyway. I think the word he used was *Mischling*."

"As in 'half-breed,'" she said. "Like a dog, you know." She reached into her bag again and pulled out a magazine, opening it to the page she wanted him to see. "Look. This is an exposé about a game that someone has been circulating, in discos and schools. The board is a six-pointed star; each player chooses a color as his target: purple for the gays, red for the Communists, yellow for the Jews. The goal is to gas as many as possible. Its purpose is to teach contempt, and contempt is something to which we Germans are susceptible. Whoever that was, on the train, the psychological reality is that he was trying to build up that sort of contempt inside himself."

The magazine was on newsprint, with smudgy black-and-white photos. Alex looked it over, then passed both magazine and passport back. Cynthia's hand covered his, seeming to linger longer than necessary. Alex had a sense like what he'd felt with her and the policeman the night before—something about being taken possession of. Afterward she jumped up and paced to the wall and back, in the space between Alex's bed and the green plastic curtain.

"This is not just something German," she said after a few paces. "These neo-Nazis are part of a larger mood, a racist mood, in the Western world at large. Look at your own country. Look at Reagan, who came here to make his peace with the graves of the SS. Look at Rambo, the ugliest American yet."

She stopped opposite him and fastened the snaps he had left undone, covering his bandaged wound. Alex imagined the hands unfastening instead, exploring his chest. Her chosen topic was hardly a sexy one, but he was sure that something was going on. He couldn't yet put his finger on the chemistry at work. He felt it had more to do with Freud than with Hitler.

"Nazism and anti-Semitism are officially illegal in Germany," Cynthia resumed. "But legalisms do not matter very much. Race discrimination is illegal in the United States. We have right-wing parties that officially disavow Hilter, but long for the past nonetheless. We have veterans' organizations that turn out for the funerals of Luftwaffe and SS heroes. And—especially in the next generation—yours and mine—, there are paramilitary grouplets. They have names like Army Sports Club, and Stalwart Vikings, and Steel Swords for the Defense of Europe. They shoot people and bomb buildings, too. Primarily 'guest workers' and their houses—Turks, Vietnamese—but also American blacks, and Jews. Not many, a few a year, some years none."

Alex concentrated, with an effort, on the thread of her argument.

"The police don't seem to take what happened to me too seriously," he said.

"Well, they do raid some of these groups, from time to time. Then things get embarrassing, because Nazi leaflets are discovered in the home of a small-town mayor or a police captain, someone like that. But in general, it's the left rather than the right that's seen as a danger to the state."

"I see," Alex said. "You must have been quite a teacher." It occurred to him that all his favorite women were teachers, or once had been.

She smiled. There was definitely a crookedness—a kind of squint on one side, a lifted eyebrow on the other—that offset the ruddy cheeks and the tumble of wavy yellow hair. It was the combination that appealed to Alex.

"Leaping to the big picture rather than remaining with the small is a German intellectual vice. Not only teachers exhibit it. That is one reason, I think, why we tend to hurry to extremes. But I was enthusiastic about my work, yes, until the *Berufsverbot* caught me."

"Occupational ban?" he translated.

"One of our special democratic laws." She sat in the chair again, and this explanation came out wearier than the ones before. "You can be kicked out of teaching if it's discovered your loyalty to the state might be questionable. If you ever demonstrated against NATO missiles, for instance. Or the American war in Vietnam. This conveniently weeds out people who would like to introduce ways of life that involve more than taking orders and getting rich. The younger generation is kept out of the reach of socialistic and pacifistic influences. They hope. That's why I wanted to play down our connection, you see. I'm on a good number of such lists. Apparently we are destined to be allies, in something. I don't think it will help us for the police to decide you are a wounded terrorist in disguise."

"I see," said Alex. "And after you got weeded out . . ."

"After I was fired, I went to California for a few years. When my mother got sick, I came home to Berlin to be with her. I took over the *Gasthaus,* the pension, and I got to like it."

"And your mother?"

"She died. *Krebs,* cancer." Cynthia did not look away from Alex, as many people would. She held his gaze with her clear blue eyes and added, "And now they want to light our streets and protect us from the Soviets—with plutonium, so more of us will die." Only when her point was made did she drop her eyes suddenly, and surprise him by picking nervously at loose bits of cotton on the bedsheet.

"Now I hope I've established my credentials," she said finally. "Isn't it time for you to tell me about what happened to my so-called father?"

Alex suppressed an impulse to hold the fidgeting hands that picked and smoothed at the fabric near his thigh. He wanted to make them steady and strong, the way they had been until now. He couldn't change Gerald Meyer's story, however. He delivered the facts bare-boned, without a sugar coating.

"Last Friday he mailed you something. Two men who were following him seemed to want it. He may have told them where he'd sent it, I don't know. He hired me to traipse after you and get it back. Then he met a woman, unknown, at the airport. Soon after that he was shot at close range, behind my house.

"Since then, someone has tried to implicate me with planted evidence. And a man in London named Jack Moselle has told me to do what Gerald Meyer hired me for, but deliver the goods back to him. The legalities aren't clear to me, but practically speaking, I guess these goods belong to you. You also probably know a lot more about Moselle than I do. So I was on my way to talk all this over. It still looks to me as though, whoever's a Jew or half of one, it was the idea of our having that talk that somebody didn't like."

18

Wurst and Gravy

"Your counts are fine," declared Dr. Bazargan in a flat tone. "Be sure to get them checked again at the end of the week. Don't bathe the wound until tomorrow. Watch for redness, draining, or swelling, and have the stitches taken out ten days hence." Then he stepped out, for a moment, from behind his mask. He took his right hand from the pocket of his white coat, and pointed with his index finger at Alex. The pinkie—if that was an appropriate term—and ring finger were missing.

"If I may say so," the doctor commented, "you seem to be getting in a good deal of trouble. My advice is to wait another six months before you try to show the world how fit you are to fight it."

The Shah or the Ayatollah? Alex wanted to ask. He forced himself to look at the face rather than the absent fingers. The doctor put his hand back in his pocket and turned on his heel as he had the night before. He turned again in the doorway.

"I appreciate the advice, Doctor," Alex said. "Maybe it's just that I like fighting someone my own size."

"Not microscopic, you mean? Take care, Mr. Glauberman, not to choose someone too big for you. We all have a bit of Don Quixote in us. When we get close enough to the windmill, we observe that its vanes have the edge of a scalpel. Most of us put up our lance and say, 'Just having a bit of fun, sir.' Then we turn tail and ride off, if we value our necks."

Alex ran his right thumb and forefinger along his neck. He was trying to remember whether Don Quixote's had been protected by a beard. He didn't doubt that the doctor was speaking from experience. He supposed he just hadn't as yet had a close enough look at those vanes.

At the hospital door, Cynthia waved to a man in a little white Fiat waiting at the curb. In the backseat were Alex's bag and her own, minus the white rose. Alex climbed in beside these. "Wolf," Cynthia said, seating herself in front. "Alex."

Wolf's hair was neatly parted, wavy light brown, and cut just to the collar of his tweed sport jacket. He turned and extended a hand toward Alex. A small button on his lapel displayed a mushroom cloud with a diagonal line through it. He said nothing, drove his passengers to the station, and sped off.

The sign directing them to the proper platform read BERLIN-POZNAN-WARSAW-MOSCOW. Cynthia reported in a travel guide's manner that Poznan had been the medieval seat of the Polish kings, annexed by Prussia at the end of the eighteenth century. German colonists, including her maternal ancestors, had skimmed the cream from the city and the province, both of which they had renamed Posen. After World War I, the Treaty of Versailles had made her grandparents into Polish citizens. They had sent their daughters to Berlin for schooling, and welcomed the Nazi troops when they came. The Nazis had deported the majority of the citizens, according to race: ethnic Poles to slave-labor camps, Jews to the camps equipped with ovens. Now Poznan was Polish again. She and her mother had visited once. Many of the older residents spoke German, but none would admit it.

Alex swallowed and said his own ancestors had come from eastern Poland or Russia, it was hard to know which. Probably many relatives had died in the camps, but none whose stories he knew. He asked her about the silent Wolf—was he a teacher, too?

"Oh, Wolf? No, Wolf is the proverbial gay interior decorator. He used to be a hotshot architect, actually, before he gave that all up. He credits me with saving his little brother from life at the wrong end of a needle. You'll meet Hans, most likely, in Berlin."

Alex could not work up much enthusiasm for meeting Hans or anyone else, but he found himself absurdly placated by Wolf's sexual orientation. When the twelve-thirty train pulled in from Paris, he followed Cynthia forward to the dining car—warm and shabby and pleasingly old-fashioned. Two rows of long, high tables extended from the walls, with a narrow aisle between. Cynthia placed orders with the cook, a stout man with thinning hair, clad in a white apron. Alex chose a stool at an empty table.

Behind Alex, a woman smoked silently as a man harangued her in a strong New York accent about what was wrong with her attitude. Alex was about to move, but Cynthia came toward him with a bottle of beer in each hand. He noted that heads turned to watch her move.

"To our sealed train," she said. "I see a few Russians, by the way. The men drinking at the far table, there. They book the first-class sleepers, to cut down on fraternization, but they come out here for air. That's an American couple behind you, right, the ones fighting? I don't notice any Poles. Lots of Germans, but none with a mustache and a brown jacket. Are you worried, Alex? Or are you as nonchalant as you pretend?"

Alex sipped his beer slowly. It had a bit more sour taste than its American counterparts, but was nothing to write home about. Cigarette smoke swirled past him.

"I keep telling people," he said irritably, "I fix cars. It's two parts understanding how they work, one part trial and error, one part persistence, and one part muscle. I'm confident that same guy isn't lurking behind me right at this

moment. The more you can tell me about what's going on—
and the more I can believe it—the better I'll feel about any
chances I choose to take."

Cynthia regarded him with amusement. "Very logical,
very German. Sometimes I think all men should be Germans
—even Jews. Who are you, besides a man that fixes cars?"

"Born 1947, formerly married, one daughter, about half
of a college education, widely read, moderately traveled. Cur-
rently well-attached to a British citizen, professor of literature
and women's studies." That seemed too abrupt, so he went
on. "I have tendencies toward being a hermit, but I'm getting
a little bored with spending all day among machines. I play
first base sometimes."

Cynthia swiveled on her stool and went to the counter
for the food. This time she came back with two paper plates
that might have issued from a vanished diner in the American
Midwest. Thick wursts swam in a greasy brown gravy, along
with soft, overcooked peas and slices of soft tomato. Alex
found himself suddenly delighted to be alive, and attacked
the food with enthusiasm. It was warm, solid, and delicious.
They both mopped up their plates with thick slices of dry
bread. Alex swallowed the rest of his beer. Cynthia slid her
tongue over her teeth, gathering up anything that was left in
the way of food.

"Okay," she said. "That improves my mood, and it looks
like it improves yours. *Dann Gut.* Let me answer some questions you haven't asked yet.

"I told you how I came to be running the *Gasthaus.*
Since my mother's time, I've made it less conventional. I get
more than my share of punks, antinuclear activists, non-
whites, gays and lesbians, and such. I sometimes harbor
aliens without papers and, within my limits, others who are
trying to stay away from the cops. My circle of friends is
enough to make me an obvious target for neo-Nazi threats in
Berlin. On top of that, my friends and I are active in trying
to expose these groups. You remember the magazine article I
showed you. We're particularly concerned about their influence in the army and police.

"But you believe that what happened to you last night
has something to do with the death of my father. All right. I

have not usually thought of myself as having a father at all. I have his name, because my mother never remarried. She had her share of lovers, of love, of life, but she had no more desire to marry."

Alex was conscious of her legs, dangling from the stool, in rocking motion as she talked. She seemed as though she would be happier moving, pacing, attracting an audience as she lectured. Innkeepers performed, just as teachers did. They kept in motion, clearing, serving, ushering in and out, lecturing the new arrivals, giving advice.

She stopped, unzipped the vinyl jacket, slid it off, and folded it in her lap. The green T-shirt, underneath, said in faded letters, "Reagan Go Home." Sizable breasts with obvious nipples gave a solid shape to the injunction. Cynthia brushed tousled hair back from her face.

"Jack Moselle is someone I have known since I was a child. He was an old crony of my father's. He liked to make a fuss about making up for his friend's defection—a stag demonstrating its dominance by protecting the females. He arranged the mortgage on our building, so that my mother could buy it and repair the war damage. He used to stay with us, later, when he returned on visits to Berlin. Now we move in different circles, but—excuse me—is this your first trip behind the famous Curtain?"

Alex swiveled on his stool to see a pair of green-uniformed men with caps like taxi drivers wore in the films of the thirties. "Passport," they demanded. The taller one, with a hatchet face, stared hard at Alex's Kodacolor photo and then back at Alex. The passport came back stamped with date, place, and time of entry, and the steam locomotive. Alex swallowed involuntarily and waited while Cynthia went through the same treatment.

"So, what can you tell me about Jack's circles today?" he asked. "Particularly any part that has to do with payoffs to public officials."

Cynthia watched the border police chat with the cook and then proceed through the front door to the next car. "Look," she said, pointing out the window, to the north, and back somewhat toward the end of the train.

"Out that way, in the Free World, is the port of Hamburg. In that port cocaine and heroin are unloaded, concealed among the cargo of certain ships. An official must be persuaded to look the other way. That is one of the kinds of things Jack Moselle is good at. Or maybe, to make things go more smoothly, it would be best to change which political party controls the municipal government. Jack also becomes involved in things like that."

"Interface," Alex said. "How do you know about this, if you move in such different circles?"

"Well, Jack and I find it useful still to exchange information sometimes. For instance, one way to remove or pressure a chief of police or a customs inspector is to reveal that he is also a member of a proto-fascist gun club, or that he once was a member of the Hitler Youth. These things are all right in private, but it is not good for them to be in the news. So Jack likes to keep tabs on such things, and so, for the quite different reasons I've explained, do I and my friends."

"Would Jack be above having people killed, if they double-crossed him or got in his way?"

"I doubt it."

"And so, supposing your father decided to hold on to some valuable financial paper, instead of sending it on to a customs official in Hamburg? Supposing he planned to cash it in himself—or send it in a registered parcel to his daughter?"

"It doesn't seem as if that would be very smart."

No. It hadn't been. Alex chewed a corner of his lip and then got down to what was bothering him.

"You and Jack—that seems an odd alliance to me, if you don't mind my saying so."

Blood rushed to her face but subsided quickly. Alex watched her carefully in a split second of indecision that followed. Her cheeks sagged, and for the first time a furtive quality came into her eyes. She finished her beer while her legs under the counter grew still.

"You have a daughter, but you did not say how old. I told you Jack liked to act as a stand-in for my vanished father. Teenage girls are often very angry at their mothers. I was no exception. I blamed her for the fact of my not having a father —something I am very sorry for, and one of the reasons Gerald Meyer's death doesn't fill me with sadness, whoever was responsible. As to Jack, he was delighted to help me get away from home for a while. . . ."

Alex felt a little firmer grasp on things. Particularly on that chance meeting—if it was chance—in which Jack and Jerry had caught up on their lives over gin and beer on Threadneedle Street.

"Do you mean that you and Jack Moselle are ex-lovers?"

"Lovers?" Cynthia pounced on the word, and her ironic tone came back. "Love had nothing to do with it, on either side, you can be sure. But to accept your euphemism, yes. It might be more accurate to say we hated together, for a while."

"Hated what?"

"My mother, of course. Women didn't reject Jack often, particularly those who were in his debt. Don't be awkward, Alex. Turning a knife is not generally a good way to get people to open up."

No, thought Alex, it's not. But it's often a good way to keep them on a leash.

Oh, and Jerry, Jack would have said. *Let me tell you, you have one hell of a fine daughter. What she lacks in experience, she makes up in fire.* Or better words, to the same effect. Meyer would have hated the coarseness, hated Jack for flaunting this at him, but he would have sat still for it because he didn't have any right to protest. Alex wondered just how Gerald Meyer would have nursed the grudge. Would he have done what Jack wanted, and made a profit, but also waited for a time, and a way, to get even?

19

Aunt Frieda's Tale

The West Berlin station, unofficially, is always referred to as "Berlin Zoo." The nickname comes from what's located across the street, where the big Tiergarten comes to a point like an arrow stabbing into the commercial heart of the city. Alex and Cynthia's train pulled into the Zoo just after six, when it was too late to collect registered mail if any was waiting. Alex excused himself to call Trevisone, who might soon be heading out to lunch. He wasn't surprised to find the German pay phones new, shiny, and easy to use.

"Glauberman," Trevisone said. "Nice of you to call every day."

"I thought you might want to know about the daughter. I checked her passport, and she's clear."

"Is that so? And this thing Meyer mailed before he got shot, have you checked into that?"

Alex couldn't help feeling that Trevisone was more sarcastic, and less curious, than he had been the day before. Something had happened to change the chemistry, he feared, but he couldn't tell what. "Not yet," he said. He tried to make his next statement dramatic. "Last night, somebody tried to keep me from getting to it."

"Glauberman, look," Trevisone replied. Now he just sounded tired. "I talked to your lawyer. For a guy that works with a wrench, you've got a pretty fancy one. I talked to your doctor. I talked to the girl you got to follow Meyer out to the airport, and I even talked to your ex-wife. My advice is, come home. If you won't come home, stay the hell away from this Meyer business."

"Wait a minute," Alex said. "You mean I'm not a suspect anymore?"

"Disappointed? If I could get hold of you, I'd slap you with something just to keep you still. Like the weed the Somerville police force found when they looked around your shop. But as far as who pulled the trigger next to Meyer's head, right now I've got a suspect that's a lot better than you."

Uh-oh, thought Alex. There goes our beautiful relationship.

"You mean the airport mystery lady?"

"There's no more mystery."

"Who is she?"

Trevisone might have hesitated, or it might have been the time delay.

"It's none of your business, but she's just Meyer's girlfriend, all right?"

"Oh. Well, did you check into the suggestion I made about the bank?"

"I called, yeah. New York bankers don't exactly bare their souls to a guinea cop from out of town. They raised their eyebrows over the phone and said they'd investigate."

"Sergeant," Alex said, "do you remember our little conversation about names? I want to tell you where mine comes from, if you don't mind."

Alex could see Trevisone narrowing his sharp eyes and stroking his Billy Martin mustache. Whatever he had figured out, or thought he had, he wouldn't be one to throw away any loose ends.

"If it's quick. As long as you're paying for the call."

"This story comes from my Aunt Frieda. My great-

great-grandfather, or whoever it was, worked in the slaughterhouse back in the time when they were handing out last names. His job was to make sure the animals got killed in the kosher way. He was the—I don't know what it was called officially, but he was like the umpire. If he said it was kosher, it was. If he said it wasn't, it wasn't. There was no appeal, he was it. So they named him Gloibermann, from *gloiben*, it means 'believe.' It got changed from Yiddish back into the German somehow, when my grandfather came over. But I'm still the Glauberman, Sergeant, do you see what I mean?

"No."

"Death-by-mistress may be nice and neat, but I'm telling you something's not kosher. Now I've got some names for you to dangle in front of those closemouthed bankers: Interface, Incorporated, in London. And the head man, whose name is Moselle. Originally Mazelli. See whether those names make any bankers jump."

"And supposing I say that security frauds, or whatever you're driving at, aren't in my jurisdiction? Supposing I tell you I already got a call from a federal government agency, reminding me of this?"

Knowledge, persistence, trial and error. Alex smiled almost shyly to himself. He remembered the customer who'd brought in the last ailing Volvo, pleading for a quick repair job before Alex's vacation. The man had been certain the frightening noises meant a bent push rod, a demolished bearing, or worse. But Alex had listened, placed the tip of a big screwdriver to the gear cover, and listened again. Then he'd loosened the fan belt and given the crankshaft pulley a little twist. He'd felt the give, and he'd known what it was. Now he saw his hypothesis about Meyer confirmed in the same way.

"Thank you, Sergeant. Of course they did. That would mean your federal agency had already been looking into the funny paper that went across Meyer's desk. Which might explain one of the things Meyer was afraid of. Okay. I gave you the names. I can give you a supposition, too, and maybe that'll be the excuse you need to follow them up. Suppose I don't take your advice. Suppose I keep messing with this, and I screw it up, and somebody pulls a trigger next to my head.

143

Won't that be your job to look into? If you do what I suggest now, you'll have a head start."

"Yeah," Trevisone said. "I appreciate you thinking that out for me. You're a really generous guy."

At this hour, on the Ku-Damm, the neon was just coming into its own. Cynthia gave the commercial sprawl a dismissive wave.

"That's the *real* zoo," she said. "Everything for sale, and everyone looking to buy or to sell. I am taking you to see a different Berlin, the other way, toward the Wall. The Kreuzberg, where I live, is the . . . the Haight-Ashbury, I used to say, but that's not really it. We are an old respectable neighborhood that is now also a beacon for squatters and foreigners and the alternative culture. While it lasts. This is a city with no room to expand, and the specter of no place one can afford to live threatens us all. *Berg* means 'mountain,' you understand, though the district is mostly flat. Our *Gasthaus* is at the foot of the hill, close by the Victory Park."

"Which victory?" Alex asked when she paused. He knew how to be star pupil, when appropriate.

"Over Napoleon. It was the Russian winter's victory, really. The Prussian army fell on him as he retreated from that disaster. But the monument will not tell you that."

In Berlin, entrance to the U-Bahn was by the honor system. Some passengers shoved tickets into an automated orange pillar to be punched. Others, including Cynthia, did not. The station where she and Alex exited, two trains later, was decorated with grainy enlargements of black-and-white photographs. On one wall, an elevated railway ran on stone arches past nineteenth-century buildings, pseudo-baroque. On the next wall, the buildings were reduced to shells and the railway bridge had collapsed. Half the arches were gone. Twisted steel rails and a mangled, windowless car dangled from the wreckage.

Alex and Cynthia climbed the stairs to the surface, where a scene greeted them that bore no resemblance to either photo. Across a traffic circle rose a mammoth poured-concrete structure, surrounded by high chain-link fencing and topped with radio and microwave towers.

"*Polizeipräsidium*," Cynthia said. "Central police headquarters. Behind it is the military airport. Site of the Airlift, you know. Maybe the pictures are supposed to remind us of the folly of war, or maybe the error of defeat. Come on. I'll take you by the scenic route."

The scenic route led past a small shopping district and then up a winding blacktop road through surprisingly dense woods. Alex's breath came harder, and the weight of his bag seemed to pull at his stitches. Cynthia stopped in a clearing, near the top, where a stream burbled out of a concrete pipe half-camouflaged by shrubbery.

"The brook isn't natural, of course. It was built by a famous engineer in the last century. From an engineering point of view, why waste a hill? But it's a very pretty park. We have a community center down at the bottom, in the old caretaker's building. They don't give us any funds, but we've managed to set up a coffee shop, and some rooms for classes and meetings and films. We're hoping to start offering some child care. There's a small zoo, even, that's been there forever. It gives the place a certain friendly smell of shit. Like a farm."

Alex tossed a rock in the stream, watched it splash and disappear under the surface. It was nice to be here, on the scenic route, where nobody but Cynthia could know where he was. It was pleasant to listen to her ramble on about these community details, these mildly brave facts of daily life. In the twilight, in the artful tranquility of this wooded spring, the scene did not match his image of Berlin. It was not the Prussian capital, not Hitler's city, not the headquarters of the Holocaust.

"Cynthia," he interrupted, "could there still be a Jewish cemetery, *Jüdische Friedhof,* somewhere in Berlin?"

She tossed a rock that landed close to where he'd landed his.

"One that I know of, where I've sent Jewish visitors quite a few times before. It's in the East Zone. You can go quite easily. You have to be out by midnight, and you have to fork over twenty-five marks."

"I'd like to see it." He tossed a last pebble into the flow.

"Your father told me I'd find something interesting there. The identity of his killer, maybe. Does that make any sense to you?"

"None," she said, standing. "But I think that it's getting to be time to go on."

Alex gave her his hand, to be helped up, but this time he kept hers as they walked. They came out into the setting sun, on a grassy hillside with a partial view of the city to the west. Cynthia pointed the other way, to a wooden fence surrounding a stone tower at the hill's summit. Spray-painted graffiti covered the fence, among them, in black letters, the rallying cry *Turken Raus!* Fifty years earlier, it would have been painted with a brush. *Juden Raus!* it would have said.

"You know what this is?" Cynthia said. "It's a frightened city. Under all the showy stuff, Berliners are frightened of so many things."

Right, Alex thought, and the bloodhounds are asking your home address. You and I are both frightened, though we don't say so, about what we find ourselves in the middle of. His hand tightened on hers, and as they turned and kissed, Alex felt suddenly that maybe this was what Gerald Meyer had sent him to do. He had sent him to stand in, a generation late. Or, somehow, to repeat his follies, in a shiny new Berlin that was back on its feet. Or . . . Alex closed his eyes and slid his hands up into Cynthia's hair, cradling her head, exploring her mouth with his tongue, trying not to think at all about any corpses, or any *whys.*

Footsteps made him open his eyes and glance sideways at a man with a brown beard, a dog, and two children. The children pointed and shouted some kind of singsong rhyme in German. The father tried to quiet them, but grinned. The dog, however, came as close as it dared. It barked and barked, and, despite the father's commands, it would not stop barking until they moved on.

20

Even Cowgirls

Mockernstrasse ran due north from the bottom of the park. It was a street neither wide nor cramped, running straight as a rail. The houses were three stories, narrow, of graying, square-cut stone. To Alex it felt almost like Brooklyn, in the forties, say—when Brooklyn boys like his father rode in tanks or trucks, or trudged, rifle in hand, across a muddy Europe eastward toward Berlin.

Number 58 did not stand out from the others. Its large wooden door was opened by a thin, white-haired woman in a dark skirt and sweater.

"*Cynthia, so spät,*" she said. "*Wir erwarten auf dir.*"

Her German was musical. She did something with her *r*'s—a combination of a trill and a swallow—that Alex had heard actresses do in Fassbinder movies. Literally, her welcome did not translate as much: So late—we've been waiting. The tones translated as caring, reproof, and an underlying fear.

"I wanted to show Alex the park," Cynthia said lightly.

"Alex, this is Marianne, who has known me since I was a baby and put up with me, too."

"*Guten Tag,*" said Alex, shaking a hand that was crisp and lively. He stepped through the street door toward a steep, stone stairway paralleled by a large green arrow painted on the wall. Red letters with black shadow declared the *Gasthaus* to be one flight up. A smaller wooden door, before the steps, seemed to go to a first-floor apartment.

"That's Marianne's," said Cynthia, and indeed the older woman disappeared behind it. "Come on up."

Upstairs, the *Gasthaus* entryway was decorated with pop and political posters in a profusion of languages. The dining room, however, might well have been unchanged since Cynthia's mother's time. China cups and saucers sat on white tablecloths, each table adorned with a single candle in a brass holder. Oil paintings of country scenes looked down, rich but sedate, from the walls. A small spinet piano seemed to be waiting for a woman in a high lace collar or a man in a black bow tie to bring it to life. Only the dark-skinned man with long, curly hair, no collar, and a bushy mustache seemed out of place. He swooped a hand-painted pitcher of coffee down in front of a few guests still at supper. He wrapped Cynthia in a bear hug and covered her neck with kisses.

"And this," she said, laughing, "is Cenap, the master chef and well-known agitator of the Kreuzberg. This is Alex, who fixes German and Swedish cars in America."

Cenap embraced Alex too, planting a formal kiss on each cheek. He disappeared to the kitchen and returned with two skewers of kebabs and two servings of baklava. Greeks and Turks—like Israelis and Arabs—enjoyed the same food. Alex sat at a table by himself, picking at the food, while Cenap recounted the doings of the past few days in rapid if strangely accented German. The narrative seemed to revolve around the personal crises, political meetings, and social gossip of a sizable community. The guests, two Japanese men and three Caucasian women of undetermined nationalities, finished their coffee and drifted out. One of the women, with a choppy hairdo tinted orange, greeted Cynthia fondly. When Cenap was done, Cynthia took her plate and said she was going down to talk for a moment with Marianne. The Turk cleared tables and left.

So this is the Gasthaus am Mockernstrasse, Alex thought, this curious overlay of the bohemian on the genteel. There was a solidity, and a solidarity, that he liked very much. He was pleased to have made it here, in spite of all advice and in one piece. All that remained was to understand what for. In a little while, Cenap came back. In his odd accent he picked up the thread of a conversation that he hadn't begun. For Alex's benefit, he spoke more slowly. Helping the guest feel comfortable, Alex supposed.

"We're all refugees here, one way or another," Cenap said. "Marianne came from the East Zone long ago, before the Wall, and Cynthia's mother took her in. When my turn came, Marianne put me up in her extra room until I got my feet. I lived in a squat, when I first came. A big old building, not so bourgeois as this. They'd painted murals on every inch of wall, inside and out. But the police finally cleared us all away. Soon apartments will be renting there for two thousand marks."

Alex wondered whether Marianne had hidden other fugitives, in other eras. She reappeared then, as if on cue. "Cenap does not mention that he was a wanted man for the first month. He kicked a policeman who had taken aim with his nightstick at a pregnant woman." She gave the Turk a look of exasperation, but a jerk of her white head toward the next story showed that the sentiment was not directed at him. "*Sie ist solch eine . . . ich weiss nicht wass*," she began, then paused and looked around as if for inspiration about exactly what inappropriate thing Cynthia insisted on being. "She is such a. . . ." Apparently their conversation—not for the first time—had not gone very well. Her eyes fixed on Alex and she pounced on a word.

"*Eine* cowgirl! *Sie will solch eine* cowgirl *sein.*"

Her accent did wonderful things to the English consonants, too. In addition, she provided Alex with a name for Cynthia's persona, a name that he too had been seeking, though without knowing it. "Well, go on up," Marianne added. "She wants to discuss these things with you, not with me."

Alex walked slowly down the carpeted hallway from which Marianne had come. He passed more posters, rooms with brass numbers, a telephone in a nicely hand-carpentered wooden booth. At the end of the hall, bare wooden stairs led down, and carpeted stairs led up. Alex found himself tiptoeing. Near the top he called, "Cynthia?"

"*Herein.*"

The room she was in seemed to be a study—desk, typewriter, a couch, books and papers scattered, a bright abstract painting on the wall. Cynthia stood up from the desk chair and handed him a postal delivery slip and a scrawled note.

"Both arrived yesterday," she said. "The threat is what has Marianne upset. *Mischling* again, you see. Mixed-race subversive, leading German youth to the company of Communists and *Schwarzes*. Marianne says there has been a phone call, too, just before we arrived. They asked whether I had brought the wounded Jew from Hannover. She thinks they mean business."

Alex read it over and started to hand it back.

"No, keep it," she said. "What would I do with it, turn it over to the police? Keep it, as a Berlin souvenir."

"Moselle's people said I was to use diplomacy with you, but if that failed they had less gentle ways. If I'm right about what we're picking up tomorrow, its cash value could be six figures, in dollars."

"If that's what it's all about, then you can just get in touch with Jack and give the shit back. I don't want the money, and I don't need more enemies. Neither do you."

"So, in the meantime, what do we do?"

"In the meantime we pass the time. Would you like to see Berlin by night, or listen to the album you were kind enough to bring me? Or, if you've had enough of my company, I'd be happy to show you to your room."

Alex's disappointment must have been plain on his face, because in return Cynthia flashed him a smile that was less crooked than usual. As he came tentatively closer, the crookedness came back and she said, "Do you think I embrace all the guests on top of the Kreuzberg?"

This time there was no interruption by either children or dog. From the study, the third-floor hallway led forward to a large bedroom into which the streetlamps of Mockernstrasse glowed faintly in the twilight. Their light blended with the light of an antique floor lamp with a marble base, and together these coaxed a shine out of the bars of a brass bedstead old enough to have belonged to a previous generation of Meyers.

Alex hoped that it had not. He did not try to see how this fact connected to that. He admired Cynthia, and he wished he could understand better what gap in her life he was filling. He was embarrassed, somewhat, to be just another cowboy passing by. He tried to get some or all of these feelings across, without words for once. When finally he felt her thighs around him as he had imagined in his hospital bed, he wanted to live that way forever, though of course he did not do so. When he was ready for words again he said, not very originally, "Wow. Cynthia."

She said, "Wow, yourself." She ran the tip of her finger down his belly, stopping just at the base of his warm and wet penis. "You know, there are a lot worse ways to spend an anxious Wednesday evening in Berlin."

Alex ran his fingertip down the same path on her belly, also stopping, as if it hadn't already traveled this path, just when he got to the top of the blond-brown hair.

"Tomorrow we get our work done," he said, "and . . . I feel kind of bad to be one more deserter."

Cynthia pressed her hip tighter against his, sliding her hand up to turn his head toward her, by the chin.

"The last thing I need is for you to go around being ashamed or embarrassed about the time we spend. A lot of men mix up sex with power or with sin, because those are the things that excite them. I don't think you are very excited by power, but I'm not so sure about sin."

"No—it's not that," Alex said. By which he meant maybe it was that, but that wasn't what he wanted to talk about. "I guess I just don't like casting myself in the same role as Gerald Meyer. Here today, gone tomorrow. And I do get the feeling you might have sort of a preference for picking up American Jewish men."

"Thank you." She lifted her own chin in that don't-take-on-airs way. "Other doctors with better degrees have long since helped me to figure that out. You are well-attached to a British citizen, you were careful to say. I am just a part of this little adventure, please have no doubt. As to the picking up—you called me from America to tell me my father was dead and ask me for a date." She tapped the bandage that covered his stitches. "Then you staggered off the train with a slash in your chest, and told me you needed a few stitches. On the way to the hospital, you told me that by the way you had this little cancer, too. You have a certain unusual charm that doesn't depend on whether you are circumcised or not."

Alex bit his lip, because her unasked question had been a long time in coming, and that made it, if anything, harder to answer. At the same time, her summary made him realize how many other questions she had not asked, questions she should have. Finally he took her hand and pressed it to the back of his neck, then returned it to his groin, this time just at the crease between belly and thigh. Her fingers stiffened.

"You know," he said, "it has occurred to me that I have a God-given line for seducing women. I mean, could you say no to somebody who asks you to come up and feel his tumors sometime? No one does feel them, outside of Meredith— that's the British subject—and the docs. My daughter did once, but she pretends not to find them too different from, I don't know, mosquito bites. Sometimes to me they're very different, and sometimes they're not. Sometimes I say, 'One day these are going to kill me.' Usually I say, 'Right now they're not.'"

He stopped and considered, as always, whether what he said about this could possibly give the listener a clear enough picture of what he meant.

"Okay, okay," she conceded. Her fingers did not relax immediately, but she moved them from the lump in his groin to the back of his hand. "I don't mean to be your therapist, either. Your aren't a monopolist in the country of illness, *Liebchen*. Others have been that way before. You're going to bite your lip off, too, if you aren't careful."

She guided his fingertips to her vagina, tightening her thigh against his as she opened her legs to make room. "Now, no more serious thoughts," she said very seriously, beginning to move against him as she kept up the pressure of her hand on his. Alex couldn't tell whether she was making fun of him

152

or not. He kissed her breasts slowly, all around the nipples but not touching them. Half-kosher nipples, he thought. There was something not quite kosher still. He could hear his ancestor, the slaughterhouse functionary, telling him that. But just now was no time to be comtemplating rituals of slaughter. Just now was a time to comfort and be comforted, to make love in a city that could use all the love it could get.

He took one nipple in his mouth, feeling it rise against his tongue, and buried the rest of his thoughts in the softness of her breast. From then on she guided him very nicely through everything she wanted done, and Alex—Alex responded to some deep and perhaps ancient impulse to pretend to a clarity about life that no one really has. When she shuddered with pleasure, he held her tightly and kissed her everywhere he could reach, as if kisses could seal out all the past and all the future. He whispered that he was so glad to be spending this anxious Berlin night with her. And he told her, foolishly, that they made a great team and that tomorrow . . . tomorrow everything was going to be all right.

21

Cremation

Alex showered thoughtfully while enjoying the warm water and the feel of the soap on his skin. His stitches were still tender but sealing up nicely. He found a bathrobe where Cynthia had said. Soft and long, it covered him with an intricate pattern of blue Chinese fans. He wiped steam from the window to reveal a brilliant blue day outside. When he returned to Cynthia, she was blowing dust off a framed photograph in her hand. She offered it to him, wordlessly.

Private Meyer—or Lieutenant, for all Alex knew, not being good at uniforms—stared straight into the camera. He had a bushy head of light brown hair, which made him seem taller and less vulnerable. His lips were fixed in a slight smile that could be either pride or stoicism, it was hard to say. He was good-looking in a young, untested way.

Gertrud Meyer, née Tronkel, laughed. She was thin and did not seem so young, maybe because she had just lived through a war. Her laughter was defiant, which was part of her appeal. He imagined her laughing at some wry joke by the photographer, whom he decided he'd like to be Marianne.

Between the parents, Cynthia Meyer, aged perhaps a year, sat primly on the sofa, hands folded in her lap.

Aged perhaps forty, hands loose in her lap, she watched Alex. She was wearing the "Reagan Go Home" T-shirt again, sitting up with her back resting on the brass bedstead, her legs extended under the covers. In the morning light, the brass bars had a dark shine to them. She said, "I dug that out because I thought you might want to see it. Now you are giving me an evil and suspicious look."

"I want to know why you haven't asked me a single question about your father," he said. "What did he look like when I met him? Did he ever remarry? Was he happy or sad? What did he tell me about you or your mother? Why do I think he sent you the goddamn treasure that belonged to Jack? Why do I think he changed his mind and wanted it back?"

"Oh. So that's it. I didn't need to ask about the man, because I met him myself this past spring." She pointed toward the hallway and the study beyond. "In there. Believe me, Alex, after that I didn't want to know any more."

"When were you planning to tell me about this?"

"When you asked, and not before. Come on, sit down, don't stand there taking notes like that cop in the hospital. All right. I answered the door to find a woman, an American. Younger than me, I suppose, though she seemed older. Straighter, as you would say. *Echt* suburban American: a velour running suit, hair just so, a Fodor's guidebook under one arm and a gift under the other."

"A gift?"

"Yes, I asked if she was looking for a room—she didn't seem the right type—but she said no, she was looking for Fräulein Meyer. The gift was for me. An art book. She had bought it at the Dahlem the day before. The art museum. The Museum of Prussian Cultural Possessions is its official name. An expensive present but impersonal, like a bottle of fancy cognac to a client at Christmas. She stuck out her hand like a queen's to be kissed, and announced she was my half sister. She said our father—emphasis on the pronoun—was in Berlin also."

"Really? He implied to me that his second marriage didn't end so differently from his first."

"That was supposed to give us something in common. 'I've got more reasons to hate the bastard than you do,' she said. 'You're clear of him. But our father's our father, even if he is a prick. He wants to see you, but he was afraid to come like this, out of the blue. So he sent me to do his dirty work.' Words like that, anyway. She claimed that now he was growing old and wanted to patch things over with us both."

"What happened?"

"I didn't like her manner. It didn't feel . . . sisterly, not at all. It felt like she was his . . . his robot, I don't know. I said if he wanted to talk to me, that was up to him."

"And he came?"

"The next evening. We went in there to catch up on old times over two cups of tea. He began to ramble about how it felt to be back in Berlin. He tried to tell me his version of what it had meant to him the first time, after the war."

"What did it mean?"

"It might matter to you, but I have to say I didn't listen. There was something about the city being a combination of horror and possibility. What was I supposed to make of that? That my mother filled him with horror? The 'possibility' I understood. The occupying army has rights to the women of the conquered people. The Russians raped, people say. The Americans bought with chocolate."

"I thought he and your mother were in love, at the time."

"Oh, probably. I'm talking about the man I met in the spring. It seems his idea was to buy my love, or my forgiveness."

"Did he say anything about that? About providing for you in a material way?"

"I didn't give him much chance. Now you tell me that this was just a tactic in some sordid power struggle with Jack? Stags locking horns until the loser dies. I don't want any part of it, except"—she looked down and picked at the hem of the T-shirt—"except I suppose I do want the pictures."

"The pictures?"

156

"Oh yes, I think that part of what he told you was true. That picture I showed you, that's the only one I have." She reached for it, studied it, and shook stray hairs from her face and stray thoughts from her mind. "The family saga, as told by Mother, agrees with yours. He took the other pictures with him, God knows why. Do you know what Sitting Bull is supposed to have said—about the Americans?"

Alex shook his head. If she'd been about to reveal more, she'd retreated behind history once again.

"He said, 'The love of possession is a disease with them.' So now we might as well go and find out if he got cured of that disease. I think you will find that Marianne has delicately left your bag at the bottom of my stairs. We should stop and visit her on our way out."

Alex crept down the stairs, collected his clothes, and crept back up. He dressed as an inconspicuous tourist, in corduroys, a striped dress shirt, and the windbreaker with bloodstains only on the inside. Cynthia emerged, hair wet from the shower, in baggy white pants and a black sweater.

Down the two flights, the stairway door opened onto a modern, Formica-topped kitchen where Marianne, Cenap, and a young German man waited over fresh cooked rolls and empty coffee cups.

"Alex," Cynthia said in German, "from America. Hans, Wolf's brother, a former student of mine from Frankfurt. Turned carpenter"—she waved around the room—"and Berliner."

"Very nice job," Alex told him, shaking hands. He nodded credit to Marianne, as well. "Um, is the house very old?"

"Not very, but more than a century." Marianne spoke slowly and precisely for his benefit. Her inflection once again made the harsh edges of the language silvery and smooth. "When Gertrud got it, it was bombed out. Over the years we have done nice things. I raised my children here, when I came from the East Zone."

"Alex would like to visit the Jewish Cemetery," Cynthia said. "He believes that my father left some sort of secret message there."

Alex flashed a quick look around the table to see how that went over. Cenap didn't meet it, but Hans was watching him with open curiosity. Had he never seen a Jew before? Alex wanted to know. Or a man who looks for messages left by the dead?

"It is on the Schonhauser Allee," Marianne said. "Just down from the Kollwitzplatz. It's a quiet neighborhood, residential, a peaceful place."

Hans laughed a young laugh. It welcomed knowledge, but protested seriousness.

"If you find a neighborhood on the East Side that's not quiet, Alex, you tell me. Marianne takes children to the puppet theater, and she drags all of us to the Brecht. Nobody goes across for the lively atmosphere."

"I go," Marianne said, "because to me it is all still Berlin." She gathered coffee cups for refills and added, "A very bad recipe. Equal parts Prussian culture and Stalin's revenge, plus a pinch of what was left of the German workers' movement after the camps. You may have my story this evening, if you like. Now I wish you two would stop being polite, and take care of your business instead."

The Kreuzberg post office was only a five-minute drive away, on the Mehringdamm, the main commercial street. Yet Cynthia and Alex had trouble filling the time. She explained that Marianne's parents, Communists, had died in a concentration camp, of hunger. Marianne had been taken in by less exotic relatives, who stayed in line. Alex, suddenly not wanting to know this, attempted to chat about the mechanical history of Cynthia's VW bug. She parked the bug in front of a vacant storefront on whose soaped-up window competed graffiti of the right and the left: a black *Turken Raus,* and a peace symbol in green. It was half a block to the post office—a quaint brick building sandwiched between a furniture showroom on one side and videocassette rentals on the other. The sidewalk in front was crowded with shoppers and loafers, Aryan and not.

The remodeled interior reminded Alex of a suburban bank at home. Everything was glass, plastic, and hushed. He stared up at a photo of Chancellor Helmut Kohl. He wondered whether Kohl was surprised, staring down, to find in the pristine lobby this bearded, wandering Yid.

Cynthia presented herself at an opening in the glass. Alex watched her sign a form, offer identification, and receive Gerald Meyer's flat corrugated box. She stepped aside, resting the parcel against the white countertop and a pane of clean, sparkling glass, while she slit the strapping tape with a penknife from her bag. She opened the flap and looked inside. Only then did she turn toward Alex, and surprise him with the tears welling from her eyes. They glistened in pouches and then dripped onto her round cheeks. He kicked himself for being surprised. She brushed at the tears, not very effectually, with her soft black sleeve.

Alex found tissues in his jacket pocket and went toward her, but she shook her head no, sniffled once, hard, and handed him a manila envelope like the one in which Gerald Meyer had sent him his fee.

"Here's your treasure," she said. "I guess. The rest really is the pictures, and, oh shit, a spoon, *verdammt, meine Kindermütze,* baby bonnet, more pictures. . . . " She stood, sifting down in the box with one hand, more tears coming. "Jesus," she said, "I don't believe he saved all this, all these years. . . . Alex, you go. Call Jack, call your policeman, go chase clues in the cemetery, whatever you must. I need to be alone with this . . . these relics for a while."

Alex reached out again but she shrugged him off. He turned and walked out of the building, down the three wide stone steps and into the early-afternoon crowd. He leaned against the furniture showroom window, envelope still unopened, waiting for her to come out. She turned the other way, toward the car, a tall, rounded blond woman pushing her way past a knot of skinny teenagers in leather and army-surplus drab. She blended slowly into a stream of shoppers, women on their way to and from work, men getting in and out of cars, a haze of exhaust from the parade of cars down the wide, divided street. She became nearly as invisible, as anonymous as she had been when Alex had stood daydreaming in line in front of her father the past Friday.

Now he opened the packet that seemed to have cost Gerald Meyer what had been left of his life. He thumbed through a pile of forms that looked like oversized cashiers' checks. They bore computer-generated names of commercial firms and banks, labeled as drawees, drawers, and payees, as well as invoice and shipping numbers. They bore dollar amounts, none less than $25,000. The words and numbers were obscured, here and there, by darker letters overprinted at right angles with a rubber stamp. ACCEPTED, the stamp said, and below this was a line labeled AUTHORIZED SIGNA-TURE. In every case, the authorized signature was that of Gerald E. Meyer.

The market value of this pile of checks was impressive, as Alex had guessed. Behind the wad of acceptances, however, was something he had not guessed: several sheets of white, thick, high-grade paper, clipped together, covered with nota-tions in Meyer's neat, precise, fountain-pen hand.

The notations were dates, serial or identification numbers, banks and brokerage houses, and the names and titles of individuals. Alex did not recognize the names, but the titles placed them in public positions in West Germany, Holland, and Great Britain. It slowly dawned on him that this information, to Interface, Incorporated, would be worth guarding at least as closely as the money itself. Alex groped to an understanding of what kind of dynamite Gerald Meyer had changed his mind about sending to his eldest daughter. His concentration was shattered by the explosion down the street.

He ran toward the sound, knowing as he ran that run-ning would do no good. Other bodies were running the same way as he was, and the opposite way, banging each other as they crossed. Alex forced a path, head down and elbows flail-ing. He fought his way through the tight crush of onlookers. There was a faint, familiar whiff of gasoline in the air.

Alex forced his way into the space—not comprehending why there was so much space—between the edge of the crowd and the car. The windshield was shattered, the maze of cracks hiding the inside from view. But the passenger door was open. If her legs were working, she was out already. Even so, out didn't mean safe. He tried, frantically, to pick her out of the crowd.

Then he got a step closer, and he could see around the

open door. Cynthia Meyer was inside, slumped over both bucket seats. Her face, toward him, was streaked with blood. More blood made an intricate, irregular red pattern on her white pants. One hand, the index finger torn to the bone, hung out the door toward him. As Alex sprang forward, somebody screamed harsh, meaningless, high-pitched syllables. From behind, something hit him so his knees buckled. He couldn't reach her. He fell backward, away from the car. A shock wave rolled passed him, and his eyes closed against scorching heat. He smelled acrid black swirling smoke. The roar of flames was joined by a siren's scream.

When he opened his eyes, he was crawling after the retreating crowd, the manila envelope still clutched in his right hand. He reached the edge of a building, sat on the envelope, drew up his knees, and watched what was left of the car slowly burn. He didn't know who had tackled him, but he knew that whoever had done it had saved his life. The fire was cremating Cynthia's body inside her car. Tears trickled down Alex's cheeks, as they had washed down hers only moments before.

The siren became a fire truck, from which came firefighters who hosed down the wreckage with chemical foam. Another siren wailed, and this became a police car, from which two policemen emerged. One of them set about persuading the crowd to move on. The other, following a slew of shouted advice and pointing fingers, advanced toward Alex.

"She was my friend," Alex explained in a simple declarative German sentence. The policeman's answer was the equivalent of "You'd better come with us."

22

Keep Your Temper

Alex gave the victim's name and address, which the policeman duly radioed in to his dispatcher. The order that came back made him hang a quick U-turn, siren blaring once again. He shut the siren off as he approached the central Police Presidium, near the railway overpass that was no longer there. He made a sharp turn into an underground vehicle entrance, then came to a stop. Alex waved his passport and demanded an English-speaking officer. A new cop took him to a room with a desk and two chairs, and told him to sit.

The chairs were new, with aluminum alloy frames and plastic seats. Alex felt the twice-folded manila envelope in one back pocket as a lumpy wad between himself and the plastic. In the other pocket, when he replaced the passport, he found the death threat Cynthia had told him to keep as a souvenir—just before she had invited him to her bed. He tried not to think about what she had looked like then. He tried not to think about what she had looked like in her shattered VW bug. He tried to focus on the mechanical details of how the explosion had happened, and the factual details of why.

Those who are gone live on with us, in the memory of their dear ones. The sentence rose in Alex's mind unbidden. It was a line from the section of the Jewish worship service set aside for mourners. It was the kind of line that lay inside, dormant, because you had absorbed it by osmosis, dozing through your friend's bar mitzvah. He wasn't sure he qualified as a dear one, but if he did, then Cynthia lived on in her off-center smile, her clear eyes, the white rose pinned to the brown strap. The feel of her tongue in his mouth. Yet those memories happened to survive only because blood still carried oxygen to Alex's brain. And that—he was sure—was sheerest accident. He was sure the bomb had been intended for him as well.

Did the planter of the bomb know that these memories, and Gerald Meyer's dangerous gift, survived? If Alex had stayed in Boston, intent on putting nothing right but chipped teeth on timing gears, would the result have been any different? If he had plunged the switchblade into the neck of the man on the train, would there have been someone left to place the bomb? These questions had no answers, not yet. Nor did the others that circled about, snapping like voracious scavenger fish. Especially there was no answer to the great, implacable white shark of a question: Why is it that she is dead and I am not?

Finally a square-jawed, silver-haired officer came in, cassette recorder in hand, to place simpler questions of his own. The officer sat on top of the shiny metal desk, adjusting the crease of his gray slacks. He plugged in the recorder, and pressed a button to get it rolling.

"Sorry to keep you waiting, Mr. Glauberman." His English was British, not American. "They had to rouse me out of a conference, you know. Could I take a look at your passport, please?"

In exchange for the passport he handed Alex an embossed card. Hauptmann Gerhard Schultheiss.

"Hm." Schultheiss returned the passport, intertwined his fingers, and cracked his knuckles in a self-satisfied way. "And where were you between the time you entered Britain at Heathrow on Sunday and the time you crossed the DDR border, by train yesterday?"

The precision of the query brought Alex back to the present. *Hauptmann* meant "captain." Captains were not hauled out of conferences to interrogate witnesses just because of linguistic skills. It was time for another duel with another cop—and not by long-distance telephone this time.

"I stopped over in London and in Hannover."

"Could I have the addresses where you stayed in each of those cities, and in Berlin?"

"Excuse me, Captain. Am I a suspect, is that it? My address in Berlin is Gasthaus am Mockernstrasse. What does my address in London matter to your investigation?"

Schultheiss straightened his tie, which was red with gold lions rampant.

"That depends. How long had you known Fräulein Meyer?"

"Since early yesterday morning. I'm staying now at her *Gasthaus.*"

"The witnesses say you headed for the car to drag her out, milliseconds before the gas tank blew. You would have gone up with her, except somebody got in your way. They say you were rather broken up afterward."

Schultheiss regarded Alex steadily for a minute without putting his observation into the form of a question. His silver hair was fashionably long, maybe longer, parted back over his ears and held there as if by spray. When Alex did not comment, he raised his eyebrows and his voice.

"Bed-and-breakfast sort of affair, Mr. Glauberman?"

Alex tried with all his might to hit the captain on the point of the square, close-shaved jaw. He lashed out with his right fist into empty air. Schultheiss slid easily off the side of the desk, out of reach.

"Keep your temper," he warned, straightening his tie once more. "Your record is clean, as far as our files are concerned. We have no evidence you are involved. You just picked the wrong dolly, maybe. What do you think caused her departure to Valhalla this afternoon?"

Alex sat down. Sharp steel tools kept their temper; so could he. It wouldn't do anybody any good to get himself locked up. He took a deep breath and then answered.

"I think somebody wired an explosive into the starter

switch of her car. In those old bugs, you just have to open the trunk, in the front, and yank out the cardboard divider. The switch is exposed, and you can just leave the bomb in the trunk. The gas tank is right underneath. It looked to me—" Alex shut his eyes and took another breath, in and out. "It looked to me like it was a fragment bomb, and whatever was in it went right through the dash. Or else it blew the dash to pieces, and the pieces went into her. She was bleeding a lot, all over. That first explosion must have put a small crack in the gas line or the tank. I guess the fumes ignited from the heat."

"You seem to have this all figured out."

"I've had time." The rest of Alex's answer was his stock one, hollow in the circumstances. "And I fix cars, besides."

"Then I pardon your ingenuity. I wouldn't put much stock in your theory, though. My guess is it was her bomb, that she was carrying in the boot, and it went off ahead of schedule. We'll see soon enough, because right now your pleasant little *Gasthaus* is being raided. We've only been waiting for sufficient cause. I expect we'll find the makings of quite a few bombs under the pretty furniture. You're a very lucky chap, Mr. Glauberman. You picked a quite subversive dolly, and the wrong time to go riding in her car. She didn't say anything that might give us a lead about where she was heading, did she?"

"No," Alex said, staying put with an effort. "She said she was going home." He thought of Marianne and Cenap and Hans, or whoever else of Cynthia's makeshift family might be around. Raid first, the police procedure would be. Explanations afterward. Thus far, they wouldn't even have revealed she was dead. He did not expect much from Schultheiss, but he would do what he could with the captain, for them.

"You're Red Squad, I guess, or whatever you call it around here. So you won't want to think about what I have to say until you don't find any bombs under the furniture. But I have a few leads that you can pass on to the appropriate officer. One—Cynthia Meyer had been receiving threats from neo-Nazis. I have one of the threats right here."

He handed the note over. The policeman looked at it quickly, then looked up and spoke airily.

"This is not the 1930s. I grant you, there's a lot of feeling in this city against whole neighborhoods starting to smell of garlic. I've heard that, even in Massachusetts, there are rotters who don't like to see their neighborhoods invaded by other races. But do give us some credit for being one jump ahead of that sort of thing. I grant you a slight possibility of a sort of gang war, right versus left."

He started to hand the note back, then thought better of it.

"Thank you," Alex said. "If you're one jump ahead, maybe you'll know where to look for the killer. Now, two— if you've got files anything like the FBI, I bet you've got a big one on Cynthia. You'll see in the file that she has a father in America. You probably won't see that Gerald Meyer was murdered, gangland-style, as they say in the American papers, last Friday night in Cambridge, Massachusetts. You'd want to speak with a Sergeant Trevisone there."

"Is there a three?" Schultheiss interrupted with an ironical smile.

Yes, Alex said silently. The evidence for lead number three is in my back pocket. But I don't want to trust you with that, just yet.

"No, that's it. I'm sorry I got angry, but I didn't . . . well, I'm sorry. Are you going to let me go now? If not, I'd like to call the American consul, please."

The detective sighed. "If you're a terrorist, your country breeds sentimental ones. Otherwise you wouldn't have waited around to be picked up. Yes, you may go. If you change your address—which I would strongly advise—be sure to let me know your new one immediately. And don't leave the city. That would look suspicious."

"Yes sir," Alex said. A patrolman showed him to the street door. The sky was still blue and clear, the air comfortably warm, the traffic steady. But Alex felt his adrenaline dripping away, replaced by dogged, gritty sludge in his veins. This sludge was a grimy, abrasive substance that mocked the cheeky performance he'd just put on. The grit was made up of images: Cynthia's friends, spread-eagled against the wall while cops made ghoulish, cryptic jokes. Cynthia slumped over, possibly alive, while the fumes built up and nobody pulled her out. Cynthia by his hospital bed, hands on hips, a woman to all appearances in control of her destiny. The sludge hurt, but it had power.

Alex entered the subway, as she would, without a ticket. He studied the map, rode two stops to the north, and got off where the Mehringdamm met Friedrichstrasse. This was a busy intersection next to one of Berlin's myriad canals. He found what he needed—a phone—inside a bar, smoky and hot. The smoke felt like airborne death in his lungs, but somehow talking here was less lonely than it would be in an open booth on the bustling street. In German, he negotiated details about the number and credit card. In English, the desk man told him Trevisone was busy. Alex felt all the lonelier, hearing this.

"This is Alex Glauberman," he insisted. "About the Gerald Meyer murder? Meyer's daughter has been murdered too. This time I was a witness. I'm calling from West Berlin." Alex began counting, silently, to pass the time. Trevisone got to the phone on eight.

"Glauberman," he said. "What the hell was that?"

"Somebody just blew up Cynthia Meyer's VW. She was in it, and I think they expected me to be in it too. Soon they'll find out they were wrong. It may be that all this killing is about race, religion, and politics, but I doubt it. What Meyer sent his daughter was somebody else's money, as I thought, but it was also a long list of names, numbers, and dates. Meyer must have figured Cynthia could use that to blackmail Moselle. It turns out she wasn't the blackmailing type. Do you think the names, numbers, and dates would interest that federal agency you mentioned? The Treasury or the SEC or whoever?"

"Maybe." Trevisone's voice was matter-of-fact. Just one more killing to him, and very far away at that. "Off the record, you were right. They say they've been closing in on Meyer for about the past six months. But you haven't convinced me that stuff explains why he got killed. A lot more often there's a garden-variety motive involved."

"Right," Alex said. Tell me another one. "Did you arrest that girlfriend yet, then?"

"I can't arrest somebody I can't find." The sergeant sounded peeved for the first time. "You trying to tell me this Cynthia was put out of the picture by the same hand?"

"We'll see. Right now I'm trying to tell you that you might get a call from a Captain Schultheiss, who seems to be in charge of the investigation here. If you do, I'd appreciate it if you try to talk some sense into his head. Meanwhile, I'm going to run one more errand, where I hope nobody's expecting to find me."

"Uh-huh. I'm not going to waste your money giving you any more advice. Just maybe drop me a hint about where that might be."

"Sure," Alex said, his mother's tongue rushing to the fore. "If I don't come back, I'd like you to know. It's in walking distance. To get there, I head up along Friedrichstrasse and then on through Checkpoint Charlie."

"Aw, fuck, Glauberman. I hope the damn Russians keep you."

23

Knives Sharpened

It was three o'clock, building toward rush hour. Walking up the street he had named, Alex left all the bustle behind. This had been Berlin's Fifth Avenue—once. Now it was desolate. Its only reason for being, in the West Zone, anyway, was that it led to one of the few breaks in the Wall.

Across vacant lots to his left, Alex could see other kinds of walls. On two apartment buildings, maybe eight to ten stories tall, the sides had been left exposed by demolition of adjacent structures. The exposed surfaces were painted in huge surrealist murals. One featured melting shapes of missiles and doves. The other depicted clouds, planets, human shapes, spires—and likewise doves, for good measure.

"Those are squats," Cynthia's voice told him. "They'll be knocked down soon, or renovated. We can't have people living in rundown buildings, much less painting pictures on them. Anyway, they might smell of garlic."

The words weren't right. The real woman was already slipping away beyond Alex's ability to conjure her up. But he knew that if she'd chosen to drive him to the crossing point, she would have given him some kind of self-assured, ironic commentary along the way. Except there wouldn't have been any along-the-way, because shortly after she turned the key they would both have been dead.

Walking up the deserted street, Alex counted up the things done wrong, the angles not figured, in the interval they'd spent together between sex and death. What did you do, he asked himself, during the time you could have been planning a few simple precautions? Like, I'll stay outside and keep an eye on the car. He had slept, asked pointless questions, drunk coffee, been polite to her friends. Then he had walked with her into a trap, with both eyes closed.

A block later he came to a collection of low, rusty fences and small, decrepit buildings. The buildings seemed make-shift and badly kept up—flaking gray paint, cheap corrugated roofs. There were crossing gates for cars, zebra-striped, like the ones at railway crossings. There were floodlights. On either side of the assembly of gates and fences rose a bare concrete wall, rounded at the top.

Checkpoint Charlie looked like World War II surplus, because that's what it was. At this place, after joining forces to defeat the Nazis, Russia and America had flexed exhausted muscles and stared each other in the face. Forty years later, they were still flexing and staring. In the meantime, you could pass through to visit the East if you lived in the West, but not the other way around. The East German authorities called it the Anti-Fascist Protection Barrier. In his own case, Alex thought grimly, the term might have its first claim to being accurate.

Death was a kind of checkpoint. A valve between two reservoirs. You could go through in one direction, but not the other. Alex found that it made very little sense to believe Gerald Meyer had anything more to tell him from beyond the grave, via Jewish cemeteries or any other means. It made very little sense that the man's daughter, one moment such a complex organism of body and brain, should be nothing but ashes and police records now.

Alex told himself, aloud, to cut that shit out. He got a curious glance from the bored black sentry in his Plexiglas booth. Across the road from the soldier, a sign warned any unwary travelers they were now leaving the American-controlled zone. Beyond the concrete barrier, Alex could now see, there was a second fence, barbed and electrified. Beyond it rose several blocks of white, faceless high-rises. Alex joined a knot of foot-passage seekers like himself, shoving passports across a waist-high chain-link gate at an East Zone guard.

When his name was called, he imitated those who had gone ahead of him. He leaned over to press the mechanical latch that opened the gate. After the mandatory exchange of Westmarks for Ostmarks, he was admitted through a steel door into a gray-walled interior with a locker-room emptiness about it. A green-uniformed official, middle-aged and yawning, stamped a form and gave him a copy that he would need to get out.

Then it was just a matter of one more door, one more gate, and Alex resumed walking north along a more populated Friedrichstrasse. On this side people came and went busily, but most did not linger on the street. A policeman patrolled, with a walkie-talkie and a pistol on his hip. At the corner of Unter den Linden, once the center of the German empire, Alex stopped to buy a map.

Unter den Linden was a dead end too. Alex could see it petering out at the Brandenburg Gate, a monumental set of classical columns that now led only to the Wall. He studied the map and asked the tourist guide in her booth where he could board a bus to Dimitroffstrasse. She pointed across the street, where a billboard proclaimed a government message: WE WILL DEFEND THE PEACE BY STRENGTHENING OUR DEFENSES.

Alex reflected that his own President couldn't have put the argument any better, or any worse. He was glad he did not have to wait very long for the bus. At Dimitroffstrasse he transferred to a crowded streetcar. The passengers did not look so different from those in the West, but more of them were white and middle-aged. More of the teenagers wore their hair hippie length, and they affected denim more than leather. A few years behind the times. He felt as if he had stepped out of time himself, as if time had stopped when he crossed the checkpoint, and time would pick up again when he got back. At the third stop, he got off and walked down Kollwitzstrasse as Marianne had described.

The street was quiet, all right. Flowered windowboxes, where the upper stories caught sun, were the major sign of life. The apartment buildings were old. Looking closely at their weathered walls, Alex realized they bore the scars of streetfighting, bullet holes gouged like oversized fingerprints in the stone walls. The holes were left over from the death throes of the Reich, when the Red Army moved slowly westward, block by block.

His map showed not only the cemetery along this street, but also a synagogue. A decade before the Russians, who might have walked these quiet streets, close by the cemetery and the old *shul*? Wouldn't there have been some goodly number of the vanished Jews of Berlin?

Images of evacuation nagged at him. He thought of railroad cars, cattle cars, rumbling east through the city's dawn. Lettering above a shuttered shop window stopped him for a moment—archaic, faded German letters, an old shop no longer open for business. He had to fill in missing characters, where paint had long since flaked away. "Knives sharpened," the writing said.

The fact was, no one could have understood, really, what was about to happen to them. Suppose "authorities" came one sudden day, in Boston, and put Alex Glauberman and his daughter on a train. Suppose from that moment on he learned, and learned, and relearned the lesson that he was powerless to do anything for himself or for her. His child's pleading eyes would remind him that he had once seemed all-powerful, but he was now, like her, powerless to do anything except endure the unraveling of every last shred of security.

"Knives sharpened," he said out loud to break the spell. If this was survivor guilt, at least he'd picked an appropriate place to experience it. He hurried on down the block to the Kollwitzplatz, a pleasant square of park and playground, where in one corner stood a reproduction of a drawing by the artist Käthe Kollwitz, after whom the park was named. Charcoal silhouettes raised their small human fists in silent, eternal defiance. It was sobering and yet cheering at the same moment. Alex turned away from the poster to watch a man, probably a father, watching a little girl climb a jungle gym.

The father's golden Buffalo Bill hair reached past his shoulders. His beard was wispy, almost a Ho Chi Minh–type goatee. He slouched against the frame of a swing set, hands in the pockets of his white jeans. Alex wanted to tell him that he too had a daughter, in America, the same age. He wanted to call Maria and tell her again that he was all right and would be home soon. He wanted to explain that he'd wrestled and drawn blood from a man who'd said he was paid by Hitler's ghost, but that, though Alex believed the world held plenty of fascists, he did not believe they took orders from ghosts. In the end he asked whether the man could please point out the old synagogue.

"It is behind those apartments," the man said, friendly but uncurious. "In a kind of a courtyard. But there is no way in, except through the houses."

"Oh. It is just a . . . historical building?"

The man smiled at the girl, who had reached the top of the structure and was preparing to hang by her hands.

"*Ja, historisch.* Only for scholars." Alex asked about the cemetery, whether it might be open to the public.

"*Ich glaube,*" the man said. As in *Glaubermann,* in a sister tongue. Glauberman, the know-it-all. The man who knows what's what.

"*Danke,*" Alex said courteously.

"*Bitte,*" the man replied, even more so. The daughter let go with both hands and dropped to the ground, clapping fearlessly.

After one more block, Alex came to the woods on his right. The trees grew untended beside a tennis court with no net. The place had an earthy, overgrown feeling. A few feet into the woods he found a dirt path, and a bench. Behind the bench was the cemetery wall, of old mossy stones. The trees grew inside the wall, too. He followed the path to the corner of the Schonhauser Allee, where the woods abruptly stopped. The adjoining wall ran straight along the sidewalk, unhidden from the traffic along the street and the passengers emerging from the East Zone U-Bahn stairs. Alex turned right and came to the old iron gate, open. Inside it he saw a clearing with a small stone hut and several long rows of gravestones. The gravestones were crowded together like too many dominoes in the hand of a losing player. On the gate, a printed sign warned, ALL MEN AND BOYS MUST COVER THEIR HEADS WHEN ENTERING.

Alex stood, hatless and uncertain, but the moment did not last long. An attendant emerged from the hut just inside the gate. He wore nondescript brown pants and a brown jacket over a white dress shirt, collar open and no tie. A black skullcap perched on his off-blond hair.

"Leider habe Ich keine Hut," said Alex. *"Keine yarmulke."*

"Moment, bitte." The man, a young man, disappeared into the little stone building and returned with a yarmulke that matched his own. The man offered him the yarmulke with a casual air.

"Danke."

Alex placed the cap on top of his curls and looked away from the attendant, toward the headstones. When the attendant demanded nothing more, Alex wandered over to look at the names. The engraving on the old markers yielded no message to him—no Meyer, no Glauberman, only a Strauss, a Rossbach, a Hochchild. Many of the stones were chipped and some, lying flat in front of the others, were broken in half. Obviously they had at some point rested peacefully throughout the cemetery, marking the remains of the people they named—Berliners who happened to be Jews, Berliners who had died in the normal course of things.

Alex did not know about Gerald Meyer's ancestry. He knew that he himself had no actual relatives among those Berliners. But the next generation—the knife sharpener perhaps, and the shopkeepers and professors and seamstresses and steel-mill hands—had been carried off from the sedate apartment blocks and neat, street-level shops. They had gone in the cattle cars to the camps. There they had met, for the first time, Alex's relatives, the provincial eastern Jews dragged from the villages and ghettoes of the Slavic lands.

Meanwhile the cemetery must have been vandalized, in accordance with the policies of the Reich, and then, sometime since, the stones had been gathered together and righted. *Friedhof* literally meant "yard of peace." Alex wanted to wander slowly among the trees, the bits of broken stone, and the unmarked graves that testified to the flourishing and vanishing of the Jews of Berlin. Cynthia was one of those— would have been, by the Nazi way of reckoning. He wanted to pick a gravesite for her ashes, and pretend to scatter them there, and say the good-byes or apologies or requests for absolution or whatever else he had not had time to say.

He wanted to linger and to grieve a little, here out of time, but the attendant had followed him quietly, waiting to be of service.

"Are there many visitors from America here?" Alex asked, half-turning his head toward the man. "Many Jews, like me?"

The attendant smiled again. His face reminded Alex of some movie or television actor, not very famous, even-featured in a strong but innocuous way. It was the fat that made the face innocuous—enough to keep the features from being hard, not enough to make them piggish. Baby fat. Alex wondered what was happening to him, that men in their mid-twenties appeared as babies.

"*Natürlich,*" the man said.

"*Ich meine, vielen?* Very many? Every week? Every day?" Alex had thought that perhaps not so many Americans crossed into East Berlin.

"Groups come. They tell us in advance, so we can be prepared to make a little talk about the history."

"But not so many on their own? Alone, like me?"

"*Natürlich,* not so many."

Ah—but when they came, did they feel a need to talk, to make human contact with someone, friend or foe? Had Gerald Meyer unburdened himself here, with this man, or another?

"I want to know about an older man who would have visited here, in the spring maybe, I'm not sure when. . . ."

"*Nicht sicher. . . .*" the attendant said doubtfully. "Not sure when?"

Alex turned his back now to the graves, looking the attendant full in the face, and then gazing past him, toward the hut. He wondered what relics it might contain.

"I think a friend of mine visited here," Alex began

again, locking eyes at last. The attendant's eyes were brown, mild, yet also veiled. Alex considered the possibilities as to how he might find out. He wrestled with webbed-over memories of the German subjunctive. *"Sei möglich,"* he tried, *"dass es ein Register, ein Besuchsbuch gibt?"*

"Ja, ein Register, dass stimmt." The attendant's eyes narrowed, but he remained polite. "Would you like to look for the name of your friend there?"

"Bitte."

Alex followed the attendant into the hut, ducking his head under the low stone doorway. This must once have been a place for keeping tools, where perhaps a caretaker sat and smoked a pipe, when the cemetery was a working place. Now he could make out in the dimness a spade, a rake, and a pair of shears resting in one angle of the stones. The hut had the same earthy, mossy smell as the woods. In another corner, a battery-operated fluorescent lantern glowed over a bookshelf filled with looseleaf binders, sealed in plastic. Were these genealogies of some kind, for the foreign visitors to consult? Rubbings of the crumbling, broken stones? On the flat top of the bookcase rested a register and a ballpoint pen. The attendant turned toward Alex and then ducked past him out the door.

"Stay as long as you like," he said. "I will be outside, pulling *Unkraut.*"

"Unkraut?" Alex asked. Literally, "not-cabbage." In America, a kraut was a German, or used to be. What was a not-kraut, here?

"Weeds," answered the man in English, treating the *w* as a *v*.

Weeds. A weed was a plant that was undesirable, or not of use. Alex, bent over and squinting in the strange light, began slowly turning the pages of the register, weeding through the tangle of names. Like an aged man nodding over his Talmud, he thought. Puzzling new meanings from old words.

There were visitors from New York, from Rome and Paris, a few from Israel, a few even from Boston, some more from L.A. But no names meant anything to him. None told him whom Gerald Meyer had awaited, drinking himself silly, or where that person might now be. None told him whether the same or a different hand had casually opened the hood of a battered VW and wired explosives inside. None pointed a finger at jilted lovers or racist fanatics or hired muscle or smooth moneymakers who smuggled goods across the border between legitimate business and the other kinds. Alex continued to leaf backward, in the earthy, silent hut, until suddenly, there it was. Gerald Meyer, no city, just "U.S.A."

So? Meyer had been there. So what? Alex could go show the attendant, and come up with a plausible reason for wanting to know whether this one man had lodged in his memory. But first he focused his eyes on the names above and below. Natalya Peretz, Lyon, France. Joanna Conner, U.S.A.

Joanna Connor, U.S.A. Joanna. Joanna. Himself, holding that silly, half-dead houseplant, in the process of getting a door shut in his face. A man in sweatpants and a T-shirt. A woman in a purple bathrobe. Himself, feeling that he had gotten them out of bed. The man: *What the hell is this, Joanna?* The woman slammed the door, at 91 Old Mill Circle, the return address Meyer had put on the package of memories and bankers' acceptances and dangerous names. That was who Meyer had met at the airport. And she was his girlfriend and killer, Trevisone had said.

It was just possible, though the timing would have had to be close. While Alex had been hearing Kim's story and telling his own, changing the gears, putting the car back together, resting underneath, making out the bill, buying the ridiculous plant. Would that have been enough time to meet, talk, kill, and go home?

At the sound of footsteps, Alex tore the page from the book. He folded it quickly, and added it to the crumpled evidence building up in his back pocket. The footsteps were only the attendant again, coming once more to be of service.

"Ich kann den Name nicht finden," Alex told him. The attendant said he was sorry and followed Alex slowly back out the Schonhauser Allee, extending his hand silently for the yarmulke. Alex imagined him closing the cemetery up, forcing shut the rusty iron gate, folding up his own yarmulke and slipping it in his jacket pocket like a bureaucrat pulling off his tie as he leaves the office. *"Gute Reise,"* the attendant told

Alex. Have a nice trip home. Alex left the cemetery behind and descended into the U-Bahn against a tide of commuters coming home from work.

His knees felt unsteady under him, and he realized that he hadn't eaten all day. He needed a place to sit, to eat, to study documents, and to think. He was tempted to do his business in some quiet, out-of-the-way restaurant, with wurst swimming in gravy and overcooked peas. But he knew that for a maudlin attempt to go back to yesterday, with a living Cynthia on a moving train. What he needed was someplace nice and bright, modern and efficient, where above all they had good telephone connections to the West. Down in the U-Bahn station, he asked the ticket seller where foreign businessmen went to eat and drink.

The ticket seller looked up, a flicker of surprise showing on his face. Then he nodded, with assurance, as if he had sized up his customer well.

"Alex," the man said.

24

So Does Ophelia

Pure instinct made him turn and run. The panic that had not set in at the time of the explosion overwhelmed him now. He fled up the stairs. This time he was with the tide, but faster, a rock flung forward out of the sea. Stunned faces grasped at him as he pushed through the orderly crowd toward the sunny street.

Faces grasped—but no hands. Just before the top, Alex managed to get a grip on himself. It was simply not possible for the ticket seller to have spoken his name. It had not happened, or it had not happened the way he thought. He turned and, as politely as possible, excuse-me'd his way down. *"Verzeihung,"* he said, and then, on the platform, *"Verzeihung"* again. The last excuse-me was addressed to a young woman reading a paper, one of the few passengers waiting for a train toward the city center.

"Excuse me." He unfolded his tourist map in front of her. "Can you show me on here where Alex is?"

"Alex, ja," the young woman said. She pointed to a

black rectangle that announced, in white letters, **ALEXAN-DERPLATZ.**

"*Danke,*" Alex answered weakly, but with renewed confidence in his ability to think. "And is that where you would go for an expensive dinner?"

"Why?" she said in English. "Are you inviting me?"

"No, I didn't mean . . ."

"Oh," the woman said. She wore high boots, designer jeans, and an expression Alex could not read at all. "I thought you were. I might go there, yes. But I think I would go to the *Palast.*"

"The Palace?"

"Of the Republic. You are American?"

Alex nodded.

"The Congress. The Capitol. And a playground, too. Food and drink, theater, sometimes rock music, Dixieland."

"Telephones?"

She looked at him strangely and tossed her head as if to say she didn't like being made fun of.

"Of course. Telephones, they work very well, escalators, toilets that flush, and beautiful waitresses who expect to be tipped. Where do you think you are, Mr. Jones?" She tossed her head again. "Havana?"

"No, um, thank you. I'll take your advice."

Alex didn't know whether he'd just talked to a rapidly rising civil service professional or a high-class prostitute who catered to foreign businessmen. When the train came, he figured out the nearest stop to the Palace of the Republic. He got out there, and walked along the River Spree, in the gathering darkness and the oncoming chill. He tried to figure out what he did know.

In a certain way, to come full circle to the woman he'd found at the address in Melrose made sense. Gerald Meyer may not have been a man who could stick to his decisions, but he was also not a man who did things at random. He had chosen that address in case the package was returned unopened, or in case investigators tried to trace it back to its source. That made Joanna Connor a partner, or a fall guy, or both, on top of what Trevisone knew.

In any case, Meyer had gone to meet her, Friday night.

He wasn't pleased with what he'd done that day, and he wasn't expecting her to be pleased, either. And drinking, alone and morose, waiting for her, he had remembered that her name rested next to his in the cemetery book. Only here, maybe, and nowhere else. He had found it pleasing, when pressed by Kim, to hand Alex that information, in the form of a small puzzle. Then she'd arrived, and he must have told her about his arrangement with Alex. Maybe she'd marched him down the LaFarges' driveway as a warning, like Trevisone had implied. Maybe just because she found Alex as good a red herring as any. That was a sentiment, it occurred to Alex with a shock, that she most likely shared with Gerald Meyer. Now Meyer was dead, and Joanna was apparently on the run.

By the time he'd worked that out, the Palace stood before him, gleaming with light. Near the entrance, tour buses unloaded guided groups. Alex approached on foot, between buses, and pushed through a revolving door into a bright, surreal lobby that covered, at minimum, a city block. The lobby was studded with coffee and liquor bars full of well-dressed patrons. In the spaces between, teenagers in jeans loitered on the benches, near placards that announced Shakespeare and Schiller and, indeed, Dixieland. Alex approached a stout older woman behind a coat-check stand, offered his windbreaker, and asked where he could get something to eat. She directed him to a "Continental" restaurant one flight up —restaurants on level two, theater on three, legislation on four. In the restaurant he chewed mediocre pasta until he felt he'd taken in sufficient fuel.

That chore over, he finished his meal with very good German chocolate cake and a *kannchen Italien,* a silvery pitcher of double espresso that did its job well. While he sipped, he pored over financial paper like any businessman, cross-checked the computer-generated acceptances against Meyer's notes. The notes recorded payoffs over a period of eight years. The latest ones seemed to be the people he'd been supposed to pay off, but hadn't. The acceptances represented some of the missing payoffs. Others, presumably, had already been converted into cash. At length Alex paid, tipped heavily, and used a bathroom outside of which another stout old woman collected tips on a small tray. War widows, he thought. A half-century before, their husbands had marched off in the Wehrmacht. Now, as a matter of social policy, they had to be employed. A row of phones stood nearby. The war widow told him the operators would accept a British credit card, and that he could certainly dial England direct. Meredith's voice answered on the fourth ring.

"It's Alex," he said.

"Alex," she echoed. Her voice sounded flat, noncommittal. A voice requesting information from the unknown. "Where are you? Berlin?"

Alex looked around him. A uniformed usher was guarding the entrance to an escalator next to a sign proclaiming *Hamlet*. The line of Shakespeare fans formed, patiently, between plush purple ropes strung from gilded poles. Putting all the shows under one roof was an idea that might catch on. Alex imagined the headline of a travel article, sandwiched between the airline ads: SOLONS MAKE SPEECHES, AND SO DOES OPHELIA.

"East Berlin. I think."

"Are you all right? How did things go with Cynthia?"

"About as you predicted."

A strange city, she had predicted. A mysterious woman. A mission. A frosty silence met his comment now.

"But it doesn't matter," he added. "She's dead."

"Very funny, Alex." Meredith didn't like him being cryptic, he knew. "You've fallen in love with the dead, so I won't take offense, is that what you mean?"

Alex tried to pull it together. He didn't know how to begin to explain.

"How long has she been dead?" Meredith asked. "And why did he send you to her, in that case?"

"No, dammit." Once he found his tongue, the story took care of itself. "She was alive when I met her. When we went to get the package, someone assumed we and it would both get back into the car. Or maybe not. Anyway, she got back in, and I didn't."

"And?"

"They blew it up. I tried to get her out, but I was too late. I don't know, maybe other people had already tried. The gas tank went up. Somebody knocked me down. Too late for her. Just in time for me. That was this morning. Since then I've been to the cops, and the cemetery."

Meredith's tone was no longer frosty, but it didn't exude trust and confidence, either.

"Where are you, exactly?"

Right question, he thought. Where now, and where next? Back into the stream of time. Still tilting at windmills, perhaps, but better grounded and better armed. Peace Through Strength, he reflected bitterly.

"I'm in the Palace of the German Democratic Republic. A showcase of democracy if I ever saw one. I think I know who killed Jerry Meyer, or who the police have decided killed him, at least. I'm sure I know what Meyer was up to for Jack Moselle, more than I should. I need to get out of here, and I need to see Jack. Tomorrow. I need to see him before any of his friends see me."

"Not alone," Meredith said.

"What?"

"I said 'not alone,' God damn you. Not this time. I explained this already."

"I'm okay," Alex insisted. "I can do it." He pictured the color risen in her cheeks, the cool, level stare projecting from her eyes. He didn't even convince himself.

"No."

"All right," he said. "We. We can do it." He felt, absurdly, like Popeye handed a can of spinach. "But the cops have your address, and I don't know who's giving out what information to whom. So meet me at Moselle's hideaway, where I told you it is, at ten o'clock in the morning. Or, wait, is there someplace near there, public, not too near, where we can meet?"

"Victoria Park. By the goats."

By the goats? Victoria Park? Victory Park, by the zoo.

"All right. I can find that. Has anybody been looking for me?"

"A policeman has been here inquiring. Your Sergeant Trevisone may be getting impatient. But you don't seem to be hunted, if that's what you mean."

"Okay, good. I'm not going to have any luggage, I don't

think. Just a few papers. Will that raise questions at customs?"

"I doubt it. But a briefcase and a tie wouldn't hurt."

"Okay," Alex said.

"Suppose Moselle isn't there?"

"Call him and make me an appointment. What time is it there? Maybe somebody takes messages, after hours. Or call first thing in the morning. Give my name and say I'm interested in buying some shares of—hold on, I've got to check Meyer's list. Say I'm interested in, um, Siebert Industries. That ought to do it."

"Do what?"

"Let him know I'm coming, so he doesn't have to send anybody after me. And let him know I've got his package, and I understand what's in it."

"I see. Take care, Alex. Ten A.M."

"Right." *I love you* wanted to come next, but it stuck for a while before it worked its way out. When it did, it sounded rather like a rasp.

"Yes," Meredith said. "Well. Let's get through tomorrow, shall we? Then we can go back to talking about things like that."

Okay, thought Alex. Let's. He called Lufthansa and booked the last flight from West Berlin to London, at ten. He made the reservation under the name of A. Platz. Then he did not want to make his last call, so he took the escalator down again, and detoured to a sunken bar not far from another set of phones. He ordered Russian vodka and drank it down, straight, with apologies to his stomach lining. He got some change and dialed once more.

"*Gasthaus,*" a male voice said.

"Alex Glauberman *hier.* Cenap?"

Let it be Cenap, he requested silently. Cenap would be best. A man, a foreigner, like himself. Let him not have to explain himself to Marianne, not yet, not now.

"*Polizei, Herr Glauberman. Wo sind Sie?*"

Gestapo, Alex thought. Why can't you leave those people in peace? Then for an instant he wondered if Schultheiss could have been right. But no. Cynthia and her friends were

184

not terrorists who bombed train stations and department stores.

"*Ich bin wo ich bin,*" Alex told him. "Could I please speak to one of the . . . to someone who lives there, or works there?"

"*Nein, Herr Glauberman. Wo sind Sie?*"

"Well, fuck you," Alex said. "You know that much English, fuck? Whose phone is it, anyway?"

"*Wo sind Sie, Herr Glauberman?*" the polite police voice repeated.

"Moscow." Alex said. "Beirut. Jerusalem. Johannesburg. Washington. Where the terrorists are. Go fuck yourself, okay, and tell Schultheiss, too."

He banged down the phone, went back to the bar, piled a second vodka on the first. There was nothing more to do today. He wanted to get on a vehicle, any vehicle, that would take him directly to the chi-chi rehabilitated firehouse in Bethnal Green, London. Instead he reclaimed his jacket, left most of his remaining Ostmarks for a tip, and caught the bus that the appreciative widow said would get him to Friedrichstrasse.

On Unter den Linden, the bus stopped in front of the Memorial to the Victims of Militarism and Fascism. An everlasting flame burned, and an honor guard of the DDR patrolled. The honor guard goose-stepped. The bus moved again, and at the next stop Alex got off and retraced his afternoon steps between high-rise apartments and ministries. Somewhere around here, he had read, would be the buried remains of Hitler's bunker.

At Checkpoint Charlie he showed his passport and turned over his unspent Ostmarks, now on permanent deposit, in his name, in the National Bank of the DDR. On the American side, nobody wanted to see anything. The black GI in the booth had been replaced by a white one. Just beyond was a German cabbie, looking for customers. Alex climbed in, said, "Tegel Airport, *bitte,*" and took refuge in sleep.

When he woke up, the panic came back. The streets outside meant nothing to his groggy brain. But the driver pulled up in front of Lufthansa as nice as could be.

A tie and a briefcase cost nearly as much as his ticket. There were no rock posters, and this was not the place to shop for excellent wool sweaters. So he bought Maria a Swiss army knife instead—one with nail file and scissors as well as can openers and blades. He bought a picture postcard, which he addressed to Hans Heidenfelter's shop in Grand Island—or where Hans Heidenfelter's shop in Grand Island had once been. "Dangerous town," he wrote. "Love, Alex."

He passed up newspapers in several languages, but he did leaf through an English-language tour book on Berlin. He learned that along the Ku-Damm, near the Berlin Zoo, one could find pickup lounges in which customers sent confidential messages from table to table via pneumatic tubes. He liked the idea of the pneumatic tubes. When A. Platz boarded without interference, Alex felt he was entering just such a device. He visualized himself as a very confidential message for Jack Moselle.

25

Under Glass

Traveler's checks paid for a sterile, expensive room at the airport hotel. For fifteen pounds more, Alex badgered the night staff into photocopying the contents of Meyer's package. He mailed the copy to Bernie with instructions that it should be opened only if Bernie didn't hear otherwise from Alex. He mailed the page torn from the cemetery register to Trevisone.

With sleep, the elephant dream recurred. This time the flaming elephants did not die. Charred, blackened by the fire from his weapon, they rose again after each blast. There was infinite sadness in their liquid eyes. They stepped forward, crumpled, struggled laboriously up, and came closer. The smell of fried flesh clogged his lungs.

Alex woke, showered, and forced down a hearty British breakfast. Then he rode for a long time underneath London, turning over in his mind what he was about to do. It was not so much a matter of turning over, though. It was pushing and shoving—trying with all his might to force what he wanted into the mold of what he could get. That explained the dream, perhaps, because it was without doubt a hard, bitter thing to do.

When he emerged from the tube, in Stepney, he had just a short, chilly walk to Victoria Park. The park proved to be a big, pancake-flat, green place with scattered groves of trees and a hint of formal garden here and there. The entrance was deserted except for a trio of gardeners at work in a flower bed, digging. Alex watched them for a moment, then asked what they were doing.

One gardener leaned on her shovel and said they were digging up the bulbs. The flowers would be kept alive in hothouse for the winter. She gave Alex a quick once-over and added that tourists were rare in this park. It was a pretty park, Alex said. The gardener explained that it been planned, originally, to separate the rich from the poor—"You know, to stop the spread of disease." Alex asked her to point him toward the goats.

The goats ran back and forth, nibbling at the sparse grass in their pen. They made irritated old-man noises at Alex as they went by. Alex turned his back, watching a few figures come and go along the black-paved path that wound through the green of the park. He recalled how once, long ago, he'd made an appointment to meet a man by the buffalo pen in Golden Gate Park. That appointment—an AWOL soldier from the Presidio base—hadn't showed. But soon he could see Meredith in her red leather jacket, flanked by a black woman in long, beaded cornrows and a gangly white man whose blue jeans were shredded. These escorts slowed down as Meredith came up to Alex.

"I know you don't like to ask for help," she said. "I brought some anyway. This is Paula, and Stork. This is Alex."

Alex shook hands with them and kissed Meredith on the cheek.

"Are these a few of the panting groupies?" he whispered.

Meredith did not smile, but only nodded and brushed the straight dark red hair from her face.

"These are my students, yes. Paula grew up in a neighborhood that's as tough as they come. Stork is an expert in kung-fu. I thought they might sit over pastry with me and keep an eye on matters."

"Oh," said Alex. "Thanks. Why not?"

The four of them left the park, marching past stately row houses newly spiffed up. Stork wore a bleached tail down his neck and strode forward like a tin man in seven-league boots. Paula was equally silent but steadier, watchful, catlike. Alex remembered what Meredith had said about her students —her disturbing feeling that to them it was all some kind of game.

Nearing Moselle's building, Alex described the soft-faced man in the cap. Other than that, he found he was grateful for Meredith's presence but had no advice to give. He waited for the brass cage to come to him, riding its shiny pole down the transparent shaft. When it arrived, he opened the glass door, pressed 2, and slid easily upward. No alarms went off to signal his arrival. He stepped out and offered the receptionist his name.

This receptionist was not the young, wide-eyed one who had sent him to Lady Jane Friedhoff. She was closer to Alex's age, a small, skeptical woman in a dark blue suit. "Mr. Glauberman, is it?" she said. Her accent had an affected quality that grated on him. So did her attempts at flamboyance—big designer glasses, and exuberant curls unnaturally blond. He wanted no preliminary battles with gatekeepers. Armored in what he now knew, he wanted to fight with the man himself.

"That's right," he said haughtily. "I believe I'm expected."

She looked down at something on her desk, pursed her lips, and finally consented to press a button on the intercom. "Mr. Moselle," she announced without intonation. "A Mr. Glauberman is here."

"Alex." Moselle's voice crackled with contrasting enthusiasm. "Fast work. Come on in."

This time Moselle was behind his big, antique desk. He sat with his accustomed healthy ease in an old-fashioned wooden swivel chair. He was wearing a soft cashmere sweater with leather patches at the elbows. His hands rested calmly on the uncluttered top of the desk. Alex plopped his Tegel Airport briefcase onto the green blotting-paper surface. He snapped open the lid to reveal the envelope that Meyer had sent.

"I let Cynthia keep the family memorabilia," he reported. "I brought you the rest."

Moselle looked the papers over, then slid them into a drawer. He opened the drawer below that to get a checkbook. He wrote Alex out a check for fifteen hundred pounds.

"You're an honest man, Alex. Depending on the market for sterling when you cash this, my payment ought to match Jerry's, or better. Let's treat it as a gift rather than a payment, though, shall we? The paperwork to escape double taxation can use up a year in itself. Most of us don't have so many years to waste."

"Cynthia," Alex said, "didn't have any."

Moselle turned his palms up, dropping his eyes toward them as if their lines held wisdom. "Cynthia tangled with the wrong people." His hard eyes came up to meet Alex's through the dark-rimmed glasses. "I protected her while Jerry was alive, because she was useful to me. I can't be expected to protect her forever."

"Meyer wanted to give her a hold over you," Alex said. "It was his awkward way of taking a bit more revenge. It was his way of making up for her dependence on you when she was young. Maybe he didn't realize all he was doing was setting her up for trouble. Then he panicked, and told your boys where he'd sent the stuff, am I right? Meanwhile, I came along, and he decided I was nice and expendable. Maybe I could undo what he'd done. If not, maybe I could draw fire away from his daughter. But let's go back a step, can we? Why was Meyer double-crossing you after all these years? Because the feds were closing in?"

Moselle blinked twice behind his glasses. On the second one, his left eye gave that little tic that might have been a wink. Nothing else moved—not his hands on the desktop, not a strand of his handsome gray hair. Alex felt loose, disorganized, by contrast. He wasn't sure he was making enough of an impression.

"You seem to be doing the talking," Moselle said.

"Okay. Let me tell you what he did for you. Say you own two dummy firms. Let's call them Siebert Industries and

Mannheim Gesellschaft. Siebert places an order with Mannheim for, what was it, warehouse cranes? They send Mannheim a letter of credit from Meyer's bank. Mannheim goes through the motions, pretending to ship the cranes, and the papers end up on Meyer's desk. Meyer accepts. Only he doesn't return the acceptance to Mannheim Gesellschaft, for them to cash in. Instead, Meyer forwards it to, say, the Minister of Justice of the state of Hesse. The Minister is happy, because that piece of paper is as good as gold. Mannheim Gesellschaft doesn't mind, because it never really shipped any cranes. Meyer's bank will be happy, as long as Siebert Industries makes good on the loan within the ninety days. And Siebert is happy, because they don't need any cranes, they only need to get a sum of money to the Minister of Justice. The thing I don't understand is why you didn't just have Siebert Industries write a check to the Minister, the way you just wrote one to me."

Moselle made a show of examining his checkbook, then smiled, shut it, and put it away.

"Because the Minister of Justice might get his finances looked at closer than yours," he explained calmly. "What you don't understand is that this was nothing new. It was a new riff on something Jerry and I used to do together a long time ago, in Berlin. I wanted concrete, okay, and a certain supply sergeant was in charge of the concrete. Jerry was a desk soldier, in the paymaster's office. Jerry paid the supply sergeant off, legal as could be. I got Jerry the money to make up the deficit in his accounts. Same idea, higher society."

"And you weren't afraid your dog would turn on you someday?"

"Sure, but when a dog gets old, and sick. . . ."

"You have it put to death."

Moselle said, "What is it you want, Alex?"

Your neck, Alex said silently. But, unfortunately, that wasn't what he'd come to get.

"I want evidence that'll convict Cynthia's killers, and clear her and her friends of any bomb charges. I don't expect this evidence to implicate you. Just the ones that did the work."

"Or else?"

"A copy of Meyer's list is already on its way someplace safe. If I don't get what I want from you, the copy goes to the feds investigating Meyer's irregularities. In case I'm not around to go with it, the list is traveling with an explanation of how I acquired it, and where I was headed this morning. I think that adds up to a lot of hot water you'd rather avoid."

"Maybe." Moselle leaned his chair back on creaking springs. Alex expected him to put his feet up on the desk, but he didn't go that far. "Hot water washes off me like— what was it I said?—like whiskey off a duck. But I don't like trouble. What happens if I manage to give you what you want?"

"The copy goes up in smoke. Believe me, I know better than to double-cross you."

Moselle plopped flat again. The springs creaked, and wood met wood with a solid, resonant sound. Moselle linked his hands in front of him and cracked his knuckles.

"You ought to *sell* cars, my friend. You got yourself a deal. I'm not anti-Semitic. I sold Nazis east or west, depending on the bid. East, they got a big, showy trial and jail, usually. West, they sometimes got a deal and a job spying on the Russians."

"That was a long time ago," said Alex. "Now you'll expose them when it's useful to you, the way Cynthia said. But you're just as happy employing them to run your errands —like blowing up people that get in your way. With luck, the cops don't go after the bomber at all. If they do, you're still covered. The victims are a known left-winger, half-Jewish, and a visiting American Jew. It's terrible to learn there are still such Nazis about, but the case is open-and-shut. You probably staged the business with the knife on the train, too, just to set things up right."

Moselle held up a warning hand. "I said we had a deal. Don't go peddling stories I don't want to buy. And remember, switch-hitting is what made Mickey Mantle great. When Cynthia became a hindrance, her enemies got wind of a rumor that she was about to expose some of their most important friends." He stopped suddenly, with a boyish grin that admitted he'd said more than he'd meant to. "Now. What am I supposed to do with this evidence?"

"Forward it to a Captain Gerhard Schultheiss, West Berlin police. And to Cynthia's friends, too, or their lawyers, to make sure there's no cover-up. Get somebody to whisper a few words in the ears of one or two of Schultheiss's superiors."

"Your wish is my command. I assume you don't need my help with your own local police?"

"I don't think so. When they find Joanna, that will take care of itself."

"And would you mind telling me what you know about Joanna, as long as you're showing off?"

A small not-kosher sign began to appear in the far corner of Alex's mind's eye, a reminder that there were many things about the circumstances of Meyer's putting-to-death that he still did not know. But he was feeling power now, too much power to pay the sign much mind. The more he seemed to know, the more Moselle might tell him. The more Moselle told him, the greater the chance of a slip that somehow might give Alex a new handle—a handle that could make this smooth, parasitic creature pay for Cynthia's death.

"I know Meyer met her at the airport Friday night. I know she and he have been an item for a while now. I know he had her pretend to be his second daughter when he wanted to see Cynthia but was afraid to go himself. The cops know all this. More important, they've got an eyewitness who saw her and Meyer leave together Friday. I think they've got more evidence they haven't told me about. I don't know what hand you had in that, Jack, but I expect you were happy to see Joanna put your sick old dog to sleep. That way your two American employees who caught up with Meyer the day I met him didn't have to do it. Maybe if I had gotten blown up with Cynthia, Jerry's death could still have been pinned on me. But not now. I wouldn't get in deeper by protecting Joanna now, if I were you."

A laugh crackled from the speakerphone. The electronics made it even more mirthless, more bitter, than it already was.

"You should be thinking about protecting *yourself*, hotshot," a woman's voice said.

As Alex whirled, the receptionist in the blue suit appeared in the doorway. The blond wig was gone, along with the false British accent. Her own hair was dark, shiny, short, and shaped to her head. The big glasses were gone, too. Her eyes were big but not wide—experienced, angry eyes— under eyebrows penciled into sharp angles. They were set in a face that was round yet severe, a face Alex had been trying to call up since the Jewish cemetery, the afternoon before.

"Excuse me, ma'am," she whined in a high-pitched little-boy tone. "I have a plant here for Mr. Meyer." She carried a pistol, a big one, like a police revolver, in her hand. She raised the gun toward Alex. Alex grew warm all over.

He knew he had been foolish. He felt a fool's urge to stare stupidly at the evidence of his mistakes. But he told himself that Joanna did not call the shots here, or fire them without permission. He forced himself to turn his back on the woman and her gun.

"You don't want me dead in your office," he said.

"It's not Jack who's facing a murder charge," Joanna Connor rapped out behind him. "I think you made that perfectly clear. It's us small fry that have to look out for ourselves."

"What's she to you?" Alex demanded of Jack. He hoped ignoring the woman would make her mad. Not mad enough to shoot without Jack's go-ahead. Just mad enough to make a mistake.

"What's she to me?" Moselle leaned back in his chair again, stroking his short, handsome, pepper-and-salt beard. "Let's go back to your Minister of Justice in, where was it, Hesse? Right, Hesse. He can't waltz into his broker's office and say, 'Hey, somebody laid a *sehr guten* instrument on me, a hundred thousand G's—would you mind turning it into cash?' He doesn't want to make his broker suspicious. The thing has to come like any normal acquisition, from a broker in, let's say, Boston. So Jerry needs a partner who works in a place like that. Then let's say—as you did say, Alex—that the feds start to close in. So Jerry and his partner decide to grab what they can for themselves, while it lasts."

"Let's say, everybody shut up," commanded Joanna. In the moment of silence, Alex had time to wonder what charms the late Meyer had retained that would raise the hopes of a woman like this. Maybe it was not so much Meyer's charms as her own history. Unfortunately he knew nothing about her, except her home address, her manner with alleged delivery-men, and the one moment when she pushed Meyer through that narrow checkpoint into death. When Jack picked up his story again, she did not interrupt.

"I found out that some payments weren't ending up in the right place," Moselle said. "Joanna had the good sense to see it was time to change sides again. Double-cross the crosser, you know. I was willing to let bygones be bygones."

"Sure," Alex said. "You're generous. On the condition she got rid of Jerry for good. But now I don't see why you need her. Just like you don't need my body in your office."

Moselle made an easy swivel in his chair, once around, like a carnival barker spinning his wheel of fortune.

"I don't know. I think you overprice that little list, just like Jerry did. With his testimony, or Joanna's, it might be worth something. Even with Cynthia's, maybe. Not with yours. And believe me, not all by itself. The folks looking into all that, their job is to keep the banking industry pure of criminal influence. With Meyer gone, that's pretty much taken care of. As for your local police, if they could touch me I wouldn't deserve to be here. But you, Alex, you were Meyer's errand boy. You got big ideas, you shot him, you cleaned him out. If you turn up dead, somewhere in London, that's just another falling-out among thieves. They may have a better suspect, like you say, but if they can't find her they'll settle for you. Dead suspects don't talk back."

He looked down at his hands again, then straight at Alex. "All in all, I'd rather have Joanna working for me, with you out of the picture, than Joanna singing for her life, with you pulling the strings."

"Sure," Alex said. "And once I'm gone, you can always turn her in for two murders, if you need to."

Get mad, lady, Alex prayed. Now is the time to lose your cool. He turned, hoping to see the gun waver. But Joanna's eyes were harder than Jack's. They had seen too many bad decisions already, and too much bad luck. Now they exuded loathing, and the points of the brows punctuated the emotion. The set of her lips was tired, but sure. She took two steps sideways, out of the doorway. Her thumb caressed the hammer of the revolver.

"I want you to walk to the elevator," she said. "And get in."

"One last question," Alex rattled out. "What the hell did you see in Meyer? Besides money, I mean. That big guy you rushed home to bed with, after you shot Jerry . . . that guy looked a lot better to me."

This time Joanna Connor took two steps toward Alex. Her finger flexed on the trigger. But Jack said, "Don't," and she stopped. She hurled words at Alex from where she was.

"That man was my husband, asshole. Jerry wasn't my lover, or whatever it is you think. Jerry was my father. Jerry was my father, and he was ruining my life. He ruined everybody's life that he touched. He talked me into this thing, a little money on the side. Then it started to blow up. So he talked me into the next move, double-crossing Jack. Finally I smartened up. Now do you understand? I've got two kids to think about that mean a lot more to me than you do. I didn't like killing Jerry, though I had enough reasons. But believe me, I'm going to like killing you."

Alex cast a last look at Jack, but Jack had swiveled again, turning his back. So Alex backed slowly out the door, his thoughts whirling and then straightening out. Gerald Meyer's second daughter followed him with hatred in her eyes. He backed across the reception area. The elevator was waiting, its door open.

"Jack had your sister killed," he said. "Cynthia was your sister, and she didn't deserve to die."

"Sister!" Joanna's knuckles whitened on the handle of the gun. "She was a figment of his imagination, and his bullshit silly pride. I had to go with him to find her, because he got principles all of a sudden, when everything started to cave in. Didn't she tell you he was going to take good care of her, finally? Now shut up and get *in*, or I'll shoot you right here."

She motioned with the revolver. Alex went.

"And in the end," he said almost to himself, "Jerry cleaned *you* out. He sent everything to her, because he guessed you'd gone back over to Jack. The deserving daughter, the selfish daughter. No wonder he quoted *King Lear* at me."

"Yeah." Joanna stepped warily into the elevator cage. "Jerry understood a lot. In books."

She punched a code into the security system, and the elevator door closed. She turned sideways to Alex, gun hand under her suit jacket. The butt was hidden behind her wrist. The mouth of the barrel made a slight bulge in the jacket, in front of her left arm. Alex raised his hands against the brass bars, like a stickup victim in an old Western. What he had to do was keep her mind on his words, not his pose. The words didn't have to make sense. They just had to keep her thinking. He swallowed, and she pushed the button marked *B*.

"What are you going to do after you shoot me?" he demanded. "Hide out forever, wherever Jack finds to shut you away? What about your husband and your kids then? You didn't convince anybody with those little tricks about the gun and my card, you know. It might almost have worked, except Jerry told me you shot him. He told me right there against the trash can, before he died. That's what brought me to your house so quick. I didn't know what to do about you, but I wanted to get myself a look. My mistake was giving you time to get away."

The elevator glided down between glass walls. Alex raised his hands higher. He edged along the rim of the cage, trying to put the fire pole between himself and the gun. Not that the slim, gleaming pole would do him any good.

"Shut up!" she rapped out. "And stay still. I mean it. Don't fucking move."

Alex stayed still. Eye level was just a foot off the reception area carpet now. The bottom half of the elevator would be visible from below. His legs and her legs, but no story would they tell. He waited a second to see whether she was going to respond.

"You're lying," she told him, but her eyes doubted that. "He couldn't have. . . ."

"It was short and sweet, you mean, a bullet to the brain? Oh no, Joanna. He lingered long enough. And do you want to know how your half sister died? Thanks to your friend Jack, upstairs. She died stuck in a car, conscious, counting the seconds till the gas would catch and burn her alive."

God, let that not be true, Alex told himself. Let her

have gone out in an instant, as Meyer must have. And let Meredith see my hands in the air, and understand.

As the elevator sank, the herbal store seemed to rise at his feet and then levitate upward. The pastry shop was behind him, out of his sight. Then everything disappeared, and the shaft was concrete instead of glass. A ceiling lamp gave a dim light inside the darkened space. Alex was tempted to crumple and roll, but he didn't. A switchblade in the dark was one thing. A pistol would be another. And this was no airport lobby, and Joanna was no hired gun. She brought the weapon out from under her jacket. With her free hand, she pointed to the knob of a steel door.

"Get out," she ordered. As he opened the door, Alex saw her finger press a series of the little buttons, and then the big one marked 2. Express to Jack, that would mean. No escape route. No reinforcements. She stepped out after him, gun at his back. "Over by that boiler," she said. "And kneel down."

It was a new boiler, probably put in when the renovations were done. Besides the boiler, there were just banks of gas and electric meters, odd pieces of lumber, and an exit door. The exit door wasn't bolted, but that didn't mean it wasn't locked. The basement was much smaller than the upper floors, for some reason. Alex told himself that the cellar of a no-longer fire station would be too crazy a place to die. He reminded himself that, unlike other people, he knew where he should look for death. It was like being in a prophecy: the doom couldn't come before its time. Prophecies were tricky though. Sometimes you had to give them some help. Over by the boiler, he knelt down and then sprang around it, keeping low.

"It's gas, Joanna," he shouted. "You don't want to shoot wild. If you spring a leak, we'll both go up this time. I lied to you, yes, but not all the way. He was dead, you're right. But he told me anyhow, in a different way. I know, and the cops know. Now stop and think. You can quit while it's still a family crime. He fucked up your life, he led you into his crooked racket. And then you were in fear of your life from Jack. And it was all his doing. A jury might understand that. They wouldn't feel the same way about you killing me."

From the elevator shaft came a quiet *whump,* and then

another. In a flash, he knew what these sounds had to be. He peeked around the boiler and saw that Joanna knew it too. She was backing against the wall, near the exit, trying to keep both him and the shaft covered. Groping behind his back, he found a piece of two-by-four and hurled it at her head before she could try putting a bullet through the sheet steel of the door. As she ducked, he threw another, yelling, "Now! She can't see!"

Then the door burst open, and Alex and Paula and Stork all charged at once. Alex went along the wall, where she'd have to turn the farthest, where an erring slug would miss the gas supply line—he hoped. Otherwise it would be one last bang, and they'd all go the way Cynthia had. Joanna turned, and Alex saw the hole at the end of the barrel. He dove just before he heard the shot.

The bullet did not lodge in his body or in the pipe. When he got up from the floor, Stork had Joanna and Paula had the gun. The elevator door showed the empty shaft through which they'd come—like firefighters to the rescue, down the pole.

"You okay, man?" Stork asked. Joanna stared dully at Alex, the fire dying in her eyes.

"Yeah," Alex said. "Thanks, both of you. What about Meredith?"

"She probably got cut a little, busting the glass." Paula imitated the motion of swinging a large object with two hands. "The door doesn't open unless the car is there. She's a fast thinker, Meredith. You owe her a few. Now is this all over, or what?"

26

Alex at Home

It wasn't over, quite. There was the task of forcing the exit and climbing the service stairs, gun in hand. There was the task of cementing the deal, all over again. For better or for worse, Alex learned that a loaded gun gives you no leverage unless you are prepared to use it.

He was severely tempted, once. Jack offered him an extra fifteen hundred pounds as compensation for mental anguish. Right then the trigger felt very functional under his index finger—poised to strike, coiled and ready, in a way the switchblade on the train had not been. He understood why guns lent a hand to so many lethal impulses that might otherwise come and go without result. But he didn't shoot. He wasn't built that way, or perhaps Cynthia's death did not cut him all the way to the bone that would demand revenge, no matter how. In any case, Jack stayed alive and promised to get on the phone to Germany right away. The only one to lose under the terms of the new deal was Joanna. The terms required her to call the police and request to be sent to America to stand trial. Who else she was going to implicate, when her moment of truth came, was going to depend on her calculation of the odds.

Meanwhile, Friday morning was gone. In the afternoon, Alex got his stitches checked and his blood drawn at the clinic of Meredith's university. His white count was down to the low side of normal, but the doctor assured him this would not inhibit his ability to fight off normal infections. His platelets were fine. He ought to be ready for his next round of chemotherapy in a week and a half, no need to fear.

The idea of another round advanced like a distant thundercloud—the kind of dark cloud that spreads ominously while you walk a mountain trail or a remote beach. You can tell yourself that getting drenched won't be the total disaster that it seems; it will be followed by getting dry. Yet there is no solace in this telling. The only solace is in trying to ignore the approaching darkness and the muffled booms.

Friday evening, Alex was visited by a British policeman bearing a message from his counterpart in America. Joanna Connor had waived extradition proceedings and was on her way, under guard, to Sergeant Trevisone. If Alex did not return voluntarily to present whatever evidence he had, steps would have to be taken to bring him home under duress. Alex bargained for one more day; the policeman said he would be there tomorrow afternoon, as a courtesy, to pick him up.

Saturday morning, Alex talked to Marianne by telephone. It was a long and difficult talk, made much longer and more painful by the process of constructing inadequate sentences in each other's languages. Alex concluded that Jack was keeping up his end of the agreement. The hands that had actually placed the bomb had been cuffed for now. Marianne invited Alex to visit if he was ever again in Berlin. She did not invite him to make that visit soon.

After the telephone call, Alex and Meredith shopped for an excellent wool sweater for Maria, and posters for Maria and Elizabeth and Matthew. Then Meredith took him on a historical tube-and-walking tour, long promised and a week delayed. The tour began in the low, crowded East End, where working women had fought for suffrage. It ended high on top of Hampstead Heath, not far from Marx's grave. They looked down on the city in a cold October wind.

"The first night," Alex said, "I came downstairs to see what was happening. Sunday night, the day I got here. You and Janice were up late, drinking and talking, so I went back to bed."

"I remember," Meredith said. "Red red wine, it made me feel so fine."

"Janice wanted to know if I was planning to stick with you after I got certified as a temporarily normal person. In remission, ready to go on to bigger and better things."

"I don't think that's what Janice meant."

"Yeah, okay. But I am planning to. To stick."

"I believe you. But what Janice meant was, how much should I count on your plans? Do even you know *who* you'll be, once you've got that far?"

"What did you tell her?"

Meredith smiled but did not face him. "I said you'd probably be yourself, only—for better or for worse—more so." Then she turned and asked, "Who you are now, that you weren't a week ago?"

"Somebody that's seen a lot more death."

"Yes. How does that make you feel?"

Alex didn't know how to answer that, so he put his hands in his pockets and faced into the wind, letting it tug at the weakened roots of his black, bushy hair. The wind or something also forced tears out of his eyes. He was tired of tears, so he turned back to Meredith.

"Sadder," he said. "More determined. More philosophical. And, I guess, sort of at home."

It was time to go with the helpful policeman to the plane. Airborne, Alex watched the red light on the end of the wing blink on and off, on and off. He tried to meditate on this, to breathe in and out, neither censoring his thoughts nor holding on to them. His memories of Cynthia Meyer were going to come like the lights, on and off, blinking red, for quite a long time.

At Logan Airport, the INS man's face grew guarded

when his screen responded to Alex's name. Alex told him not to worry, that a man with a badge was here to meet him. Trevisone accepted delivery, and asked where Mr. Glauberman would like to go for a little talk. Alex suggested Petros's.

It was about midnight by Alex's biological clock, but by local timepieces it was almost exactly eight days ago at this hour that he'd last sat at the little Greek shop. This time he was able to drink his own coffee.

"Here's the way it is," Trevisone told him. "You concealed evidence from our department, and you possessed narcotics on the turf of the department next door. Meyer's daughter confesses to shooting him because he got her involved in a securities scam that was coming unraveled. She says she knew in her bones that he'd turn her in. Also, she was temporarily unhinged because he'd just cleaned out the merchandise and sent it to the other daughter, who never did anything to earn it. Plus a lot of other grievances that are nobody's business but hers till we get into court. But patricide, or parricide, or whatever the hell you call it, was weighing on her soul. So, after she ran away, she caved in and decided to confess.

"The Berlin police say that's got nothing to do with what happened to the other daughter. They say she died as part of a gang war between the extreme right and the extreme left. They say the perpetrators were members of a small group of Nazi nuts who'll be in the joint for a good long time. They say witnesses confirm the daughter did pick up an overseas package just before she died, but whatever was in it was destroyed in the explosion.

"Our own investigation told us that Meyer had a daughter who lived in the area, and when we went to talk to her, we found she'd suddenly skipped. Her picture more or less matched the description from the bartender at Logan. Also, it occurred to me to check whether Meyer had a safe-deposit box at any of the banks in Davis Square. If there was anything to your story, there had to be a reason why a guy from New York would pick an outlying post office in Boston to do business in. They had to be keeping the merchandise nearby. In fact, Connor and Meyer had a box in both their names, which wasn't too smart. And then it turned out some of her neighbors thought the Connors lived better than they had a right to.

"So that more than covers most of the loose ends. My question is, do you want to tie them in a tighter knot?"

Alex considered. The opening threats had been the wrong way to get his cooperation, but he appreciated the information that followed. And he assumed Trevisone needed some way to save face.

"I've beaten possession charges before," he said mildly. "And now it'll be easier, because I can plead chemotherapy to a jury that knows someday it'll be three out of the twelve of them. I only concealed evidence long enough to get off the ground, then I called you up. Why did you tell me your suspect was Meyer's lover, not his daughter?"

The ghost of a smile fluttered under Trevisone's mustache and through the crow's feet surrounding his eyes.

"I don't think so quick on my feet, so that was as good as I could do. I wanted to make sure you didn't get to her first somehow, and stir up all the shit the wrong way. Now, uh, I wonder how the hell did you find her, and what kind of persuasion did you use?"

So much for face, Alex thought. He drank his coffee until there was only mud at the bottom. He thought of his daughter, the past summer, making mud pies at the beach. Tomorrow he would call Laura and try to explain why the police had been asking about him. Then he'd tell Maria he was back early, and try to have a good reason for that, too.

Alex studied a luminous print of the Acropolis over Trevisone's right shoulder. The air conditioner wasn't running now that the weather had cooled, and snatches of other conversations came by while he thought about what he wanted to say, and how. "My tendency is somewhat different. . . ." someone said. Someone else said, "I think to some extent that that is a positive thing." Cambridge, Massachusetts, early Saturday evening. Plans made, events rehashed, words wasted saying simple things in complicated ways. Alex tried to say what he meant with honesty and without sarcasm.

"The way I see it, I wouldn't say the crimes aren't connected. One connection is Meyer's trouble with wives and daughters. What that was about could keep us all busy for a long time. Besides that, there's history—fascism, Hitler, the war, the occupation, you name it. And then, thanks to all this, like I told you, there's Jack Moselle. Moselle is in a position to make a lot of things happen, or not happen.

"The problem is, none of that would be in your jurisdiction, would it? None of it would change who could legally be convicted of either murder, in any country's court. I could tell you the whole story, but none of it would be admissible evidence. If I did have evidence, the best thing for my health would be to bury it deep."

"Uh-huh," Trevisone said. "Well, that's what I thought." He left Alex looking at his departing back, and he left Alex to pay the bill.

In the very, very, final analysis, there was one person whom Alex most trusted to give him advice and explanations of things. He didn't know whether this was true of everybody, or of most people, or only of Alex Glauberman. But he was happy enough to watch the sergeant disappear, and then to ask that person—himself—how he should reckon it all up.

He first thought, involuntarily, of that dark approaching thundercloud. It gave him a weak and dizzy feeling down where Greek coffee sloshed around in his stomach. Nonetheless, there was something rather wondrous about his treatments. The wondrous thing was that they were so effective. They killed malignant cells as fast as—well, without getting into distasteful comparisons with weapons, they killed them pretty damn fast. A few more rounds, it appeared, and they would kill them down to the point where there wouldn't be any evidence that anything was wrong with him.

There was just one problem about that. Somewhere inside him would be a last cell, hiding out, still in business. Soon that cell would get back to work at the thing it was best at. Therefore, after who knew how long a while, the tumors would come back. When they came back to the point where they caused significant trouble, then it would be dark thundercloud time again. And so on, and at best there would again be a surviving last cell, and so on. This was a merry-go-round on which Alex's mind had already amused itself many times.

But murder, he supposed now, was a lot like that. Whatever you felt about the victim, however much you loved or admired or pitied or hated him or her, the same thing was going to be true. You could put murderers, some of them, out of the picture. You couldn't really get at murder. That was a truth Trevisone must have known without Alex making speeches at him. Maybe the root was a conspiracy, or a kingpin, or a family, or a war, or something quite different from any of those. You could get close to that root, but you weren't likely to get rid of it. You couldn't take it apart and hold it still and fix it, the way you could fix a machine.

Alex left payment and tip on the table, and crossed the street to deposit Jack Moselle's check in the automatic teller machine outside the bank. He'd leave the money in the bank while he tried to find a way to use it against the man, effectively and not suicidally. If he couldn't find one, he'd give the money away someplace appropriate. It was too dirty to keep, and Gerald Meyer had already paid him for his costs and his time.

Still, there was a ghoulish feeling in Alex this night. It wasn't from the money. He knew he could tear up the check and the ghoulish feeling would still not go away. It had to do with a final thought that came to him—a strange thought that he didn't even want to put into words. He remembered what he had said to Meredith in their little summit conference on top of the heath. He was troubled by the thought that murder—even more than machines—had a way of making him feel at home.